F. START

SANTANA KNOX

Crossed Over © 2024 Santana Knox

All rights reserved under the International and Pan-American Copyright Conventions. No part of this book may be reproduced or transmitted in any form or by any means, electronic or mechanical, including photocopying, recording, or by any information storage and retrieval system, without permission in writing from the publisher.

Warning: the unauthorized reproduction or distribution of this copyrighted work is illegal. Criminal copyright infringement, including infringement without monetary gain, is investigated by the FBI and is punishable by up to 5 years in prison and a fine of $250,000.

This book is a work of fiction. Names, characters, places, and incidents are the product of the author's imagination or are used fictitiously. Any resemblance to actual events, locations, or persons, living or dead, is coincidental. This book is intended for mature audiences 18+.

No part of this book/cover was created or facilitated by Artificial Intelligence.

Head Editor/ Copy Editor: Alexa @ The Fiction Fix

Dev Editor: R.N Barbosa

Final Proof: The Havoc Archives

Cover/Interior art: B. B., @FlashFryed

CONTENT WARNINGS:
POSSIBLE SPOILERS AHEAD

Active addiction, consumption of prescribed narcotics, on page consumption of illegal substances (Snorting) (heroin/RX narcotics), suicidal ideation, intentional OD, accidental OD, mentions of abuse (historical), driving under the influence, mention of parental suicide, death of a loved one, mentions of cancer, misgendering by a piece of shit cis-het man, history of nonconsensual touch, boot stuff, relapse, withdrawal, physical assault.

AUTHOR NOTE

This is a book about loving someone through active addiction. If this is a triggering topic for you, please do not risk your mental health. Every way out of addiction is a valid way out, whether for ourselves or for our loved ones. The author does not believe that sex can heal drug addiction. **This story is fiction.** <u>Addiction is incredibly personal, as is any illness, and every experience is individually unique.</u>

There were parts of this book that were so incredibly difficult to write while prioritizing my own mental health and recovery that the only way to get through it was to detach myself from the writing. These are not formatting errors. They are intentional.

> This is a story about two people healing from the same wound. This is a story that shows how one cut can scar many ways.

PLAYLIST

Available on Spotify

Help I'm Alive - Metric
Past Lives - BØRNS
Eat Dirt - CRAY
You wouldn't like Me - Tegan and Sara
Nobody Asked Me (If I was Okay) - Sky Ferreira
Such Small Hands - La Dispute
So Jealous - Tegan and Sara
Nothing's New - Rio Romeo
Portions for Foxes - Rilo Kiley
Love I Don't Have to Love - Bright Eyes
Casual - Chappell Roan
I like the way you kiss me - Artemas
Happiness Is A Warm Gun - The Beatles
Addictions - Lucy Davis
Wake Up Exhausted - Tegan and Sara
Dark Come Soon - Tegan and Sara
Vampire Empire - Kyla Ren
Combat Baby - Metric
I Like Giants - Kimya Dawson
There Is a Light That Never Goes Out - The Smiths
Let Me Love You Like A Woman - Lana Del Rey
Francis Forever - Mitski
Lives - Modest Mouse
Soon We'll Be Found - Sia
Lost Girls - Tilly And The Wall
She's My Collar - Gorillaz, Kali Uchis

For the ones who were my way out when I didn't love myself enough to find my own path.

And For JB.
Who went home too soon.

This book is also dedicated to every person who has held someone else's broken pieces. Some of you are still holding on to them even though they've made your hands bleed.
Thank you.

DEVIL'S DAME DERBY LEAGUE ROSTER -

MAD MORGAN - THEY/THEM COACH
SCOTTIE CROC - HE/HIM MANAGER

B - TEAM
NANCY SHREW - SHE/HER B TEAM BLOCKER
VENICE WITCH - SHE/HER B TEAM BLOCKER
ELECTRIC-HEEL - SHE/HER B TEAM BLOCKER
K-OTIC - THEY/THEM B TEAM JAMMER
BAE-RUTHLESS - SHE/HER B TEAM PIVOT

A - TEAM
LADY YAGA - SHE/HER A TEAM BLOCKER
DREADPOOL - SHE/THEY A TEAM BLOCKER
STARSCREAMER - SHE/HER A TEAM BLOCKER
HARVEY DENT-HER-FACE - SHE/HER A TEAM PIVOT
NIA-DEATH EXPERIENCE - SHE/HER A TEAM JAMMER

DEVIL'S DAME DERBY LEAGUE ROSTER -

NON-ROSTERED PLAYERS
RAE-GUNN - SHE/HER BENCHED
D-STROYA - SHE/HER RETIRED

DERBY LINGO:

Blocker - The positional Skaters who form the Pack. Up to four Blockers from each team may skate, per Jam. One Blocker per Jam, for each team, may be a Pivot Blocker.

Bout - a Roller Derby "game" with two thirty-minute halves.

Fresh meat - a skater who hasn't passed their minimum requirements test and is not eligible to bout.

Gear - Roller Derby equipment: skates, protective wear, mouthguards, helmet.

Hockey stop - An abrupt stop using the sides of the skates.

Jam - a basic unit of time during a bout; a jam lasts two minutes.

Jammer - the point scorer for the team, only one on the track per team.

Panty - a slip cover for the helmet to designate the jammer and the pivot.

Pivot - a Blocker with extra abilities and responsibilities, commonly referred to as the **Pivot**.

DERBY LINGO:

Quads - Roller Derby skates (two wheels in the front, two in the back).
Scrimmage - a practice/friendly bout between teammates.
Taking a knee - happens when injuries occur.
T-stop - stopping technique where one skate forms a T behind the other.
Turn stop/derby stop - stopping technique where skater turns around and stops abruptly on their toe stops.
The star - the helmet cover (panty) for Jammers, containing two stars, one on each side.
The stripe- the pivot helmet cover (panty) with a stripe down the middle.
WFTDA - Women's Flat Track Derby Association
Zebra - referee

FLAT TRACK ROLLER DERBY GUIDE

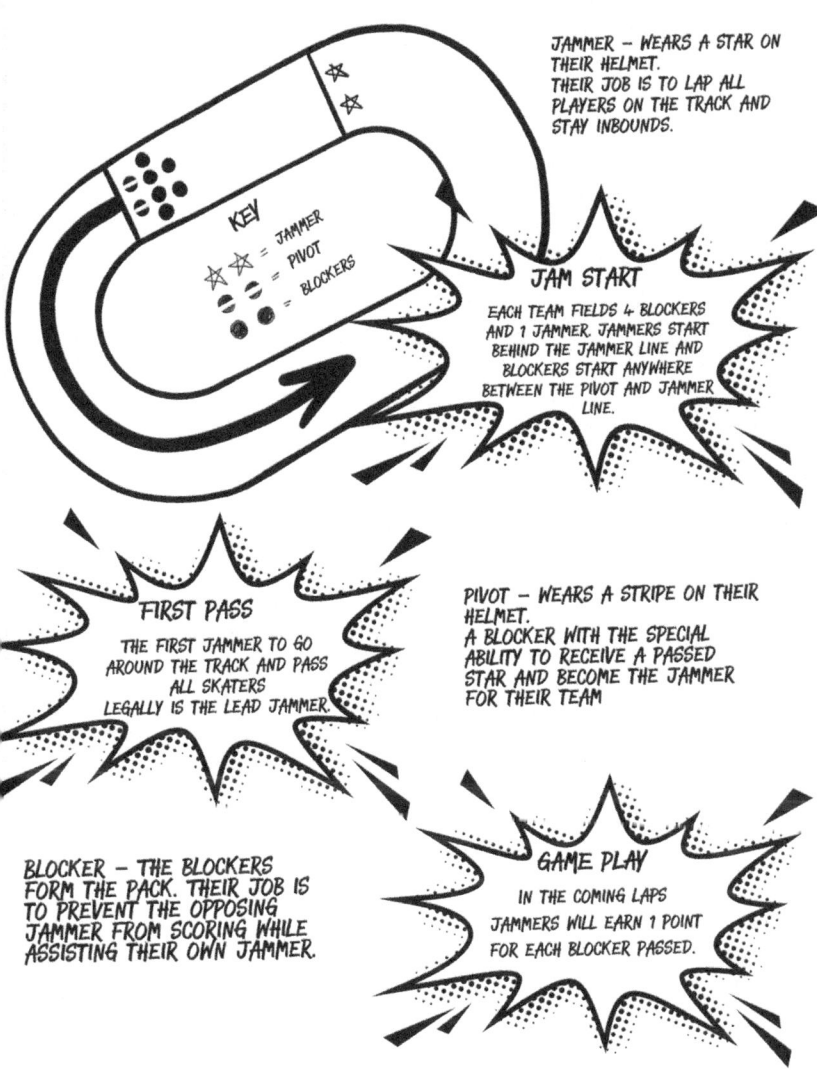

JAMMER — WEARS A STAR ON THEIR HELMET.
THEIR JOB IS TO LAP ALL PLAYERS ON THE TRACK AND STAY INBOUNDS.

KEY
☆ = JAMMER
= PIVOT
= BLOCKERS

JAM START
EACH TEAM FIELDS 4 BLOCKERS AND 1 JAMMER. JAMMERS START BEHIND THE JAMMER LINE AND BLOCKERS START ANYWHERE BETWEEN THE PIVOT AND JAMMER LINE.

FIRST PASS
THE FIRST JAMMER TO GO AROUND THE TRACK AND PASS ALL SKATERS LEGALLY IS THE LEAD JAMMER.

PIVOT — WEARS A STRIPE ON THEIR HELMET.
A BLOCKER WITH THE SPECIAL ABILITY TO RECEIVE A PASSED STAR AND BECOME THE JAMMER FOR THEIR TEAM

BLOCKER — THE BLOCKERS FORM THE PACK. THEIR JOB IS TO PREVENT THE OPPOSING JAMMER FROM SCORING WHILE ASSISTING THEIR OWN JAMMER.

GAME PLAY
IN THE COMING LAPS JAMMERS WILL EARN 1 POINT FOR EACH BLOCKER PASSED.

THE BASICS

- BOUT — A ROLLER DERBY GAME
- TWO TEAMS MATCH AGAINST EACH OTHER IN A BOUT
- A BOUT CONTAINS TWO THIRTY MINUTE PERIODS
- EACH PERIOD CONTAINS MULTIPLE "JAMS"
- A JAM CAN LAST UP TO TWO MINUTES
- LEGAL CONTACT — HIPS, REAR AND SHOULDERS
- ILLEGAL CONTACT/BLOCK AREAS — BACK, TRIPPING, ELBOWING

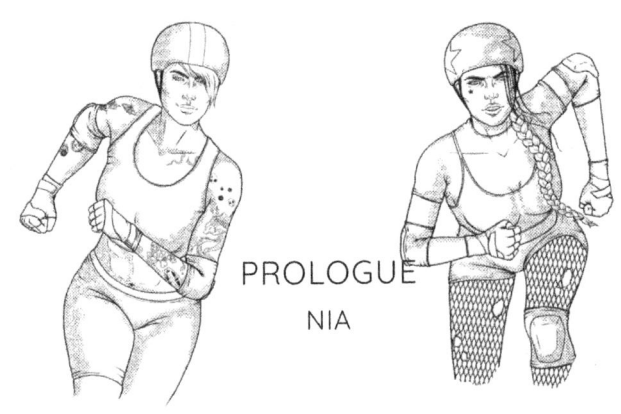

PROLOGUE
NIA

Sitting in my car, fingers clutching the leather of the steering wheel, I curse myself repeatedly. I still can't muster enough spine to do the one thing I drove to this town for.

I gave up immediately, chickened out the minute I walked through the doors of that skating rink and made a full U-turn back to my car, where I now sit, drenched in my own humiliation.

Switching on the ignition, I fight the incoming cycle of rumination the only way I can—by calling my mother. Every negative thought I can conjure about myself is on full blast, so I mess with the volume knob and the heat, as if it somehow helps. Winter in the Midwest is in fury, the roads packed with weeks of nonstop snow that have now turned to ice.

A loud honk pulls me out of my trance just in time to swerve out of the way of an incoming semi-truck.

"Crap!" I yell, taking my foot off the gas once I feel the ice under my tires steal the car from my control.

The bridge is too slippery; I spin once and then a second time before my brain tells my body to cooperate.

The brakes.

My thigh musters the shaky strength to lift my foot over the pedal and slam down on the third spin, my vision nearly black from adrenaline and my throat hoarse from screaming. The car keeps sliding, not stopping until the front makes contact with a tree.

The side of my head smacks against the glass with a crack just as the airbag explodes in my face, sending me back into the headrest violently. My teeth are the last to rattle, the sound of them clashing against each other more unnerving than the prolonged honk of my horn.

My head rings from the inside out, pain reminiscent of a sharp ax splitting my skull in half. The car alarm brays, beckoning for my attention, forcing my eyes open to find the tree has settled halfway through the hood.

"Antônia, are you driving? Antônia? I can't believe you'd be so reckless as to…" My mother's voice fades away over the Bluetooth as the ringing pierces deeper into my brain.

It's just like my mother to chastise me at a time like this.

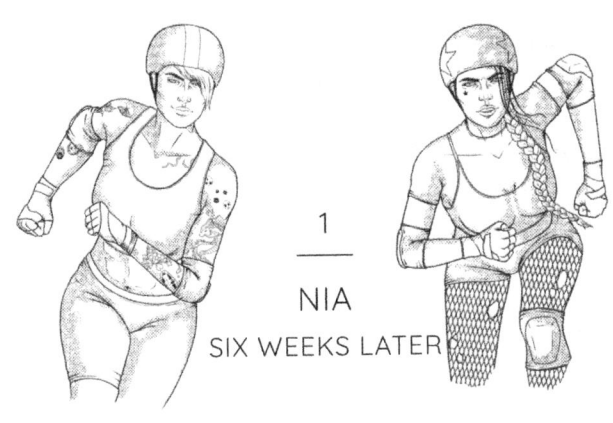

1
NIA
SIX WEEKS LATER

At this point, the ritual is deeply ingrained into me like muscle memory. A habit. A word I've spent my entire life trying to cultivate, to embody in the healthiest way possible but have never formed a positive connotation with.

Habit.

Brushing teeth is a habit for *most* people. For me, it's a painful task filled with more executive function than I can muster at eight in the morning, and even less around ten at night. Running in the mornings, drinking a daily cup of coffee, hell, even logging into an app once a week to learn a language can count as a habit.

But those aren't the ones I can form or conquer.

No. Not me.

Shaking my head, I press into the white lid of the plastic orange bottle, open the container, and give in to the admission with a heavy exhale. Here I am, in full *habit* mode.

Because habit sounds cleaner than addiction, a word

I'm having a hard time accepting, even though I'm well aware it's more chemical than psychological.

For now.

It's the nature of who I am. Get in an accident, get hurt in some way shape or form—even if unintentionally—then take the pills. Eventually, the pain stops, but the pills still come.

And I, so *good* at the *bad* habits, always continue to take them.

The clock radio in my beat-up Chevy doesn't work anymore, not since the crash. I flash the screen on my phone—nearly six in the evening, just in time for my 'coffee.'

I chortle at the thought, opening my glovebox and pulling out a CD case that dates back to the 2000s. Miley Cyrus' debut album. I smile to myself, remembering how I'd bought it sarcastically but ended up loving nearly every goddamn song. StarScreamer had to ride with Feral-Streep to practice for three whole months because I refused to play anything else in my car until I had memorized every single lyric.

And now that CDs are relics of the past, it's my favorite prop.

Checking around to make sure no one is roaming the parking lot, I place the CD case on top of the middle console and drop two pills right over Miley's face. I dig through the glove box looking for the spoon, unsure if I'd taken it out at the hotel or not. Without it, I'd have to improvise, which is fine. I can adapt.

I pull an old gift card out of my wallet and a trusty dollar bill. It's trained already, rolled up into the perfect shape, just waiting to be tightened into a little straw. I open it up, though, folding it in half and dropping the painkillers inside of it like an envelope and pressing the edges together to avoid any spills. With the CD case perfectly centered in the middle console and my one dollar envelope stuffed with pills, I press down with the gift card, doing my best to crush my medicine into a fine powder.

A cracking noise immediately lets me know this is the last time I'll be able to use Miley for the job, but I press one more time anyway, hard enough to be sure there are only crumbs left of my pills. *Meet Miley Cyrus* is officially fucked, a giant split in the center that spiderwebs off into four directions, making it an impossible table for the itch I desperately need to soothe. I sigh, picking up my dollar pouch and tossing the broken case into the backseat.

I settle for my middle console, knowing I'll never get all the powder out of the fuzzy fabric and that I'll likely be inhaling years of built up dust and cigarette ashes recirculated through my car's AC system.

Fuck it.

I dispense the powder into a perfect line, undoing the enveloped bill and smoothing out all the wrinkles before re-wrapping it into a little straw. Another glance around the parking lot, just for good measure before I put the rolled up dollar in my nose. Plugging the opposite nostril, I go to town. In one single inhale, I suck up the entirety of the line. I ignore the burn, keeping the nostril plugged as I facilitate drainage by pushing against the other cheekbone.

Full body shudders have me shaking my head like a dog, the bitter taste of the powder sliding down the back of my throat like a familiar friend. I search the car frantically for something, anything, and settle for an old can of soda, forgotten with time in the cup holder of my driver side door.

I jiggle the can side to side, checking for liquid and

feeling my heart soar at the sound of the stale soda splashing around the bottom. Turning it over, I swallow it down, pushing the astringent powder further down my throat.

Fucking wretched.

Was there anything worse than warm, flat Coke?

Yes.

Remembering I had ashed a cigarette into that particular can at least three times before the accident.

Acid rises up to my jaw, the feeling of nausea sweeping through my body in one hot burst.

Shaking my head again, I heave, this time loudly, as if it could somehow make the feeling better by purging it with noise. It works with tequila, so why can't it work with Roxys? The mellowing isn't immediate, but just knowing it's in my system is enough to give me courage, enough to ease the anxiety and make what's coming next just a little more bearable.

Nothing felt bearable anymore.

A natural consequence of writing off my Latin American mother because I refuse to adhere and function in a cycle of generational trauma that only multiplies, never seeming to have an end in sight.

I will no longer contribute.

But that doesn't mean I'm not rotting in my own pool of guilt about it.

If my grandmother was alive, I would probably be on the receiving end of three hundred phone calls a day about how it wasn't right to cut off my mom the way I did.

But my grandmother *is* dead, and I owe nothing to the departed.

Just like the first time, weeks ago, I wrap the laces of my quads around my fingers. Leaving my bags in the trunk, no plans to stay longer than a few laps and maybe have a cup of coffee with Lonnie for old time's sake, I step toward the building.

A quick glance in the side mirror, just to make sure there are no crumbs hanging from my nose, is all I need, but I catch a flash of the scar on the side of my head. It's only a few weeks old, still bright pink and raised, even more visible now that I keep that side of my head shaved. Rolling my shoulders back, I take a deep breath in through my mouth.

Fuck, am I really doing this again? As if the repercussions from the first time around weren't enough of a warning sign to stay the fuck away from Devil Town and Skateland? No, I'm delusional enough to convince myself it means the exact opposite, that getting into a nearly lethal car accident after copping out six weeks prior had been a punishment for avoiding my fate.

I stare at the double doors, ignoring every alarm my brain blares off. This isn't my home anymore, hasn't been for five years. The chances of being welcomed with open arms, finding the sisterhood and joy I not only miss but desperately crave with every inch of my bones, is nearly gone.

But I can't give up that easily.

Nia Da Silva doesn't fucking quit; shit, I don't even fucking die. I glance back at the proof, still visible on my crumpled car. With a sigh, I double back and walk to the trunk, slinging my gym bag over my shoulder in defeat. I can't do this without my protective gear. Skating without my pads would be a surefire way to fall, fall wrong, and get hurt again.

I'm already plenty hurt.

I don't need the extra help.

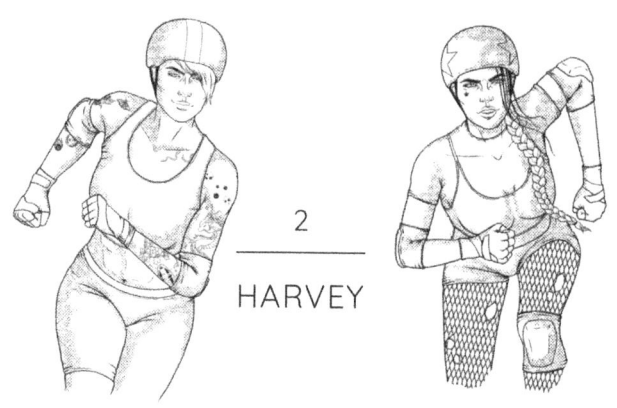

2

HARVEY

On any given Saturday, three things are guaranteed to be true.

One, I'll be covered in bruises by sunset.

Two, I'll be making at least one girl cry.

Three, there will be blood.

Lots of it.

It can't be helped. It's just the way Slam Nights work. The Roller Derby leagues come, they play, and we whoop their asses. It's the natural order of things in Devil Town, and the Devil's Dames Derby League regularly opens our doors for a beat-down.

Today is Tuesday, though. Today, we're closed for business. Our new manager will be walking through those doors, reassessing our team, and getting us ready for the "big leagues." The Devil's Dames haven't competed in any regulated Women's Flat Track Derby Association bouts in nearly five years—not since our star jammer gave up after a brutal injury, long before my time. Everything we've been doing for the last few years has simply been *for fun*, or for fundraising to keep this rink open to the public.

God knows we only make money on Fridays during *Tween Skate Party Night*. Hardly anyone shows up to a bout anymore, so the cash we make from concessions and merch on Slam Nights is practically nonexistent.

Skateland is headed for closure.

Once it's shut down, Devil Town will fight for city hall to demolish the building against the owner's wishes and force a sale of the lot. Eventually, they'll put up some chain grocery store in its place.

Lonnie, our coach and the owner, knew this day was coming and prepared for it. They signed away the rights to our league to some washed-up basketball team manager to try and dig us out of this hole, to make something of the Devil's Dames again.

There's nothing but excitement drumming through the veins of every skater on that track—because they have hope. If shit hits the fan, if the worst comes to fruition, then we'll have to dissolve. The skaters who *don't* live in our little town will have to find other derby teams to skate for, and those of us stuck here will have to abandon the idea of skating or start traveling for it.

The closest league to us is the Wolverine Dream Team, at least a fifty-minute drive to their city from here.

I sure as shit can't manage the back and forth multiple times a week for practices, so what will the skaters with more demanding jobs, families, or no car do?

Losing Skateland would practically be a death sentence for some of us.

Because if we aren't skating, we're likely making a shitstorm out of our lives.

I, myself, am a fucking bulldozer.

I've wrecked my way through life, plowing over

anything that doesn't serve me until all that's left is curated, especially in my favor.

The repercussions of being too much and not enough all at once.

We're mid-stretch on the track when he comes in. He's the sleazy type, impossible not to judge when he walks into a run-down skate rink in seemingly-Dolce and Gabbana shoes and a salmon-colored suit.

This guy thinks his dick is too heavy to carry between his legs, I know it.

We're about to clash so hard.

See, *my* dick is much bigger, and men like him don't do well knowing that. They don't tolerate the idea of a woman being in charge, knowing more, giving him guidance, which is everything I need to do to make sure we *stay* winning.

We just require a *little bit* of his money.

This guy has no clue what Roller Derby is about, and from the way his eyes bulge out of their sockets while scanning the room, I know he's way out of his element.

"Scott!" Morgan waves him down from the center of the track, where they stretch their hamstrings with the rest of the skaters.

They give me a quick look, using their forehead to gesture in his direction, as if to beckon me over as well. I sigh, feeling uneasy about this entire thing. I trust no one anymore, and this particular situation makes me feel like a wild animal, being lured into a cage by the promise of a juicy steak.

There is no other option, I remind myself, looking back at every skater with hope-filled eyes. This is their home too, not just mine. We're doing this for them.

"Ladies." His smile reminds me of a hungry cartoon crocodile, waiting above the water for the main character to let go of the branch. His yellow-blonde hair is short, gelled up like it's the early 2000s, and sunglasses sit above his head.

Designer, I'm sure, and I hate him for it.

"Skaters," I correct him, crossing my arms over my chest.

He furrows his eyebrows like he's not understanding.

Morgan clears their throat uncomfortably. "We're not all ladies here. *Skaters* is preferred." They hit me with a look that's nearly lethal, telling me to back off and not ruin this before it has a chance.

"Ladies, skaters, whatever," he chuckles. "I don't care what you want me to call you, as long as you're making me money."

Sleazy fucking reptile.

"Whatever?" I can't help it; I've already decided this guy is gonna be the end of my peace.

I can fucking feel it.

He doesn't respond. Instead, the double doors swing open, and both he and Morgan whip their heads in that direction, their eyes glued to the five-foot-nothing brunette with a single braid hanging down to her waist.

Nia fucking Death.

God is real, because this kind of bad timing has to be the work of a higher power, punishing me for all of my mistakes.

She looked tiny the first time she came here almost two months ago. No muscles, frail, like she was completely out of shape, not at all like the legend this team had painted her out to be. Today, she looks one step up from dead—

sunken cheeks, dark circles under her eyes, somehow more skeletal than before. One swing of Nancy-Shrew's hips, and half her bones would be broken.

So what the fuck was she doing at Skateland, her quads dangling from her fingers?

Morgan's eyes grew ten times in size, the *oh shit* look on their face impossible to mask, but thankfully, Scotty Crocodile isn't looking at Mo. No, he's locked in on the former Roller Derby Star who has no business crash-landing into a closed practice.

Or whatever the fuck this is.

A high-pitched shriek comes from the gaggle of skaters, who are no longer stretching but standing in a small circle together. StarScreamer dashes past us in a frenzy, one foot after the other slamming against the wooden track until she crashes into our unexpected guest.

"Nia!" she shouts, squeezing her into a death lock and lifting her until her feet no longer touch the ground.

Bae-Ruthless, Venice Witch, D-Stroya, and Lady Yaga take off from the crowded circle and skate in the direction of the girl, piling on top of her and StarScreamer.

The whistle blows directly in my fucking ear, and every hackle on my body raises, ready to go a round with this impossibly frustrating man.

Who the fuck gave him a whistle? I don't say it, but I guess the look on my face is enough to make Mo shrug, as if they can read my thoughts.

"All right, ladies," he calls out from where he stands. My blood pressure skyrockets, the sound of my pulse pumping in my ears too impossible to ignore. "I wanna see you warm up, and then everybody is doing assessments."

A roar of displeased comments erupts from every skater.

Nobody wants to skate twenty-seven laps in five minutes, but it's necessary to qualify under WFTDA regulations. Every skater here can probably do it with enough fire under their asses, but that doesn't mean we want to be surprised with it, and it especially doesn't mean we want to do it for this jackass, who isn't even asking nicely.

Preparation is important; building up stamina is crucial.

Not passing the speed test can be the kind of ego-killer that keeps good skaters from coming back.

You *never* test before you're ready.

He whistles again, this time less in my ear and more directed toward the incoming crowd of skaters, the sickly-looking girl awkwardly standing to the side, still in converse shoes. Star grabs her by the wrist and drags her into the rage pit, where nearly every skater in the Devil's Dame league points their finger directly into the crocodile's face.

He blows the whistle once more, this time on an extended drag that quiets every contrary voice and forces all the skaters to plug their ears for protection. "You're under the impression that this is a democracy, and maybe that's how Lonnie Green did things around here." A flat expression covers his face as he dishes out the next round of insults. "And that's exactly why Lonnie signed you all away, why Lonnie couldn't make successes out of you."

A grumble of protest rises again, but the whistle is far more powerful, starting to go to his head.

"If you disagree, you're welcome to leave." He points to the door. "To meet Women's Flat Track Derby Association regulations, all skaters must pass their skills and speed tests. *No one* is exempt."

We go in turns so as not to crowd the track. Four at a time, five minutes. When eight out of all twelve skaters have tested, Morgan, myself, and Star strap our helmets back on and get behind the blue line. Mo has been our assistant coach for the last year. When I first arrived in Devil Town, they'd been positioned as pivot, and there was hardly anyone who could get past them unscathed. Time gets us all, though. Eventually, you either retire, or you find a way to make yourself useful.

"Nia." StarScreamer whistles. "Get your ass over here." She looks up at Scott to explain. "Nia-Death here is *still* the all-time highest scoring jammer per bout in the entire Women's Flat Track Derby Association." Pride practically drips off her tongue, as if her friend's accomplishments are her own.

"Get behind the line." Our new manager doesn't need convincing. He even gives her the extra time it takes to get her skates and gear on.

Nia looks around the track awkwardly, like she's waiting for additional permission. It comes in the form of Lady Yaga pushing her in the back, propelling her toward the track. StarScreamer catches her by the wrist, whipping her in a circle until she steadies herself on her toe stops.

The two grin at each other, bumping shoulders until Star almost knocks her down. Scott gives us a hand signal to prepare us.

I would fear my ability to make it if I didn't have confidence in my own hard work and my body. There isn't a day my skates aren't on my feet, even if it's just for a stroll around the park. I'm not some tiny little thing; speed doesn't come to me easily. I'm five-eleven, and the velocity of my skates depend solely on the strength of my thighs.

And those bitches are toned to perfection.

He whistles us off, and the four of us move in perfect synchronicity, left knee over right, crossing over as we make our first turn around the track. By the fifth lap, Morgan is severely behind, and I'm starting to reach them from the back. I pound my skates harder on the wooden floor, the noise enough to alert Mo and force them to fight for their speed.

At the tenth lap, the braided brunette makes her way to my left, tight on the curve, passing me with ease. Quick little crossovers are all she needs to get a good distance ahead, but I know I'm still fast enough to meet the challenge. Star's blonde low-ponytail sticks to her sweaty back as she passes Mo on the right, an encouraging grunt from her as she hypes up our assistant coach.

My lungs burn at twenty. At twenty-four, I can no longer feel my feet, just a wave of nausea that's impossible to fight. *I only have to hold it back three more laps.* I'm just behind Nia-Death now, the tail end of her braid practically in reach as it whips behind her, almost teasing me to yank it.

Another lap, then one more, and my shouts to Mo to push harder are the only thing I can hear above the sound of our wheels on the track.

Nia passes the line, a 180 turn on her toes marking a classic derby stop before she rolls out of the track and collapses to the ground. D-Stroya, Venice, and Lady Yaga hover over her, fanning her with a laminated flier. I cross the line, rolling out of the track and dropping to my knee pads.

Sweat drips from my forehead down to my skates, but I keep my eye on Mo and Star until they cross the starting line. The croc blows his whistle just after, and the two practically fall onto each other, nothing but exhausted breaths coloring the air.

Mo is sobbing. They rarely bout unless the roster demands, and in the four years they've been here, I've only seen them skate the twenty-seven in five once. I understand just what those tears mean, the emotional exhaustion that sweeps over once victory has been achieved, the body's cry of conquest.

Our new manager doesn't let us revel in the moment.

Scott begins to assign positions, one skater at a time, until they've all been given their roles. He begins with the blockers on the B-team, the ones who stay on the bench during bouts unless a substitution is made. Nancy-Shrew and Venice Witch are named, followed by Bae-Ruthless as pivot. K-Otic is a substitute jammer like before.

Then, the A-team is formed: the ones guaranteed to be bouting unless injured, tired, or somehow missing. Lady Yaga, DreadPool, and StarScreamer for blockers—obvious, a given, our usual set up. Then, he calls my name for pivot. I think I hear him wrong, but then he announces the little one's name instead for the position of jammer.

My position.

"What? No, *I'm* fucking jammer." My chest is practically touching his, sweat forcing my shirt to stick to my sports bra.

"You *were* jammer. She's faster." He says it like it's nothing, like he isn't changing everything I know.

"She's not even a Devil's Dame!" I counter, absolute disbelief being the only thing I can feel while this guy fucks with the entire dynamic of our team.

It's as if the whole world is spinning—maybe from dehydration, maybe from exhaustion, or maybe from these two assholes fucking up my entire life in a matter of seconds.

"You can block, or you can get benched as a sub. Last I read, only one jammer per team goes out on the track. Your call." The look on his face is of pure satisfaction, like he can't be more fulfilled at giving me the news. "You." He points at the girl my siblings-in-wheels call Nia.

She turns slowly, an apprehensive look on her face. "Yes?" The word is barely audible.

"You a Devil's Dame?" he asks her.

Dead silence surrounds the rink, anticipation growing, like standing on a precipice, as she chooses her answer carefully. She looks between the skaters I've called my best friends for the last four years. Aspiration glimmers in their eyes, and they nod their heads in unison, StarScreamer clasping her hands to her chest like the perfect vision of hope.

"Yes," Nia-Death says, a little more courage behind her voice this time as she bites back a smile, her eyes darting over to me just long enough for me to catch.

They all scream, and the crocodile laughs a cold sound.

Clenching my molars together, I grind my teeth as every feeling between loathing and outrage courses through my veins.

"Fine. You want a blocker? I'll fucking block." I slip my mouthguard in and move to the pivot line for scrimmage.

The whistle goes off again, this asshole far too trigger happy with the thing, and it makes me wonder if he ever actually coached a basketball team, or simply owned them. The two are not the same. "Practices are Monday, Wednesday, and Fridays from now on," he belts out. "See you all tomorrow, bright and early. Those who didn't pass will have three more chances. After that, you gotta find yourself a new league."

Ass wipe.

He knows we practice Tuesdays and Thursdays, because here we stand, on a fucking *Tuesday*, with our skates on. These are all power moves, shows of dominance, pissing on Skateland as if he fucking owns it.

Well, *he doesn't*. He might own the name of the Devil's Dames, but he doesn't own us. He doesn't own the skaters, and if we organize, we can still come out in charge of our shit here.

"That's it?" I ask, forcing him to freeze in place.

He turns around slowly, raising a single eyebrow in question.

"Not gonna assess our footwork, our individual strengths and weaknesses?" I snort.

"I've seen what I needed to see." Turning to Mo, he adds, "I'll hold open auditions to fill the final spots once the last of the grandfathered skaters get their chance to finish their speed tests." He walks out without another word.

My anger consumes me. I worked my ass off for nearly half a decade and now it's all been taken from me in less than five minutes. I spin toward Morgan for some sort of support, finding nothing but a vacant stare, as if they too are still recovering from the whiplash of the last hour.

Enough is enough. I need answers.

"Who the fuck do you think you are?" The words come

out of my mouth before I even get a chance to stop in front of our new *teammate*.

I'm half a head taller, and even my bones look twice her size. Every blocker on our team is going to crush her in scrimmages. Sure, she's fast, but fast means nothing if she can't take a hit. And by the look of her, one check of my hip will send her flying.

"W-what?" she stutters out, clearly uncomfortable with confrontation. "I'm Nia. I-I was here a couple months ago." She tries clarifying, like I wouldn't remember when she chickened out of skating weeks prior.

"I know your name, princess. What are you doing here? Messing with all of my shit?"

She looks like she's shrinking by the second.

"Harvey," Star chastises.

"What? I'm supposed to be Eager Beaver over here because this chick rolls out of nowhere and bumps me from my position, and it's *totally* okay because she's your long-lost friend?" I turn back to face Nia-Death. "*Why* are you back here?" Arms crossed over my chest, I wait for an answer.

"I came back to Devil Town to skate." Her voice is still meak, quiet, like she isn't sure she really wants me to hear her.

I say nothing.

"I came back because this was my home." Her eyebrows scrunch in the middle, her frustration showing while still trying to appeal to me.

My expression is a stone mask.

She lets out a heavy exhale and speaks again, "I came to see Lonnie."

Bae-Ruthless gasps.

"Lonnie's not here, and *you* don't belong anymore," I

warn her. "Go back to wherever you came from before you disrupt any more of our lives."

She looks around, confused, but she doesn't miss the somber expression on all of her friends' faces. "Where's Lonnie?"

"If this was your home, you'd know Lonnie Green is dead."

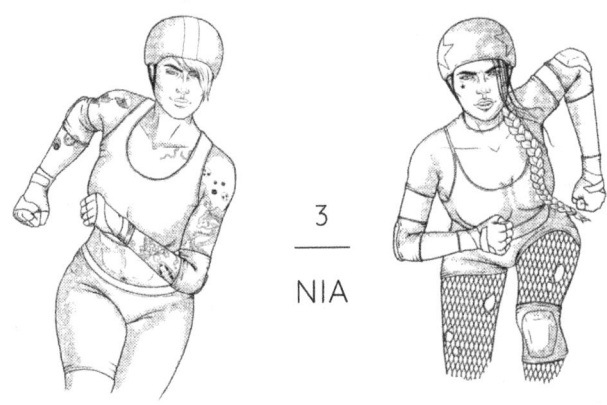

3
NIA

She drops the bomb on me, casually skating away like she didn't just destroy my reality.

Lonnie is dead. Lonnie is fucking dead.

Lonnie, the only person in this entire world I felt closer to than family. Lonnie, the one who cared for me without judgment, who tolerated all my adolescent bullshit, who pulled me from the path I'd catapulted myself down, heading nowhere fast. Lonnie, who protected me when my mother tore me to shreds. Lonnie, who sent me off to college after my injury, who told me to take time to heal before I hurt myself worse than before.

Lonnie, my voice of reason.

Lonnie, who I came home for.

Who I spoke to three months ago, with the promise of seeing each other again.

Six weeks. I lost six weeks in a hospital, recovering from a head injury. Almost two to wake up, and four more to rehab.

And in that time, I lost everything.

The buzzing in my brain intensifies, my heartbeat far

too labored from the narcotics traveling through my veins at rapid speed. Skating high seemed like a fun idea. Skating twenty-seven laps with two crushed Roxys in my nose under five minutes was borderline suicidal.

Star is saying something, but I can't hear her past the chaotic noise inside my own head. My feet move beneath me, confusion, need for clarification, and an unforgiving pattern of self-deprecation already taking root within. As if swept by a current, I'm pulled in only one direction.

I feel a squeeze on my wrist, and I find Lady Yaga's hand tight around me. "Just let her cool off." The words are barely audible, but the shaking of her head is clear as I read her lips. "Harvey's kind of intense."

It's not enough to hold me back.

I *have* to talk to her.

Shaking off one of my oldest friends, I make my way to the locker room. I'm drawn to this girl, and I can't explain why. Pausing at the door, I look back to see only anxious faces watching me. I roll my shoulders, raising one hand to the wall to combat the lightheadedness fighting to take me down.

With a trembling fist, I knock.

"Fuck off," she barks immediately from the other side.

"I'm coming in," I announce, like it would somehow make it better.

The girl named Harvey is sitting on a bench, legs spread wide with her elbows resting on the tops of her thighs. Her head is dropped, a dark spot staining the concrete where her sweat drips from her clasped hands to the floor.

With her helmet off, I can see her short blonde hair, trimmed close around the ears and the back but long in the front, spilling over her eyes. I think they're green, but I'm not sure. They look red now. An eclectic array of anime tattoos cover her muscled arms, down to the scorpion on her hand.

Her chin raises slowly, her eyes narrow and hard, scrutiny burning from them as they gaze into me.

She's fucking breathtaking. Every sharp edge of her features is softened by the glow of her skin and the fullness of her lips. My heart drums faster when the furrow in her eyebrow grows deeper.

"What the fuck do you want?" Her nostrils flare, the silver hoop glinting in the light.

Standing here now, I am well aware that my brain has abandoned me to my stupid decisions.

"Lonnie is dead?" They're the only words I can manage coherently.

She doesn't say anything, but the confirmation isn't necessary.

"When?" It becomes harder to take each inhale fully, my lungs struggling to do the work.

"Little over a month ago."

The words feel like cinder blocks around my skates; my knees buckle and beg to drop.

I brace myself, holding onto the wall and feeling the weight of them on me. "I-I don't understand. I just spoke to them—"

"Don't you have *friends* you can talk to about this?" She's already up, skating towards the door, her shoulder bumping against mine and nearly knocking me the rest of the way down.

The door slams behind her, leaving me with the echo of her words in the damp room.

I let go, falling to my knee pads and letting the tears roll down my cheeks. Everything is wrong.

This isn't the life I was supposed to come back to.

This wasn't part of the plan.

Everyone has cleared out, only Star staying behind, knowing me well enough to suspect when a breakdown is imminent.

"You okay?" She tilts her head to the side.

I shake my head but skate toward her anyway, with no attempt to stop on my part as I crash into her. She's strong enough to take it, lowering her center of gravity and wrapping her arms around me in an embrace. The tears fall, as if dehydration hasn't already set in from the buckets I've sweat and the pills I snorted. A wailing spills from my chest that I don't recognize as my own.

My friend holds me, sinking to the ground while letting me have this moment of mourning without judgment or rush.

I cry until it's no longer sustainable, until the tears burn my skin and my throat begs for water. It's not enough to make me move; it's only when the cold floor registers beneath me, when the headache begins to settle in, that I dry my face and stand.

Minutes pass, and I've gone silent, my lips splitting and cracking when Star finally speaks again.

"What's your plan? Come stay with me tonight?"

I look up at her, nodding with no hesitation. I've been staying at Lorraine's dinky old motel on the side of the highway. It's fine—nothing smells and it's cheap enough not to leave a big dent in my savings, which is just enough for a couple of months until I can find a job.

In a big city, a BA in social work is a guaranteed promise of a job. Out here in Devil Town, though, where I detoured my entire life for what I can only label as a "call from the universe" to come home? I'll be lucky to find work at a coffee shop, let alone in my designated field.

"You still live with your mom?" I smile, remembering how Star's mother had been the first person to supply us with alcohol underage.

She chuckles like her mind went to the same place, dropping her arm over my shoulder as we skate toward our things still on the benches. "Yeah, but she's a cranky grouch now. All those White Russians ended up giving her cirrhosis. She didn't do too well after the liver transplant."

"That's... terrible." I drop to the bench, undoing the laces on my skates and removing each piece of my protective gear. "Are you sure I should come by?"

"Yeah, definitely. She'll be stoked to see you; she still talks about the night you got hurt." She slings her bag over her shoulder, always much faster at removing her skate garb than me.

Grabbing my helmet off the bench, she gives it a once over. A giant smile stretches from ear to ear as she appreciates the fact that her *To Punish and Enslave* Decepticons sticker is still proudly displayed on it. It's been nearly a decade since she first slapped it on there, just moments after I completed my first speed test and became a Jammer for the Devil's Dames Derby League.

She tosses the helmet in my skate bag and slings it over her shoulder, not taking any arguments from me as I try to convince her to let me carry it myself.

"Girl, you look like this bag would knock you the hell over—no offense." She side-eyes me. "Is there a story behind why you look like the Grim Reaper, and where that scar on your head came from?" Gesturing to the shaved half of my head, she emphasizes where it cuts its way from my temple all the way past my ear.

I take a deep breath, knowing I can't hide the truth from my friend, but that she'll make far too big of a deal about it if I don't. "Stella…" I try deflecting with the use of her government name.

"You don't have to tell me now." She lifts her hand up to stop me from possibly lying, the thing I taught myself to do when the truth is too uncomfortable to stomach or share. "When you're ready, yeah?"

"Yeah," I agree with a nod.

I try to argue my way into showering at the rink, for my own personal need to be clean as soon as possible, but Star is against it, promising me that her bathroom at home would be far more accommodating.

I hate feeling like a burden, but I'm trying this new thing where if someone offers, I won't turn down their help. Maybe one day, I'll grow enough spine to ask for it.

A laughable concept to anyone who truly knows me.

Star knows me, and she spent the entire ride back to her house eye-ing me suspiciously.

"What happened to your car?" she finally asks, referring to the once crushed and then half-uncrushed metal near the driver's side.

"I hit a tree a few weeks back." I shrug it off like it's nothing, my fingers wrapping tighter around the wheel of my beat-up Subaru.

"Looks like you tried to become one with it. How the fuck is this car even running?" She laughs, toying with the sound system, only to find that it doesn't work.

"I know, it's tragic," I explain with a huff, "but East End Garage got it running for me with a used engine."

"Damn." She gives up, leaning back into the passenger side. "Is that what happened to your head?"

"Stella," I warn, not ready to fish that bottle from the ocean quite yet.

"My bad. Looks wicked, though." She stares at it some more, a grimace painted on her face.

The reality is, how am I supposed to talk about something I can't explain? Something I haven't fully processed, that changed the entire fabric of my being. How do I try to make someone understand that I'm not supposed to be here, but somehow, I just am?

Every doctor said I was a miracle, that even waking up shouldn't have been enough, because my brain activity had been so low, they expected a vegetable.

But I'm here.

Somehow.

The drive back to her house is filled with silence when it should have been filled with memories and catching up. I missed my friend. Stella—StarScreamer—was one of my closest friends in grade school, and when Lonnie Green opened Skateland, we were the first two in line for tryouts.

Right now, it feels like there are miles stretched between us, forged from years apart and distance.

We pull into her driveway. The early 1990s style craftsman home is just as I remembered it: white siding stained by time and a picket fence that looks recently power washed. My brain buzzes with regret, second thoughts and insecurities drowning me with the need for reassurance, the kind I desperately sought from Lonnie.

She opens her door and begins climbing out, the action

turning on the motion sensor outdoor lights that force her dog to appear at the window. Even his bark is recognizable.

"Jesus Christ, Monty is still alive?" I laugh, shocked that the miniature poodle is still kicking it this long.

"He'll be sixteen this year, don't worry, he's only *a little* incontinent." She grabs her bag from the backseat and then reaches for mine.

"Actually…" I start. "I was thinking I'd come by tomorrow?" I lift a hesitant brow her way.

"I don't think you should be alone tonight, Antônia." She gives me a look filled with parental concern, a look that says she knows better.

"I have all my things at the motel, and I have to run a few errands before I fuck off for the night anyway." I try my best to awkwardly fumble my way out of this one, but Star gives up first, knowing that I can't be forced into any social situation I don't want to be in.

Even if it's just a simple sleepover at a friend's.

"Tomorrow, yeah?" She holds me to it, shutting the passenger side door but leaning into the still-open window.

"I promise." I grin, nodding her way.

I need to crumble tonight. I need to shred down every fiber of my being, decompose and come back into my own by tomorrow morning, and there is only one person in town who can help me do it.

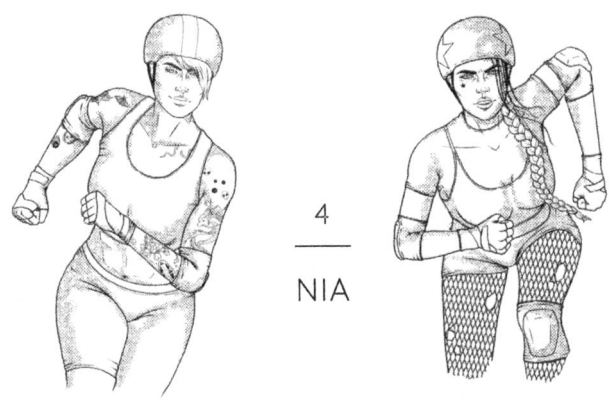

4
NIA

Here I am again, at the *most* familiar part of Devil Town. The very street I lost myself to as a teenager, the very street my mom fought tooth and nail to pull me out of. I look down at my empty prescription bottle and squeeze it tight in my hand.

This is fine.

I just need a little more to wean off, and then I'll be back to normal again. I pull my phone out of my pocket and text one of the few numbers I still know from memory.

> I'M OUT HERE

I don't know why I bother; the man never looks at his phone. I unbuckle my seatbelt, anxiously looking around as I pocket the empty bottle and feel for the wad of cash. The door opens before I can reach it, a brunette in a black pantsuit combo looks me up and down before sliding past the half-shut door.

I put up my hand to stop her from closing it behind her, returning the same stale stink-eye she'd given me, before pushing it open the rest of the way and walking inside.

"He—Hey, squirt." It comes out almost like laughter, amusement for sure in seeing me again, no doubt surprised that I'm still alive.

Ditto, motherfucker.

"Ryan fucking Lee." I grin, finding him sitting on the same torn up leather recliner I'd spent many teenage nights sleeping in.

He's only six or seven years older, but he carries with him wisdom from being on his own for so long, and at times, it appears the same as old age. When I was seventeen, he was twenty-three and running an ecstasy operation right out of Devil Town.

The first time we met, a friend convinced me to skip school to trip on acid. I had never done LSD before, nor had I any idea what it would do, what to expect. Clueless, I followed, and I spent the majority of the day rolling around in the grass, staring at the clouds in Devil Town Skatepark. Our dealer had been Ryan Lee, and he soon became one of my best friends.

Now, the skatepark is a parking lot.

Ryan Lee still looks the same, maybe a few lines around the corners of his eyes that wasn't there before, but the overall image hasn't changed. I'm nearly twenty-eight now, and he, thirty-four. He's donning the same shaggy, mousy-brown hair that some beauty school dropout probably cut in exchange for a teener of coke, and wearing the same cargo pants with just enough pockets to hide everything he needs.

Not bothering to take my shoes off at the door, I run to him and jump into his lap, gracing his cheek with a sloppy, wet kiss.

"Motherfucker," he grumbles, wiping it off with the back of his sleeve. "Where've you been, squirt? You disappeared."

"Ryan, it's been five years. I went to college." I laugh, pushing off him and walking toward his kitchen.

Cups in the second cabinet to the left, plates on the right. Bread in the drawer for some reason, and pills under the microwave. Hard drugs in the bedroom, of course—the cocaine in a fake version of *Little Women*, the hard stuff in a *Lion King* VHS. Those are only his personal stashes; the stuff he sells he keeps in the walls, inside safes hiding in plain sight, disguised as paintings and family portraits.

"Could have visited." He huffs, propping his foot up on the opposite knee as he watches me open the fridge and grab a can soda.

I'm probably the only person alive with the balls to walk this freely in his house, the only person who can do it without being accused of stealing.

"I wasn't sure this was still home. My parents moved to New York the same year I left for school," I try justifying.

"I'm not family?" he taunts, a disingenuous hurt look on his face.

I deadpan, unblinking as I pop the tab on the can, "I texted you a million times without an answer, and you know how I feel about rejection."

He furrows his eyebrows, the line in the middle growing deeper by the second before he pulls his phone out to prove me wrong. Scrolling, the wrinkles on his nose soften as he bites his lip, trying to mask any sign of defeat.

"Told you." I chuckle, dropping to the couch across from him and propping my feet on the coffee table. "I thought you were in prison, honestly."

He gives me a scolding look, like the insult might have actually hurt him.

"What? You didn't answer me! What was I supposed to think?" I set my can down.

"That I'm a better dealer than some shithead who'd get caught and go to prison." He crosses his arms over his chest.

"Sorry. Didn't mean to offend, buddy." Batting my eyelashes, I try to charm my way out of a tussle between old friends. "But you never answered."

"You know how I feel about pointless talk." He grabs his glass off the table, whiskey, neat, probably something standard like Jack, but if someone was visiting, he'd tell them it was Johnny Walker Gold Label.

No one in this town can tell the difference anyway. He doesn't bother spending money to impress others. It's not his style.

"Should have visited," he deflects.

"Ass." I chuckle, reaching across and grabbing the remote from his hand to switch the show.

"Proud of you." He says it quietly, like he's not sure if it's an okay thing to say.

Weird relationship to have with your drug dealer, but if I'm good at anything, it's parentifying anyone a day older than me. It's almost like they can sense my mommy issues from a mile away, can't fight the biological need to nurture me, even those who don't have a single nurturing bone in their body.

"Don't be." I snort. "Why do you think I came to see you?"

He sighs, not acknowledging me yet somehow not ignoring me either. Reaching under the coffee table, he pulls out a mirror about the size of a book. On it are already four lines, measured out perfectly equal alongside a small pile of the powder.

"What's your poison these days?" he asks, knowing my first addiction is escaping reality.

"I just ran out of Roxys," I confess, always feeling icky when we interrupt personal shit for business.

"The fuck for?" He grimaces, his disdain for prescription pills still stronger than ever.

"Car accident." I turn my head to show him the scar.

"Yikes," he grumbles, putting the mirror back under the table and walking into his room. In just a few minutes, he's out again, holding *The Lion King* VHS in his hand.

"No way, dude." I wave him off, knowing damn well I don't want that shit. "Just give me some narcos to take the edge off, something with codeine."

"That shit is bad for your liver." He shakes his head. "Tiny bumps, never more than enough to get rid of the pain," he instructs.

"Ryan, it's all drugs," I muse, never tired of the way his brain processes things.

"Yeah, and one favors big pharma. The other supports the local economy." He grins, opening the VHS and pulling out the clear bag.

The powder is a light beige color, looking more like something I'd cook with than something I'd put up my nose.

"I don't know," I drag out my words. "I feel like, once upon a time, I had a hard limit, and *this* was it."

"Hard limits are for people whose drug dealers don't know them by their full names, Antônia Da Silva. If I remember correctly, your birth certificate's original copy is still in my *important documents* safe." He gives me that damn parental look again.

Except I've never bothered to ask *him* for his last name. Ryan Lee always felt like enough, and maybe by not telling me, he protected me, in his own way.

You never want to know too much. That's one of his many rules. In typical Ryan style, the rules are for everyone but him.

"Are you kidding me? I've been looking for that thing for at least three years, Ryan! I blamed my mom for losing it." I get up, running to the black and white framed photo of this very house that hangs above the fireplace.

"You brought it over after the homecoming dance fight," he reminds me. "You were gonna start over, remember?"

I exhale all the air out of my lungs, an autonomous response to the memory.

That was the night I'd had enough. Some petty argument between my mother and I had escalated into me telling her college wasn't my path. At the time, it hadn't been, but she, an immigrant who had worked her entire life to give me the opportunity of college in the United States of America, couldn't fathom the idea that I'd throw it all away.

For *Roller Derby*, of all things.

After threatening to send me to Brazil for *correcting*, I exploded. Packing everything I deemed as necessary to become an independent adult into a small bag, I set to camp out at Ryan Lee's house. *Still a minor then.*

I lasted two weeks before she goaded me into

responding to a text, somehow using that message to help the police track my location. Ryan and I had been at the local Waffle Station getting breakfast when the police showed up, his assistant at the time feeling the full force of the raid in his stead.

I lift the frame from the wall, entering the numbers I know by heart.

Fourteen, forty-one, fourteen. The guy is some weird sort of genius, but he's oddly obsessed with the number fourteen. I can't fight his logic; when he breaks it down and tells the chronological tale of every fourteen that had brought him blessings, it gets hard to argue that it truly *isn't* his lucky number.

Fourteen has kept Ryan Lee from prison many times.

The safe clicks, and inside is nothing but a thick manila folder. Opening it up, I find every single conviction this charlatan would dare try to convince me doesn't exist. Thumbing through a few Wayne County misdemeanors from the last three years—no doubt discharged by whatever judge he paid off—I eventually flip right past it, the *Silva* catching my eye before I flip back to find my full name.

I smile victoriously, folding it in half and sticking it back into the pile of papers. I don't know why, but it's been safe here for this long. Why move it? It's not like I know where I'm going next anyway. I tuck the rest of his trophies back into the folder before I close the safe once more.

"Keep it here for me until I figure out where I'm going? I don't want to lose it."

He smirks like he knows I can't be trusted with my own shit. "You good to go then?" He's obnoxiously irritating for a man his age with so many felonies.

"Don't be annoying." I slump back onto the couch. "I'm just not sure I'm ready for *that*," I confess.

"I'm not the Devil on your shoulder, I'm just the facilitator." He clicks his tongue, putting the bag back into the VHS.

"Wait." I bite my lip, and he lifts his chin up, raising his eyes to look at me. "Maybe just to try it?"

"I don't know, squirt. I don't think you're right for this shit." He stands again, grabbing *The Lion King* as if he's going to put it away.

"Ryan…" I growl. "Don't be a dick."

I know his methods well, the dark psychology he uses to get addicts from one thing to the other. It's kept him rich, regardless of whatever product he might be low on at any point in time. The man's a mad genius. Borderline terrifying, but he's undeniably *good* at pushing drugs.

"No, I'm not playing, Nia." He shakes his head, a severe expression on his face. "This shit isn't for you. I have painkillers under the microwave," he says, as if I need reminding.

"Are you kidding me?" I'm insulted and don't care to hide it.

He's treating me like a fucking kid, no better than my mom.

"I'm just looking out for you," he says softly, walking into his bedroom.

Getting mad at Ryan Lee serves me nothing except the guarantee that if I throw enough of a hissy fit, he won't be selling me anything tonight. So I huff internally, putting away all my feelings of resentment and accepting the pills as my consolation prize.

I walk toward the microwave, lifting the countertop unit just enough to slide out a flat wooden box. "Which ones?" I ask, looking at the different clear baggies and the plethora of pills they hold.

"Blue, with the thirty on them," he shouts from his bedroom.

They're hard to miss, the other blue pills clearly ecstasy with their fancy little imprints of robots and flowers on them.

"How much do you want for these?" I ask, turning around to find him right behind me.

"Hmm." His breath is hot on my shoulder as he prowls over me with his towering height from behind me. "My tub's *real* dirty, kiddo." He gives me a dark smile as I look up at him.

I sigh. "I'd say I need to hold on to what little pride I have, but I could honestly use the free shit." Reaching under the cabinet of the kitchen sink, I rummage for whatever cleaning products I can find.

That had always been his thing. I never bothered to inquire whether there were girls who fucked him for drugs, or if there were people who owed him to the point where it was dangerous. When it came to me, his expectations were always clear, always innocent. A task, a chore, in exchange for what I needed.

There were many times in college when I thought back to Ryan and how I'd made it through the most turbulent time of my life unscathed. High as fuck, almost always deathly out of it, but never *in* danger. Because, for some reason, he was, in his own way, always looking out for me. If I blacked out from drinking, I'd wake up tucked safely in his bed, clothed. If I was up too long rolling, he'd kick out any strangers to make sure I didn't get taken advantage of during the night.

It's taken a lot of years to realize the privilege that came with our friendship.

Privilege that extends far beyond free drugs.

"Can I ask you something?" I can't keep it in anymore. My brain is doing the thing it does, and I have to know for myself, have to process it outwards and not just in my own head.

"What?" He puts on the tired big brother tone he's so good at using with me.

"Why did you keep me around so long?" I ask, and a confused look spreads on his face. "You know what I mean. You never tried anything, never took advantage of me when you very well could have, never asked for more than I was willing to give." The word vomit flows out easily, like the rehearsal in my own mind was enough preparation.

"I don't rape women, Nia. There's plenty around who give it to me for free." He takes that same annoyed tone as when I made the prison joke, like he's not happy about his morals and ethics being called into question. As if he's not a fucking drug dealer.

A good-looking one at that, with all his teeth, which is fucking rare for this town.

"Okay. My bad." I raise my hands, one wrapped firmly around a bottle of cleaner and the other a scrubber.

He lets out an exhaustive sigh. "I kept you around cuz you made me look good. Because I trusted you more than I trusted my runners," he confesses anyway. "Every other bitch coming in here was blown out of their minds, trying to fuck me or fuck me over. Half of them were Xanni-ed out on my couch, head in another universe with drool pouring out of their mouths. Dealers were coming in and out of the house back then, but there you were, pretty little

Nia. My golden trophy, sitting on the chair, doing *just* the right amount of the good stuff to be sweet and social. Making a great impression. You're part of the reason I'm king of this empire now. Remember that year before you left, when I had you in charge of weighing my blow?" He chuckles at the memory. "That was hot as hell. Every minor league pusher was jealous of me, and every major leaguer was impressed."

I hold back the smile, the compliment doing more than it probably should, but I'm feeling fragile as fuck at the moment, and my vulnerabilities are starting to leak out.

"I'm not upset by any means." I tuck my hair behind my ear, trying to laugh it off. "Just something I thought a lot about over the years. How lucky I was to have had you in my life and never get caught in a situation where I got taken advantage of, or have you put me in awkward positions of having to turn down your advances."

"My advances? First of all, you remind me too much of my little sister." That confused look appears once again. "Second, why would I hit on a gay chick?"

I bite the inside of my cheek. "I didn't realize it was that obvious." I frown. "I'm just now starting to realize it myself."

"Do you not remember the night Big Ricky brought his girlfriend over and we blasted through an eight ball in an hour? The two of you made out for half the night. I thought he was going to kill you for trying to steal his woman." He grabs the cleaner from my hand and then the scrubber.

I laugh, unable to pull that memory from deep within the dungeons of my mind. "I do *not* remember that night. How is she?"

"Dead, I think. Ricky went to prison for assault." He walks around me, placing the cleaning products back under the sink.

"Fuck," I whisper, never getting more than a moment to forget just how easily life took from us.

"You smell like shit, and you look even worse, Nia. Pay me back another night." He closes the cabinet doors and walks over to the bathroom door, as if to tell me to shower.

"I can just shower at my hotel," I laugh.

"Stay the night. You can have my bed." He's not joking.

"Miss me that bad? I'm not even high yet. I can drive home." I walk past him, back to the living room.

"I can't have my neighbor thinking this is exactly what this is. Sarah Prichard is enough of a bitch without being suspicious of my daily activities," he finally explains.

"Sarah Pritchard? I think I went to school with her. She lives next door now?" She was a nosy little clarinet player who always got me in trouble for smoking cigarettes in the bathroom.

"Sure fucking does." He seems annoyed just thinking about her.

"And what do you mean? How are you making money if all your customers are spending the night?" I cross my arms over my chest, trying to figure out what the hell he was doing for money.

"I upscaled. Signed on with some heavy hitters. Now, I just *liaison* the product between them and some big timers." He emphasizes liaison like there's a lot more to it than what he's letting on. "More or less, anyway. None of the product except my personal shit makes its way to my home now. Had to make changes to the game once they gentrified the fuck out of the neighborhood."

"Wow. I'm impressed," I admit, walking over to the coffee table and swiping my keys. "Don't get in over your head," I warn him, like I'd done a million times before. It makes no difference; Ryan Lee only listens to himself. "I gotta grab my bag out of the car."

"Pull your car into the driveway. Looks less suspicious," he clarifies.

"Jesus. That paranoid? You're almost as bad as Mitch the Twitch," I joke, rushing out the door before he can react to the insult.

Mitch was a low level dealer who did way too much of his own product and always came up short when Ryan needed to collect. He ended up switching to meth and developed a twitch after enough time, and the nickname Mitch the Twitch stuck. He wound up in prison not too long after for selling meth at a school playground. Anytime he came around, he'd ruin Ryan's blinds, fingering them to death to make sure we weren't being watched by the feds.

That kind of paranoia is unavoidable when staying up three to four days at a time.

I used to like the feeling. It made me feel productive, like I could get everything done for the first time in my life. Now, I just want to sleep every feeling away like they don't matter. Back inside Ryan's, I'm in the bathroom, undressing in the mirror. My reflection is just another routine I avoid.

I don't even know who that girl is these days.

The shower is hot and everything I need to feel better after the unexpected beatdown my muscles received today. Less prepared for the hit of losing the person I loved most, but still unprepared for my speed test today. Yet somehow, my body managed to pull it off anyway. Muscle memory or something of the sort. I push the thought of Lonnie back down into the dark recesses of my mind and go back to the twenty seven laps I skated.

Maybe it was the 60 milligrams of Roxy coursing through my veins that made it somehow doable.

I'm not going to overthink this one.

Not tonight, anyway.

5

HARVEY

There's something about proving an asshole wrong that fuels me like nothing else can, and proving *this* particular asshole wrong has just climbed to the top of my to-do list. I'm the first at the rink, as always, using my spare key to unlock the place before gearing up and eating a breakfast bar. Mo comes in next and prepares the track, bringing the cones out of storage to set up for ladders and drills.

We usually don't talk anymore until the others arrive. One on one time with other skaters stopped being a part of my interests after Lonnie's passing. Five weeks without Lonnie is starting to feel like a lifetime.

How long are we supposed to keep doing this?

Keep living like we'll eventually be okay without them, when I never *want* to be okay again.

Now, everything is changing, and I'm tired of being strong. Being silent feels better. We're also both well aware there is nothing we can say that would matter anyway.

We're just here to skate.

B team arrives first, Nancy, Venice, and Bae as if they

rode together, and then K-Otic follows shortly after. None of us know much about K, other than the fact they showed up two years ago, never missed a practice, but never said a word. Their chin length hair is kept slicked back, the same shade of cerulean since the day we met them, never once fading, never a trace of the natural color growing out.

I very much appreciate their presence, especially now that I prefer silence to the sound of voices.

Scottie Crocodile walks through the doors next, donning a tracksuit that has him resembling a mafia boss, a notebook in one hand and his phone squeezed between his ear and his shoulder. He waves without looking in our direction before heading straight for what used to be Lonnie's office. It reminds me to lock the door next time.

Something about him sitting there, acting like he's welcome in Lonnie's space, bothers the absolute hell out of me. My teeth squeak from grinding together.

"You need to skate. *Now*." They're Morgan's first words to me today, and there's no kindness behind them.

It feels like we're all running out of it lately.

But I get the gist: stop obsessing over the awful man that's already making my life a living hell. I can do that; I just need to direct that hate elsewhere.

As if the universe is answering my request, Nia fucking Death walks through the double doors, biting her stupid lip and looking uncomfortable.

"Hi." She waves awkwardly, dark circles beneath her eyes as they scan over the rink, like she's yet to really take it in since her return.

`It's probably exactly the same as the day she left. Lonnie Green wasn't a fan of change, and there had never been a *need* to alter Skateland. But of course, just as I give birth to the thought, men in paint-covered overalls walk in, carrying ladders and painting equipment.

Scott is literally pissing all over us.

So like a man to arrive and, within minutes, demand we change our entire world to suit him, to force that change just to assert the fact that he can.

As he steps out of the office, Scott nudges Nia with his shoulder, gesturing to the painters as they go back and forth a few times in discussion. A weak smile graces her face before she turns away and tosses her bag on the floor to gear up.

"Stare hard enough, and she might feel you finger-banging her with your eyes." Morgan's sarcastic tone comes from behind me, thankfully not loud enough to carry too far.

It doesn't need to, though; it's only meant for me to hear, and that's enough to piss me off. I hit them with a less-than-amused look, and they move quickly, skating backwards and keeping their front to me with their hands raised in defense.

That scrawny thing isn't even my type. I like women who don't need to be looked after, who are strong enough to ask for help but rarely need it. *That* girl oozes insecurities from every single pore in her body, and I'm not even sure she can hold up the weight of her gear without falling over.

To avoid slipping into a worse mood, I skate through the track until I stand in front of Lonnie's door—the door to their apartment. It's a little studio in the back of the rink with no exit to the outdoors and just enough room for Lonnie to get by. A sofa-couch, a table to eat on, and a kitchen to cook out of. I'm pretty sure they showered in the locker rooms.

Reaching over the door and feeling for the key on the

ledge of the trim, I pull it down, wiping the dust from my fingers before inserting it into the keyhole. Stale air hits my nostrils. It's been at least four weeks since anyone's been in here to turn on a fan or open the window that vents out to the track.

There's no sound at all in the little apartment, not a whirring of a fridge or a small sizzle of a light. Everything is turned off. Even their home feels dead now. Lonnie was my best friend. From the minute I arrived in Devil Town, I clung to them, and within days of knowing me, they had thrown a pair of rental skates on my feet and convinced me to join in on a practice.

A natural, Lonnie called me.

They had this incredibly warm, nurturing energy about them, and yet at the same time, they weren't afraid to dish out the truth like it was. There was a gaping hole inside my chest without them, and it felt like I was rotting at the edges, the grief consuming me.

A type of anger that feels so empty, it begs to be filled.

Dust particles float in the air, frozen, suspended in time.

Just like me.

Everything's wrong.

I'm zoned out, staring at a floating speck, and I don't hear her coming. I feel her presence there, looming like she's not sure whether to knock with the door open. I say nothing, don't acknowledge her, though she's certainly hard to ignore.

Just being around her makes me angry. Infuriated. It's not just about the jammer position, though that has a hell of a lot to do with it.

Lonnie trusted her, loved her like family.

I fail to see why, when she wasn't here when it counted.

A few seconds pass, and she comes in anyway. The muffled tapping of her feet on the floor is barely audible with her socks on. It's the sniffling that draws my attention, inevitably forcing me to turn my gaze in her direction.

"Lonnie was my favorite person in this whole world." Her voice is shaky, and her back is to me now. "I would have given anything to say goodbye."

"I would give anything to erase the memory of them dying right before my very eyes." I stand to leave, my discomfort a burn that only increases the longer she's around.

"Just because you don't know me doesn't mean I don't have the right to grieve." The shakiness is gone now, and I turn back, hitting her with one last look before speaking.

"Grieve away then, princess." I gesture to the empty studio apartment, shutting the door behind me as I skate my way back to the track.

Fucking crocodile.

A crew of twenty men in overalls spreads throughout the track, ladders and supplies in hand as they await instructions from their boss. My heart pounds in my chest; I'm suffocating in this anger, in this helplessness, in this all-consuming rage.

Lonnie is gone, and here are the hyenas, gnawing away at the flesh of everything they had stood for, everything they had built. Funny how the right decision can so easily become the wrong one.

Mo skates my way, as if they can see the confusion on my face.

"What the hell is happening?" I ask.

"Boss guy is renovating." They seem excited.

"Not his rink to renovate," I bite back, not hiding the sharpness in my tone.

"*Well then.*" Morgan clears their throat before beginning. "You need to decide whose rink it is. No one's, or *someone's.*"

"Fuck off, Mo." I skate away, tired of feeling like everyone is an enemy.

King Shit whistles for our attention, and by the time I make it to the circle, I realize the entire team is here now. "Good morning, ladies. Thank you for showing up on time," he begins, still looking at his phone, like giving all his attention is more than we deserve. "As you can see, renovations are being made. Nothing drastic, just modernizing and cleaning up the place, bringing it up to code with the century." He laughs, but it feels like a personal dig at Lonnie.

As if he's pointing out that he is able to do in one day what Lonnie couldn't do in years.

"The workers shouldn't be too in the way the next couple of weeks, so pay them no mind, and soon, Slam Nights will look a whole lot busier." He blows that goddamn whistle, and every hair on my arm stands on end, my body fighting the urge to rip it off the chain and shove it down his throat. "Do your thing, Coach."

"Ladders, Devils. Let's go." Mo refrains from the whistle, and thank-shit, because if I hear that thing one more time, I'll lose it.

Our new jammer takes an extra fifteen minutes to join us for drills, but no one seems to mind. She comes out of Lonnie's looking like that had been the funeral she missed. Red, puffy eyes avoiding our stares, she focuses on her feet until she reaches the other end of the track, where she takes her time getting her skates on. Nia joins the pack for warmups, and Mo gathers us on Scott's behalf, passing waivers to each and every skater who completed their speed and skills test.

Standard bullshit. He's not liable if we get hurt, not responsible for our bills, not responsible for shit. Typical. There *is*, however, a fancy little section at the bottom about payment per regional win and bonuses for performance, something none of us have ever seen before.

"Holy shit. We're getting paid?" Lady Yaga beats me to the punch.

It's enough to get every skater clamoring and crowding in a big, excited circle. Too much praise over a man I can't even stomach to look at right now. As I scan the room, there's only one other skater who seems unimpressed, not so easily swayed by words on a piece of paper or the promise of a few dollars.

Nia Da fucking Silva stands on the other side of the crowd of skaters, flipping the paper back and forth, no sight of appeasement on her face, only sorrow. She waits her turn, and when the pen makes its way to her, she signs, uncaringly passing her waiver along with the pen to whoever can get it out of her face as fast as possible.

And then she takes to the bench, sitting down and waiting for what comes next.

Stop watching this fucking chick.

Croc blows the whistle, as if to wrangle my attention to where it needs to go.

I skate past her to grab my water while Mo and our new manager talk between themselves. They hand out scrimmage jerseys, mixing the B team skaters with the A team for practice purposes and separating us, red versus blue.

It feels odd, out of place, every version of fucking weird

to be standing behind the pivot line instead of the jammer line. I thrive in the thrill of the race; I'm obsessed with it, I crave it. I *need* it. But there K-Otic is, the jammer star over their helmet, standing next to Nia-Death with the other.

K-Otic is fast as hell, no doubt about it. I can accept defeat when it comes to skating against them because we're an even match. When we skate against each other, we spend so much time trying to knock the other down that we waste all our energy on strength instead of speed.

Nia is fast, with no bones or weight to hold her as a threat. I'm eager for the next whistle now, borderline giddy with the opportunity to knock this little shrimp down. Maybe then, she'll realize Skateland—no, Devil Town, isn't the place for her after all.

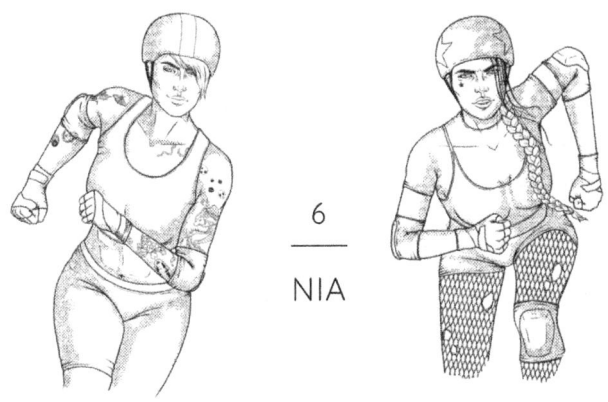

6
NIA

I've become a wretched mess of poorly composed feelings. Spending the night getting high with Ryan Lee was what I thought I needed to get my mind off Lonnie, but the minute I arrived at the rink, it all came flooding back. Every awful emotion penetrates deep and eats away at me from the inside out. Except now, I've burned through all my serotonin, and I don't have the energy to muster an ounce of social demand.

I'm not okay.

A person I loved more than anyone else is gone, and I'll never get to say goodbye.

My thoughts circle in my head like vultures, ready for their next meal—except I'm the meal, my misery their sustenance.

K-Otic slides in next to me, slipping their mouthguard in and rolling their shoulders back to prepare for the jam. They have at least a foot on me, but once they lower their hand to the track, our backs are practically at the same height. Regardless, the only way out of this jam is with speed.

The whistle blows. K-Otic moves to hip check me, but I'm too aware of my surroundings, giving them a three-pass lead to avoid the hit and grabbing Venice Witch's side to get through the wall of blockers. I'm through, but the minute I reach the open track, I feel a slam on my left from Harvey, a sharp pain in my shoulder, and suddenly, I'm thrown from the track, sliding out of play.

Hands on the ground to steady myself, I shake my head to recalibrate before bouncing back on my toe stops and diving into the track again. Just as my feet hit the line, StarScreamer sends K-Otic flying, giving me the time I need to catch up.

We're shoulder to shoulder now, just a few crossovers from the jammer line, and it's as close as it gets. I deepen my squat, damn near sitting on the ground while I skate as low as my center of gravity will allow, keeping me protected in case they try to hit me.

It's inevitable. I'm flying again, my teeth knocking against each other, and though I don't see the hit coming, I sure as shit feel the throbbing in my hip for what it is. I catch a satisfied Harvey in my peripheral, and it's all I need to know she was the one who sent me skidding on my ass through the center of the track. Mo and our new manager watch me with unimpressed looks. Grimacing, I shake it off as Mo blows the whistle and readies for the next jam.

I clench down on my mouth guard, practically piercing a hole through the plastic in frustration. Looking up to see the blonde pivot laughing with StarScreamer as if she hadn't just handed my ass to me is the same as hitting a brick wall of insecurity.

Maybe I'm not wanted here.

Maybe I *should* go.

Or maybe I'm hyper-sensitive from all the pain pills in

my system and overly aware of how out of my element I'm feeling in the only place I ever dared to call home. It's unsettling, staying in a motel when the house my parents once owned is half a mile down the street. Knowing that if I go to the grocery store, a coffee shop, or even the animal clinic I'll likely run into the parents of a friend who died too early from our bad decisions.

A reminder of exactly why I ran with my tail tucked between my legs the first chance I got.

Or perhaps I've just depleted all the good sparks in my brain.

I take my place behind the line, receiving nothing but a chin raise from K-Otic, as if that somehow counts for praise. It kind of does, giving me a little more confidence to not mentally crumble before the whistle sounds again.

I reach for Lady Yaga's hand, going for the whip as a way out of the pack of blockers skating in front of me. No chance of success. Harvey is already there, waiting in a standstill as I hit her from the front, her chest a solid wall knocking every bit of oxygen from my lungs and sending me to the ground.

The whistle blows, and Mo yells, "Take a knee," while I struggle to catch a breath, wheezing through what feels like collapsed lungs from the impact. "Goddamn, Cat. Give the girl a break."

I look up to see her skating circles around me, her gaze locked on mine even as she pulls her mouth guard out to answer. "You want a pivot, or you want me to let her win?"

"She's not wrong," our manager agrees, blowing the whistle again. "Harvey, sub for Nia until she's ready to go again." He turns to Mo. "Stand in for pivot until the rest of the girls pass their test."

I couldn't disagree, every bit of my chest aching and

begging for a break. I slip the star from my helmet and hand it to Mo, who makes the switch with Harvey while I drag my body from the track, crawling backwards until I find a wall to lean on. I make myself content with watching, realizing I've yet to examine the way this new version of the team skates.

Harvey is fast, making it easy to sympathize with her annoyance at losing her place. But she's not just fast, she's strong, and by the way K-Otic exhausts themselves jam after jam, it's clear she's nearly impossible to knock down. She's the perfect pivot, despite her feeling like I'm taking something from her. She just hasn't been utilized this way yet to see for herself.

If I'm not jammer, I'm nothing.

A weak girl with weak bones and a bunch of pins in her leg from the last time she got hit too hard.

I've been that girl for the last five years, and I'm ready to move on from the fear of getting hurt again, to get past the sight of my broken bones when I close my eyes and see visions of that memory.

FIVE YEARS AGO

The announcer's overly alert voice came through the speakers. "Nia-Death Experience passes Tonna Hips, but Reese Ender checks and—oh! That's a stumble, but she recovers, nearly tripping over the still-fallen Britney Fears. Can we get a medic on the track?"

It was a joke, but he was distracting as hell, and I was feeling that last slam. Reese Ender was a heavy hitter, and I knew I'd be black and blue before the morning. Worst of all, it was extra hot on the track tonight with all the lights set up for the film crew. They were televising this for some streaming special on the TvFlix, and our rink parent, Lonnie, was seeing dollar signs from the prospect of fame, enthralled by the idea of people coming to Devil Town to watch us play and spend their hard-earned money at Skateland.

Sweat dripped between my breasts, and my fishnets itched under my shorts at the thought of every person I knew watching, but I pumped my thighs with every ounce of energy left in me. I moved, one foot in front of the other, crossing over as I circled the track, fifteen feet away from stealing the win from the Wolverine Dreams Roller Derby team.

"Nia! Nia! Nia!" the crowd shouted to my right as I circled the track.

I lifted my fingers in the air, raising them to my head to perform a two finger salute—a little show of cockiness—as I crossed the jammer line.

I felt my brain rattle inside of my head before I'd even noticed my skates weren't on the ground anymore. My teeth clanked painfully inside my mouth, my tongue splitting from the blunt force of my canines tearing through my mouthguard and my flesh. Liquid iron pooled at my gums. Simultaneously, my back hit the floor, a sick crunch beneath me raging through my body in an agonizing wave of pain.

"Oh sh—" The announcer's microphone was still on.

"Take a knee." Lonnie's voice boomed through the crowd, and it went silent around me.

"Call an ambulance," I heard not far off in the distance.

I blinked my eyes open to see Reese Ender standing above me, a ghost-white expression painted over her face.

"Her leg," she said, a retching sound coming from another direction just as my eyes flickered closed once more.

I was in a wheelchair for seven months. It took four surgeries and almost a whole year to learn how to walk again.

While I refuse to let my fears command me, I can't deny that I'm a much more anxious skater now. It's impossible not to be extra vigilant, being always on the lookout for the possibility of getting hurt. I see them everywhere now. My brain works harder than before to recognize the patterns, as if they were tiny moments of premonition, alerting me to the possibility of pain.

Precognition induced from trauma.

My self-diagnosis reminds me I'm not my mother, that I don't need to define every little thing that's wrong with me.

They go a few more jams before I finally feel okay to rejoin the pack, forcing Harvey to pass me the star and take her place as pivot again. I don't miss her look of disdain as she's made to give up the position, but I do recognize the work she's put in. It's practically unfair, the way she completely exhausted K-Otic and made them much easier to outskate.

The jammer I can handle, but either Scott and Mo are setting me up on purpose, or they don't see the unfairness of pitting Harvey up against me round after round. With her targeting me, I can hardly get through the pack, let alone lap K-Otic, without getting hit.

I'm getting crushed between Harvey and Nancy Shrew when one of their wheels grind against mine, causing me to fall forward.

Overwhelmed with frustration to the brink of exploding, I do my best to contain my emotions on the track, to avoid taking it personally.

It's nothing but personal, though.

If this was your home, you'd know Lonnie Green is dead.

The truth of that statement is painfully uncomfortable. It stabs at parts of me that have been hiding for so long, I swear they no longer exist. Bouncing back on my skates, I struggle to catch up, but right at the last minute, I feel

DreadPool's hands on my hips, sending me flying forward, helping me take my first win for the night.

Mo blows the whistle, and I practically jump into DreadPool's arms, not caring that we've barely exchanged two words. Comradery is the only bridge you need sometimes. They lift me into the air, my skates coming off the ground as she squeezes me into a hug. I feel the heat of a stare, following the thread of the sensation to find Harvey's eyes locking onto us.

It wasn't much to anyone else, but it was *everything* to me.

My first win in five years.

Just like that, my first practice is over, and I know now more than ever that I was meant to come back. Coming home was part of my path, my journey to figure out whoever the fuck I am.

Not my injuries, not my trauma, not who my parents want me to be.

Me. Behind all that shit.

Living for me.

7

HARVEY

He's still going to start her. Unbelievable. She has no center of gravity, no muscle to hold her up, and the only way for her to win a jam is if the other team is somehow severely injured.

Bullshit.

Scott is punishing me for not smiling and playing along with his power trips. I'm not here to coddle a grown man's ego. I'm here to skate. With the announcement of this weekend's Slam Night roster, I storm off the track into the locker room. Should I be grateful that I'm skating at all? That I'm starting pivot?

It's impossible to feel that way when all I see is the opaque, blistering hate for these changes forced into my life. It's not like I'm some immovable force, unwilling to adapt and change. It's the opposite. I've been constantly molding and remolding myself to fit the circumstances of my life, an exhausting feat, for over two decades. When I moved to Devil Town four years ago, I was sure that things were changing, that being somewhere small and quiet would ease the internal noise disruption, soothe the need for chaos.

It worked for a while, but ever since Lonnie's death, this place has become a prison, and now more than ever, it feels like everyone and everything is working against me. I've never been a violent person. Angry? Sure. Physically capable of putting my hands on someone? Never.

But this girl?

This girl makes me see red.

Every time I think about the fact that Lonnie is gone and she is here, it drives me beyond reason. I throw my dirty clothes into my gym bag, not bothering to wait for the shower to turn hot before stepping in. The cold water is a startling shock, a welcome sensation against my hot skin.

Antônia was practically my baby, Lonnie would say with pride anytime a skater brought up the fact that *the* Nia-Death Experience had come from Skateland. *You would have loved her, Cat.*

Yeah. Sure. If this is love, then I can't imagine how it feels to hate her.

Clenching my fists tightly and pressing my knuckles against the cold tile of the stall as the water beats down against my skin, I wish for a dead person to come back to life. A light tapping comes from just outside my stall.

"What?" I ask, turning the water off and wrapping myself in a towel.

"You okay, Harvey?" D-Stroya's voice is quiet and meek, reminding me her confidence is likely shattered after being one of the few skaters to not pass their skills test.

She's still a Devil's Dame. It doesn't matter what Scott tries to claim. You can't take away the family we built here with something as trivial as a speed test. Still, it doesn't make it any less painful that she won't be rostered or even benched during a bout. The most she can contribute will be working merch or concession.

It suddenly makes my anger seem minimal.

"Are you?" I ask with a sigh, drying myself off as she slumps onto a bench.

"I'll be okay." She tucks a few loose locs behind her ear. "Scott's letting me test again next practice." D drops to her back, staring blankly at the ceiling while I slip on my underwear and then gym shorts over them.

"You'll pass," I assure her. Deandra's one of my longest friends on this team; skating without her wouldn't just be weird. It wasn't right.

"And if I don't, I'll be okay." She gives me a sad smile that makes me question how much of that is true and how much of it is her trying to convince herself.

I slip over my head a green Celtics basketball jersey over my sports bra before giving her a *you're full of it* look.

"I mean it, Cat. I'm turning forty-five this year. I've been skating for over a decade now. I was here when Lonnie bought this place, when Nia broke her leg. I was here the first time *you* fell on your ass." Her eyes well with tears, and she shakes her head. "I don't think I can stick around for any more changes."

"If you give me some kind of 'I'm too old to keep skating' bullshit, I'll drag you to the rink for the next ten years myself, D," I deadpan, throwing her my flattest expression and reaching for the towel to dry my hair off.

"It's not that. I'm just at a point in my life where I crave predictability. I open the boutique every day at nine, close it at four, go home to my husband and kid, and three times a week, I come here to kick ass with you bitches." She sighs. "The money, the promises of glory, the *Scott*," she emphasizes with a snort, "that's not for me."

"You said you were testing again, so why does it sound like you're already giving up?" I drop the towel into my bag, zipping up the rest of my shit with no method or reason.

"Maybe I am. I just figured you deserve to know. You're one of my best friends."

Skaters trickle into the locker room, as if practice is just *now* officially over.

I'm sure the crocodile will have something to say about me checking out early.

He can fuck right off.

"That means I'm the last person you've told, doesn't it?" I raise a suspicious eyebrow, trying to temper my mood, because I can't risk directing it at D right at this second.

"You've been off the last couple days. I didn't want to add to your list of problems." She bites her lip, her gaze looking over at Nia coming into the locker room, all smiles and laughter as she chats with DreadPool.

I can't help but blurt out, "Does *she* know?"

D frowns. "Yes. Nia is *also* one of my oldest friends. She held my daughter when she was born, Cat."

I slam my locker shut, a few skaters flinching from the noise and pausing their casual conversations. "That's actually why I was hoping to talk to you before everybody got here." Her voice gets quieter. "Whatever you're dealing with, it isn't Nia's fault."

"Are you kidding me right now, Deandra?" I'm not about to sit through this.

"Stop." She pushes at my chest, keeping me from walking away. "If Lonnie was here, they'd be handing it to you right now. I'm happy to do it in their stead." Her voice sharpens, no longer quiet and meek, but laced with authority. "You either look out for that girl like she's family, or you're going to find yourself alone in Skateland, Harvey."

The look she gives me is cold, a warning that chills me from the inside before she turns on her heels and walks out of the locker room. I feel a stare itching in my peripheral, turning my gaze just slightly to see Nia looking at me from across the locker room.

She couldn't have heard what D said, but I'm just as annoyed as if she had.

"Jesus Christ, is that from today?" DreadPool's voice grabs her attention, swinging my gaze over to where they're inspecting Nia's already-bruising hip.

"Oh. Yeah." She gives an awkward laugh. "I bruise easily."

"Harvey also hits like an MMA fighter. You're going to be purple all over tomorrow." Dreadpool laughs, slapping her on the ass before sauntering over to the shower stalls.

There's a glint of annoyance creeping up, but I shake it off.

"Learn to take a hit." I shrug, picking up my duffel bag and throwing it over my shoulder.

"I can take a hit just fine when I'm not being bullied," she murmurs.

"Excuse me?" I drop my bag to the ground once again and turn to fully face her.

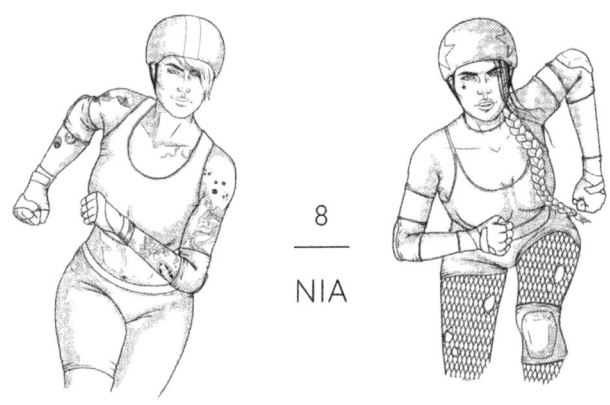

8
NIA

"Are you mad that I'm a better skater, or that I'm easier to like than you?"

A gasp to my side and a few murmurs tell me I might have gone too far.

I can't hold it back anymore, though. Being backed into a corner, pushed until there's nothing I can do but go to that terrible place inside me and reach for something cruel, a skill I inherited from my mother, honed with time under the cruelty of her steel tongue.

Nonetheless, it's a skill I both take pride in and am ashamed of.

"Everyone out." Her nostrils flare wide with rage, not a single person bothering to challenge her request, as if she owns the fucking building. In a few seconds, the entire locker room clears out.

"What, it's okay when you insult me, but if I finally bite back, you want it in private?" I scoff, tired of taking this girl's shit.

She licks her lower lip, walking toward me with hard,

narrowed eyes. She steps, I move back. Another step, I mimic again. We continue the dance until my back slams against the metal locker.

"I get it, you have a problem with me. I took your spot. I'm faster than you. I knew Lonnie in a way you *never* will, and that bothers you. But that isn't my problem, and I'm not afraid of you, Harvey." I exhale it all out so fast, there's no way it's convincing.

Maybe I *am* afraid of her.

She huffs out in amusement, like she doesn't believe me either, a crooked smirk gracing her face. "Is that so, princess?"

Her left hand slams the metal behind me, just inches from my face. I gasp, too startled to mask my surprise, but I'm prepared when the right hand repeats the action, locking me in place between her arms.

"You don't scare me." I don't dare break eye contact, watching as her gaze softens and her eyebrows lift in amusement.

"Hmm," she hums closely in my ear, the hairs on the back of my neck all coming to stand.

She's fucking with me.

I can play chicken. I can play chicken *really* damn well.

Just barely enough room between us, I grab at the waist of my spandex shorts, shimming out of the material that's nearly damp with sweat. Just a slight movement of her eyelids, but she regains control, not yet daring to move. Fingers gripping at the hem of my practice shirt, I lift the fabric up and then over my head, dropping it to the ground between us.

Her gaze betrays her, but just as quickly, she corrects her expression, laying on that mask of indifference once again. It's only when I shimmy out of the fishnet stockings that I'm granted enough space to move by her, and with the next movement, I undo the front clasp of my sports bra.

"I need to shower." Each word is sharp as I push them out through clenched teeth. "Move."

Her hands fall, and with them, so does her gaze.

I lean forward, and she backs away, giving me the space I need to walk toward the showers, where I remove my final piece of clothing. Dropping my underwear to my feet, I turn the knob, waiting for the water to become warm before stepping inside.

I still feel the heat of her stare behind me, overwhelming and nearly suffocating, but I don't turn to face her. Closing the shower curtain of my stall, I make do with a bar of soap, the only thing I managed to bring with me while my heart was too busy hammering from the adrenaline of the confrontation.

Did I just do that?

Never the kind to speak up, always the doormat. Always accepting the conditions of my life for what they are and leaping over every hurdle thrown my way as if it was custom built for me. That is the reality of being raised by immigrant parents. *Blend in. Don't let them notice you.*

Well, fuck that.

She notices me now.

The heat of the shower is enough to settle the brutal pumping of my pulse, and when I've dried myself off, I see the rest of the skaters have made their way back inside. They're continuing on in the locker room with their after practice routines as if Harvey hadn't kicked them out, as if there's no sort of lingering weirdness or humiliation for me to mull over.

Was it just in my own head?

I'm already clothed and brushing my wet hair into a single braid to the side when I hear a husky voice behind me. "Hey, uh… Nia, right?"

"Antônia," I correct before I turn around, finally having reached a point in my life where claiming the power of my name in its entirety feels healing instead of triggering.

I stare up at piercing blue eyes and matching hair. K-Otic is already dressed in fitted jeans with classic low tops and a gray v-neck, though I can't recall having seen them inside the locker room. Their hair is wet, framing their face instead of slicked back like I'd seen before.

"Cool." They look me up and down with an awkwardness that triumphs my own but somehow seems entirely attractive on them, almost purposeful. Resting their forearm on the lockers and leaning over me, their voice comes out almost like a hushed sound. "I'm Kade."

"Hi." It bubbles out of me like an awkward laugh. I never know the right way to respond to someone introducing themselves when they already know my name. I rush out the easiest brain garbage fact to pull from my head. "You're fast."

"Yeah," they acknowledge, taking it just as a statement of fact and having no issue with it being a single sentence on its own. "Wanna grab a drink?"

"That sounds great, actually." My eyes can't help but glance over to where Harvey stood at her locker.

She's long gone now, surely, but there's an uneasy feeling lingering of something being wrong. It only takes me a few more minutes to gather my things into my bag, but Kade has no problem waiting.

They open the door, and as we step out into the rink, I

hear DreadPool's voice. "I was gonna ask her out, but K beat me to it."

I follow the sound of their voice to where they stand in front of Lonnie's office, talking to someone out of sight.

"You heard K talk?" Harvey's voice is full of surprise, though I still can't see her. We walk toward the entrance where the two are talking about *us*. I can only imagine what her face looks like, but I avoid it like it's my job.

"To her, yeah." Just as DreadPool says it, we walk past them, Kade not bothering to spare a glance to their side as they push open the door and hold it for me.

They practically rip my duffel out of my hand, grabbing the passenger side door of their car before throwing my bag inside the trunk.

"Oh, I drove." I point back at my car.

"You shouldn't drive drunk." Kade stands at my side, as if waiting for me to make a decision so they can shut the passenger side door. My bag is already firmly secured in the back of their Mustang.

I'm stammering, not a coherent response that can be translated into any meaningful sentence in my head.

"I'll bring you back to your car in the morning," Kade says with a chuckle, not letting me overthink and making the decision for me.

"Okay," I sing, trying to mask my chronic anxiety but genuinely grateful to not be burdened with the paralysis that often comes with choices.

I'm only slightly surprised when we pull up to a red-brick townhouse just minutes from downtown. I can't help but wonder what they do for a living to be able to afford rent so close to the heart of Devil Town.

"I need to feed my cat first. There are a few bars in walking distance," they say, but I'm well aware.

"I know." I present it as fact, not as superiority.

I catch a smirk from just a sliver of their face. "You're from here, right?"

"Yup. Spent my whole life in this place before college." My fingers tuck into the fabric of my pockets awkwardly. "What about you?"

"I moved here two years ago. Didn't really mean to." They shrug, opening the front door to their house.

A cat nearly the size of a golden retriever greets us, their fur dramatic like a lion and a beautiful charcoal gray.

"Oh my God. I'm in love." I drop to my knees, and the kitty doesn't hesitate, brushing up against me and nudging me with their head.

"That's Tolkien." Kade introduces us, the name quite fitting for such a majestic creature.

"How did I ever live without you, sweet kitty?" I'm on the ground now, fully embracing my cat lady moment and letting a forty pound cat make biscuits on my chest.

He runs off once he hears Kade pouring food into his bowl, and I'm equal parts disappointed and relieved to not look so insanely obsessed. "Did you say you didn't mean to move to Devil Town?" I backtrack to our earlier conversation.

Kade scratches the back of their head, scrunching their nose in thought. "It wasn't supposed to be permanent. My aunt died and left me on her estate, and when I came to clean up and sell the house, I realized it was probably going to be my only shot at owning property in this lifetime. Devil Town's cost of living is manageable, so I went back to Maine for my shit and made this place home."

Had I been drinking something, I would've spit it out. "You moved from Maine to Devil Town? Incredible." I laugh, shaking my head.

And then I remember that my parents immigrated from an entirely different continent… for *Devil Town*. Well, the research facility at the edge of town, but the point remained the same.

"It's not that bad here." They shrug. "But I get it. I'd only been here a handful of times to visit my aunt. You grew up here—hometown blues and shit."

"Something like that," I agree, deciding for once not to trauma dump and word vomit my entire twenty-two year history with this town.

The truth is, this place is the cemetery that holds every mistake I made. This town is made from the bones of all my traumas and injuries and they're somehow all locked in a coffin that had once been metaphorical, but now, with Lonnie gone, seems far too real.

"You okay?" Kade asks, as if my face reflects how I feel.

I nod, searching for comfort in any way possible and giving the cat another head scratch as he eats from his bowl.

"I have to confess why I asked you out." Their tone sobers as they sit on a blue suede couch.

I tilt my head in curiosity.

"I've been…" Kade starts fidgeting with their fingers as they avoid my gaze. "I've been really lost since Lonnie. I know you really knew them well and… I just… I don't know. You showed up, and being close to you is kind of like being close to them again. That probably doesn't make sense." They finally look up, tears streaming down their eyes. "I lost my sister not even two years ago, and now Lonnie. It isn't fair."

"Kade." It's barely a whisper as I sit down, embracing them in a tight squeeze. K drops their head to my chest, a hearty sob exploding as they shake in my hold.

Grief is like that.

It can be the sticky glue that holds us together as much as it can be a searing hot knife that divides.

9
HARVEY

I'm only ten minutes late to my shift when I clock in, but it doesn't matter. Nobody here gives a fuck, just as long as the bar is prepped before the rush starts. Freddy's is the only bar in town with a pool table and arcade machines, which means anyone drinking ends up here at some point in the night.

By nine, I've already got all my garnishes cut and separated, my glasses cleaned and cooling in the fridge. I'm zoned out, listening to one of my usuals tell a story about his wife's casserole, when the bar starts filling up. That's when I see them.

It's never unusual to see my skate family here. In fact, it usually makes my nights better, because it means I can get away with fucking off and drinking with them. What I don't expect is to see K-Otic pulling Nia-Death by the hand as they look for a table in my bar.

She's all smiles until her eyes drift to where I stand. She stumbles back, freezing in place before K gets her attention and pulls her toward a table. Nia's head turns, her gaze staying locked on mine until they take a seat. She shakes her head like she's trying to clear me from her thoughts, and it's only slightly amusing.

Because same.

Somewhere, in another life, maybe one where we hadn't lost Lonnie, their presence might have bridged the gap. Maybe Lonnie *was* right. Maybe Nia and I would have been best fucking friends if they were still here, maybe even more.

But all I feel now is that ball of hatred deep in my chest, and it only grows the more she's around.

It seems like lately, she's always around.

"I need three Old Fashioneds," Freddy calls from his end of the bar.

It's going to be a long night.

I pour the whiskey, the majority of my attention still on the girl with the pink-tipped braid. They've barely sat when she gets up for the bathroom, and K comes my way.

"Harvey." They keep their voice low, hard to hear, even though it's a crowded room.

I'm bothered in every sense of the word. Annoyed, frustrated, angry, downright itchy in my own skin, and her showing up to my place of work doesn't make it any better. But none of this has to do with K. I'm not about to take it out on them.

"K." I tilt my chin up. "What are you having?"

"The Lost Thirty on draught." They turn their gaze to the bathrooms where Nia disappeared to. "And a Whiskey Sour."

I pour the beer and then measure out the whiskey into the shaker, the simple syrup, the lemon juice, the egg white. K-Otic is still staring at the bathroom door, and I'm shaking the contents of the cocktail, both of us desperate to avoid small talk.

They're paying for the drinks by the time Nia comes out, not bothering to stop at the bar and going directly to her table.

The hour moves at a glacial pace.

It's Wednesday, so there's maybe four other people at the bar, which makes it impossible for me to delve into my usual pastime of people watching when I'm actively trying to avoid one of said persons.

But she's loud, hard to ignore, and Freddy doesn't have the music turned up nearly high enough for me to even pretend to be enjoying it. She gushes over how fast K is and emphasizes that they'd likely outskate her even if she *wasn't* taking hits. I don't agree with the sentiment.

Here I've been, expecting some cocky little has-been, someone who thinks the world should get on their knees for her and grovel at her presence. Instead… She's insecure.

That's not the girl Lonnie painted a picture of.

The basketball game comes on, and a few more people enter the bar, right on schedule. I keep busy, making drinks, avoiding eye contact and the burning need to stare at the table to my left where the two sit, casually talking. I'm serving Cosmos to a few nurses from the ER who just wrapped up a shift when I catch Nia standing at my peripheral.

I fight the urge to turn my head, knowing she's likely headed to the bathroom again.

K stands and orders two more of the same drinks for them, this time bringing their phone with them and scrolling to avoid conversation. But it's almost half time, and an older guy bids for their attention, not taking the clue and asking about the game.

"I don't know anything about basketball." K shrugs the

man off their arm, grabbing both the drinks before heading back to the table.

It takes Nia a few more minutes to return from the bathroom, her eyes catching mine for just a brief moment before she sits down, this time next to K instead of across from them. The rest of the game passes, though neither of them looks up at the television the entire night.

They order cheese fries and mini sliders while I pretend to not give a fuck.

I don't even know *why* I give a fuck, but I give *so* many fucks.

The sooner she leaves, the faster I'll feel better. I won't have to see her until Friday, and maybe by then, I'll be able to figure out how to rein in all this anger.

She's on her fourth bathroom break in an hour while K still contently sips on a wheat beer, not a drop of suspicion on their face.

"Cover me?" I nudge Freddy, who nods but doesn't put down his phone.

It's a one person bathroom, but we've got three of them. The other two have their doors wide open, so I'm not even guessing when I rap my knuckles against the door.

"Hold on," she says nervously, but I knock again.

I hear the toilet flush and a soft *damnit* from inside before the handle jiggles. Nia swings the door open, eyes going wide with alarm at the sight of me standing in front of her. She stutters something incoherent before trying to walk around me, but I'm doing my best to take up all the space at the threshold, moving to my left when she goes right and blocking her from leaving.

"W-what are you doing?" she stammers, nervously stepping back as I walk her into the bathroom again.

"What are *you* doing?" I ask with a crooked smirk, shutting the door behind me.

"I'm using the bathroom." She frowns, doing her best to make the lie believable.

"For the fourth time tonight?" I cluck my tongue as I check my watch, like it even means anything. "Try again, princess."

"I am!" She's visibly flustered now, trying to push me out of the way.

I grab her wrist, forcing her to face me, and when her body slams against mine, I'm able to see the little bag in her pocket.

Not what I'm expecting.

I still have her wrist in hand, her chest pressed to mine and a lethal smirk on my face, when K-Otic enters the bathroom with us.

"Everything good here?" they check, bouncing their eyes between us.

"Is it?" My lip can't help curling at the realization that I have something on her.

"It is." She shakes her arm, and I let go of her wrist.

"I need another beer," K says without looking at me, their gaze locked on Nia.

I turn, returning to the bar, the little bag of pills safely tucked into my own pocket.

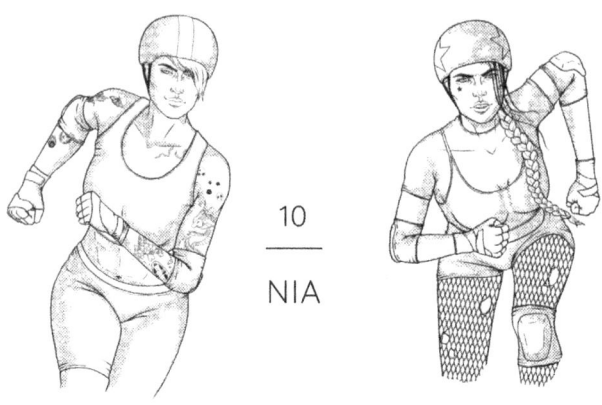

10

NIA

"You sure you're good?" Kade asks, eyeing me suspiciously, their gaze stuck where Harvey had gripped my wrist.

I nod, wiping it on my pants as if that could somehow rub off the redness on my skin. "She doesn't like me."

They chuckle. "No shit." Hands find their way to the small of my back as they shepherd me to our table. "She'll get over it."

If Kade can work like Harvey repellent this easily, I'm finding myself to be quite fond of them. But it isn't just the way they're able to nonchalantly disregard Harvey's hatred or anger toward me—it's also in the way they spent the night listening to every word out of my mouth as if they were worth listening to, in the way they didn't judge me when the topic of my mother came up and I immediately started crying, which then forced me to go to the bathroom to numb the parts of me that could feel too much.

When I decided to come back to Devil Town, my biggest fear was coming home to find everyone I loved gone. To my surprise, I still have many friends. And here, with Kade, I'm proving I'm still capable of making new ones, something I abandoned trying long ago.

With my head swimming from the painkillers and nearly three full cocktails, I hesitate once we get to our table.

"You wanna get out of here?" Kade notices, stopping me from sitting.

"It's probably for the best. I don't know that I should be in her space," I confess, feeling every kind of awkward at having invaded the place she worked, knowing she couldn't stand me.

"Sounds tough for Cat Harvey. Devil Town only has so many bars," Kade chuckles. "I'll go pay the tab if you want to wait outside."

I want to argue and maybe fight for the bill, but the thought of going up to the bar and having a one-on-one with Harvey again makes acid crawl up my throat. I'm leaning against the brick wall when it hits me just how sloshed I am.

Taking a deep breath in an attempt to clear the fog, I realize it will do me no good. I'm fucked up, and the dizziness is permanent. I don't make a habit of drinking to the point of throwing up, but I overlooked my threshold with narcotics included.

A wave of nausea sweeps over me, and I run, leaning over the nearest planter, throwing up cheese fries and whiskey across the freshly sprouting tulips. I instantly feel better, despite the world still spinning all around me. I wipe my mouth with the back of my sweater, returning to my place by the door when Kade comes out of the bar, sticking their arm out in a silent bid for me to take it.

We're only two blocks from their place, and though there isn't much in Devil Town, Kade's house would be considered prime real estate. There's a lot that wasn't here when I left five years ago—a gourmet coffee shop, a pottery studio, and some other blurry things I can't make out in the dark.

"Oh, I got you," Kade says, catching me from behind as I trip over my own feet.

"Sorry." Laughing, I cling to them a little harder as we walk back to their place.

"What are your plans? Long term?" they ask.

It's quite possibly the worst time for this kind of conversation, but I've fought through worse.

"I don't know. Get a shitty job until I can get a better job. Crash at StarScreamer's until I get a place. Maybe not in that order." I laugh awkwardly as we reach their door.

"Stay with me." They gesture inside with their head, the proposition seeming more than just for the night like we'd originally agreed.

"That's a bit forward, don't you think?" I ask, doing what I always do best and making a joke out of what I can't fully understand.

"I don't want to fuck you, Nia. I want to help you. You're cute, but you aren't my type." Kade winks, shutting the door behind me once I've committed to entering.

I'm only slightly offended at their bluntness but also fully aware that I've misread dates my entire life. I am not the queen of social cues. Kade is good looking, *really* good looking, but the minute I held them in my arms, I knew they'd been sent to me by Lonnie.

Platonic love is so often overlooked when we try to force it into something more.

Platonic love is healing.

I have friends here, *old* friends, who I love dearly with my entire heart but who also haven't grasped the complexities behind all the changes I've gone through in the last five years.

I'm not the same Nia who left Devil Town broken.

If anything, I may be a little *more* broken.

"Seriously. I have a spare room, and there's no mortgage because it's paid off. As long as you're not a slob or on drugs, I think this will work. You can help with the utilities every now and then." They give me a genuine smile, their teeth sparkling white. "If not, we reevaluate in a couple of weeks."

"Oh God, I don't know if I can handle the stress of a roommate probation review," I try to joke again, catching a grin from Kade.

The rest of the night is easy. I spend it cuddling with Tolkien on the couch and using the giant cat as a blanket. K picks an old *Transformers* movie, but my eyes betray me and fight for sleep before we get to the part where Megan Fox is doing *hot girl over the hood*. I no longer have it in me to fight sleep.

I WAKE UP ON THE COUCH, SOBER. MY MOUTH DRY AND MY head pounding, but I'm sober, my least favorite feeling as of late. Tolkien is still faithfully beside me, as if he can sense my need for company, but Kade has been in their own bed since the first sign of me nodding off.

The previous night was all spins, but I still remember most of it, even the terrifyingly awkward confrontation with Harvey. Kade's offer lingers in my mind. Staying at the motel isn't a long term option, and my next best bet will be crashing at Star's house with her *mom*. I can't drop my baggage at her doorstep like this.

I'm far too deep into this downward spiral, and I gotta see it all the way through.

Minimal rent. A roommate I can get along with.

This could work.

Optimism flows through my veins, and like a bloodhound whose specialty is seeking out my happiness to devour, my mother violates the boundaries I've set. Her name glows on my phone, and I let it vibrate, deciding whether I'm going to entertain her this time.

It's too early for this shit, so I toss the phone into a crack between the cushions.

I stretch, spreading my limbs and each of my toes, letting out a little squeal before sitting up on the couch. K comes out of their room, half their face covered by a mess of blue hair, but they muster a wave as they walk past me to the fridge.

"Good morning," I chirp, not feeling nearly as shitty as I should before remembering I threw up at least two of those drinks last night.

"Coffee?" Kade asks, holding up the empty pot.

I think about it, humming out loud while I try to decide. "Hmm, yes. I'll have coffee with you."

They prep the machine, filling the filter with some well-ground coffee in a fancy black and gold bag I don't recognize. I reach my hand out in a silent bid to pass it my way.

"Smells good." It's only a partial lie; my nose is fucked. Snorting this many pills isn't sustainable, and my sinuses are starting to feel it.

I lean over the kitchen island, awkwardly fingering the veins of the marble on the counter.

"Did you think about my offer?" they ask, sitting across from me.

"I did." I linger on the pause. "Why are you helping me?"

"Lonnie would have wanted me to." They don't hesitate to say it.

"You don't have to do that." I shake my head, unsure if it's enough reason for me to do something as drastic as moving into their house.

"They'd give you a very stern talking to for trying to reject my help." Kade smirks, walking over to the cabinet and pulling two mugs from the middle shelf.

One says *I'm mad at the government* and has a picture of a frog on it, and the other says *Don't talk to me until I've eaten this mug*. I'm not sure I understand either of them, but they make me laugh, and laughing sober is a guilt-ridden reminder that happiness is not for those grieving.

"How do you take it?" they ask, pouring the fresh pot of coffee into both cups.

"Straight to the face and I prefer it if it hurts a little." I blurt out, an amused snort from K before I translate, "Black, a little sugar."

"Psycho." They grin, passing me the frog mug and then the box of raw sugar packets.

They're grabbing oat milk out of the fridge when I decide to finally answer. "Yes."

"Hmm?" K looks back at me, stirring the beige liquid in their mug.

"I'll take the room." I smile, sipping my coffee.

It's really good—rich, bold, and smooth, with notes of chocolate that aren't muted from roasting.

"Don't let me twist your arm." Their sarcasm is familiar and welcome.

"Lonnie and I used to do this all the time," I say between sips, a stuttered inhale settling in my chest to prevent my voice from breaking.

"What? Coffee?" they ask, looking down awkwardly at their mug now.

"Yeah, but usually in the afternoon. Cafezinho. Brazilian coffee time." I stare off to the side, like my brain finds comfort in recalling the memory by focusing on the moving hands of the kitchen clock. "I'd bring my mom's frozen cheese bread balls, and we'd bake them, spending the afternoon chatting away."

"At least if it's going to hurt, it's over someone worth hurting for," Kade says, their eyes stuck on the clock as well.

"Amen or something," I reply, raising my coffee up to cheer them.

11

HARVEY

It's Friday, minutes before practice, and I'm sitting in my car, Nia's little bag of pills in one hand and my phone in the other, search engine results on my browser for what they may be. Some generic painkillers. The little Ziploc baggie tells me it's not a doctor giving these to her, though.

I have two options: I can be a narc and run inside the rink right now with the evidence in my hand that Nia is violating the contract she signed just days prior guaranteeing drug-free players.

Or, I keep my leverage.

And I *do* love a long game.

Plus, I don't trust this reptile of a man for shit, and between the two of them, I'm smart enough to lean toward the smallest of the threats here. As it stands, that's Nia.

I'm not a snitch anyway.

I pocket the pills just as K pulls into the parking lot, stopping their car just three spots away from mine. Inside their mustang is Nia, sitting in the passenger seat.

Have they been together since Wednesday? The thought

crosses my mind before I can try to swat it away. It shouldn't bother me, but for some reason, it burrows under my skin, taking root. K-Otic opens the door for her, but she looks over at me, saying something with a smile that forces them to walk on without her.

Once K is inside the rink, Nia turns to my car and stares straight at me from the passenger side window. She flares her nostrils before pulling the door open, but it sticks, the damn thing broken for nearly two years now. I reach over, opening it from the inside and allowing her into my space.

"You have something of mine," she says, closing the door behind her.

I try to contain my amusement, "Do I now?" I'm a little surprised that she's not denying it or begging me to keep her secret.

"Yes. You do." Her face is flat and her palm is sticking up, waiting for me.

I lick my bottom lip, choosing my next words very carefully.

"And what are you gonna do for it, princess?

She climbs over the middle console faster than the words are out of my mouth, straddling my lap, somehow squeezing in what little space is between me and the wheel. Her chest is pressed to mine, her face just an inch away from reach. She smells like summer, like berries and sunshine, and I want to know how soft her skin would feel against mine.

I clear the thought out of my head immediately.

"What's your problem, Kitty Cat?" she asks, her eyes narrowing in amusement.

The nickname both enrages and sparks something inside me. I place my hands on either side of her hips and try to lift her off, but with so little space to move, she has the upper hand.

"Give me my shit," she demands, patting at my pockets.

"What shit?" I taunt, her hand moving from my sweatpants to the chest pocket on my flannel where said baggie resides, but I clasp my fingers around her wrist, locking it in place.

"Let me go," she grits out.

"Nah." I grin, leaning in closer. "I have you right where I want you." I unbuckle my seatbelt, running my tongue along the edges of my top teeth.

She's startled by the motion, pulling away, her eyes going wide like she's not expecting it from me. Nia tries to break from my grip, but I'm stronger, and with the other hand, she attempts to reach into the chest pocket once more. My left hand locks the other one in the air as well, and now I'm in full control.

"Harvey!" She grunts my name in frustration, but I think I like the way it sounds coming from her lips.

"Say my name like that again." I lift my hips up, forcing her to fall onto me.

"I can't tell if you hate me or if you wanna fuck me." She says it with little emotion, like neither sounds appealing to her.

Is her little flirting game unintentional?

The locker room, the straddling my lap, the awkward glances?

"Definitely hate," I confirm, in case it isn't clear.

"Pity. I need a pivot I can trust to have my back." She pulls her wrists with a sharp jerk, freeing them from my hold before she climbs off me.

It stings more than it should, and it's from the sheer fact that she's using Lonnie's words against me.

The stripe and the star have to be impenetrable. The pivot should always be on the offensive, but the jammer should always trust that the pivot will have their back.

Back then, Mo was my pivot, and I never stopped to think how often my wins had been a credit to them, to the way they were both my shield and my sword.

Suddenly, my satisfaction sours. I fish the bag out of my pocket and toss it in her lap. Looking down, she closes her fist around it before she reaches for the handle. It doesn't open. Nia tries again and grunts in frustration when, the third time, it still stays stuck. I reach over her, grabbing the handle and pulling it up before pushing it out.

"It sticks," I explain, but she just gives me blank eyes before getting out.

The clock in my car says five till five. An hour and a half of practice, then at six-thirty, I'll be reopening these doors for Tween Skate Night, an unbearable event that unfortunately brings in far too much money for any of us to turn our noses up against it. With Lonnie gone, we all help, making it two Devil's Dame's responsibility to man the rink on these nights.

Tonight will be me and StarScreamer.

I'm looking forward to spending time with one of my closest friends. Ever since Nia-Death's return, it feels like everyone is slipping through my fingers. Not rejection, not quite that extreme, but the rift is there, and every day, it feels like it's growing.

You can stop that from happening.

Something inside me speaks, but I don't like what it has to say.

I didn't ask for this, didn't ask for my life to get turned upside down, for Lonnie to die. I didn't ask for things to change.

Death is a starting point.

Death is a door. It opens and shuts, swallowing up the joy and the light inside us.

Death is a starting point.

It wasn't for Lonnie.

Death isn't for the dead.

I scream in frustration, slapping at the side of my head with both hands as the searing hot pain of grief stabs into me again. Maybe the scrawny little shit has the right idea. Maybe numbing all of this with drugs is easier than dealing with the constant reminder that my best friend is gone.

Once inside, I realize I'm the last one in. Everyone's already geared up and stretching on the track, Lady Yaga leading with some fancy yoga poses that are supposed to help us skate faster. Nia is in a half lunge, the wheels of her skate nearly touching her butt, sandwiched between K-Otic and StarScreamer, and suddenly, I feel myself hesitating, unsure where my place is anymore.

I don't linger, knowing that I'll feel worse when given an opportunity for humiliation than if I simply pretend I'm unbothered. Dropping down next to DreadPool, I bring one arm over my chest and do a half-assed version of the stretches they've gone through without me.

"You look pissed," they whisper, doing their best to not talk over Yaga.

Venice Witch snorts. "She's *been* pissed ever since Antônia's come back to town."

I shoot her death stare from my left, and she scoots

away from me, realizing I'm not in the mood. My cried-out eyes are a sure giveaway.

DreadPool groans, causing a few skaters to glance our way. "You gotta get over this," they say in a hushed tone.

"I'm trying." I push the words through gritted teeth, like the lie alone is costing me.

"Yeah, okay." Sarcasm drips off their tongue, and the look on their face says they see through all of my bullshit.

Dread is like that. X-ray vision, capable of seeing everyone's truest intentions. They give me an earnest smile, like they're waiting for me to cave. The brown freckles over their nose are barely visible this time of the year, but in the summer, they'll be out in full force. By then, their now-shoulder length brown hair will be chopped into a bob, just under their chin. The pattern repeats yearly, on schedule without fail.

"I don't owe her anything!" I snap, the words coming out a little louder than I intend, and all heads turn our way again, including Nia's.

"Tell me how you *really* feel now," Dread laughs, clipping their helmet buckle under their chin.

Then, every skater is standing, scrambling into the pack as they take their warm up laps. I'm left lagging behind, a common theme lately that is slowly prickling under my skin, an annoying sensation I can't seem to block out.

Mo blows the whistle, and it feels like a direct call out, telling me to stand and join the rest of the team in laps. I don't hesitate, catching up with D-Stroya, who seems to be skating with extra leisure.

"You nervous?" I ask her.

"Fuck yeah, I'm nervous." She shakes her head. "But there's also a sense of peace, you know? Like, life goes on if

I can't do this." She sighs out loud, and I realize she's saving her energy for her speed test.

"Stop saying that," I chastise her. "You can do this. So can the others." I reminded her she isn't the only skater who didn't pass her speed test.

She comes to a hockey stop, forcing me to make a quick one-eighty and freeze on my toe stops in front of her. "Cat." Her voice is cold and sharp. "This isn't my first rodeo. It's okay not to pass your speed test when you're fresh meat. I'm not fresh meat. I'm *not* getting any faster, I can accept that." She looks over to Nia, whose crossovers are smoother than ever. She skates with a smile on her face, not bothering to slow down so others can keep up with her or use this as a social time. "It's time you do the same."

Deandra kisses the pads of her pointer and middle finger and then touches the top of my helmet.

In a way, I feel as if I'm attending another funeral.

Another death, another goodbye.

Roller Derby means family. We live for each other, bear the brunt of each other's sorrows, struggles, and joy. That bond doesn't end when practice is over or when we take our skates off for the night.

But that bond does break when the skates come off for the last time, when they get hung in a closet by their laces like a trophy. Moving on is easier than staying stuck in the memory. Nostalgia becomes a scab that gets picked too soon, never quite healing. Every retired skater tries to stick around, attend the bouts and cheer their friends on, but life takes precedent and eventually, other priorities win out.

There's no bitterness there. It's simply the way of life. If you aren't living, breathing Roller Derby, you aren't one hundred percent in. You can't give your all to a team with one foot out the door.

D already has both feet in the parking lot. She's just hoping to use Scott to push her the rest of the way out.

The whistle blows again, and we all know it's time for footwork drills. All qualified skaters move to the side, where ladders are taped on the ground and cones are arranged for toe-stop walking—everyone aside from the skaters who haven't passed their twenty-seven in fives.

They stay on the track, where Scott clutches his stopwatch in his hand, ready to test them. I switch my focus back to the task in front of me, tuning out every thought of Lonnie, D, and Nia as I let my feet do the work.

I count to soothe.

One two three. One two three. My feet crisscross through the ladders. One two three. One two three. I'm back in line, ignoring the sounds of everyone around me. I don't turn to my side to see how the speed test is going. It's my turn again.

One two three. One two three.

I can hear the clamoring around me, the cheers of our so-called family morphing into a roar of encouragement for the skaters on the track. I'm the only one doing ladders now. There's no line, no one else in my way.

One two three. One two three.

And then they erupt, as if something that was physically holding them back had come crashing down. My teammates rush over to the circle of the track, fanning and cheering as well as consoling and commiserating.

Turning my head slowly, still too afraid to know for certain, I brace for the impact.

It isn't D who is crying, though she's clearly not made it. It's StarScreamer, sobbing at her feet and allowing her friend to console her. It makes me feel better to know I'm not the only one feeling this way.

Rae-Gunn is shrugging, like she had expected not to make it this second time either and assuring everyone that it will be okay. She still has one more chance to test, according to Scott, and it doesn't look like this has been enough of an ego-kill to keep her from trying one more time.

Bae-Ruthless is hugging the living shit out of Electric-Heel, her skates lifted off the air as she spins her in circles, congratulating her friend in her accomplishment. It's a relief to not be losing any more of us like this.

Scott blows the whistle again, not going through any formality of congratulating Electric, moving on to the next thing like it means nothing. "Let's scrimmage, Devils."

12

HARVEY

I was seventeen the first time I watched Nia-Death skate. She was three years older, and I spent most of my teen years at a private Catholic school, being forced to pray my sins away by my mom and stepdad. Driving to Devil Town from the city wasn't what most teenagers were doing on a Saturday night, yet there I was, obsessively watching the Devil's Dames and cheering them on, counting down the days until I turned eighteen and could try out.

But then my eighteenth birthday came, and reality hit. I found myself homeless, jobless, and with no way to afford higher education. I bounced from one couch to another, saving what little I could from working at a fast-food joint until I got my own car. After that, I was able to remove the burden of my existence from my friends' lives. That kind of pressure long term isn't good for friendships.

I lived in my car for the next year. With no previous rental history and no credit score to back me, it was damn near impossible to lease an apartment. That's when I decided to move to Devil Town.

Nia-Death Experience had disappeared by then,

leaving behind a visible scar through what I remembered of the Devil's Dames league. The team I looked up to had become a shell of what I had romanticized. Lonnie still welcomed me with open arms, tossing a pair of skates my way and showering me with all of the confidence that only they were capable of bestowing. They hooked me up with a job at Freddy's bar, convincing him to hire me despite the fact that I wasn't old enough to serve at the time.

Lonnie nearly lost their shit when they found out I had been sleeping in my car for so long, co-signing my first apartment lease without me asking. I barely felt like an adult, so in need of their parenting. Now, I'm twenty-four, Lonnie's dead, and Nia is here.

In the place I've made my home.

And what a mind trip all of it is.

Seven weeks ago, I would have killed to see her walk through those doors, but she showed up a little too late. All I want now is for her to walk right back out.

There's only about ten minutes left of scrimmage when Mo grabs me by the wrist and pulls me from the track. Probably for the best. I've already laid Nia out at least ten times, and she's going to be black and blue tomorrow for our first official WFTDA bout in five years.

I'm too busy hating myself to bother with feeling anything toward anyone else. My helmet is sweatier than usual, and my wrist guards are begging for a wash but I'm probably better off just buying a new pair at this point.

"We're gonna hang out at my place tonight." I hear D's voice from a distance. "Like a retirement party." She grins, hesitation in her voice, like she's not sure if I'm ready to pretend like any of this is a good thing.

I'm not. Because it isn't.

"I'm working Tween Night," I explain, glad I have the excuse so I don't have to lie.

"Scott's keeping the rink closed tonight because of the fresh paint," she counters. "Can't keep those ten year olds from stamping their grubby paws all over the walls." While it makes sense, there's a part of me that's angry for not having been consulted about it.

The rink isn't his.

I groan, knowing I have no way out of this.

"Come on, my kids are at my parents' house tonight." She's trying her best to sweeten the deal, walking toward me, gym bag in hand, ready to convince me to party like we'd just had a win when the reality is, this felt like a monumental loss.

"I dunno, D—"

"Bullshit. You owe me more than a lie. Come hang out tonight, Cat." Her frown is carved deep into her face.

I know she's right. I know I can't let it end like this.

"Fine." I admit defeat. "Do you need me to bring anything?"

I always ask. I can't help it. Even when I'm angry I still want to take care of those who I love.

"Some rum?" She bats her eyelashes at me like it's a bother.

"I'll come over after I stop at home." I give her a nod, tossing the rest of my gear into the bag and bolting for the door before the rest of the skaters start filing out of the locker room.

By the time I get to Deandra's, the party is alive. Bae-Ruthless and Nancy Shrew are sitting on the porch steps smoking a blunt, Morgan is arguing on the phone with someone, and the music is practically making the grass dance, even with the door closed. It's a typical Devil's

Dame gathering, but for the first time in years, I'm feeling like the odd one out.

Like my place here isn't certain anymore.

My eyes search for her first, like my brain's got no say in the matter. Nia is sitting on top of the kitchen counter, holding a shot in one hand while she laughs at something DreadPool tells her.

I hate that her laughter makes my heart beat faster.

I despise how free it makes her look, how there's a piece of me that wants to know what she looks like when I'm the one forcing it from her lips. She catches me staring, and I cover it up.

"Dread." I nod to my friend before turning to find anyone else in this fucking house but her.

It's suffocating, the feeling of her being everywhere. I can't even think clearly, can't breathe without her name popping into my head.

"You came!" D shouts from the dining room, which has been officially converted into a beer-pong room.

Venice and Star are playing against Electric and Yaga when Deandra loops her arm into mine. "Thank you." She leans her head on my shoulder, and I ache from the growing crater inside, swallowing up all the good in me.

"Yeah, yeah. Play with me next?" I ask her.

"Fuck yeah. Cat and I got next!" Deandra stakes her claim, and since house rules, no one argues.

It's a bother spending the entire night trying to avoid her, to not catch her stares, to pretend like I want to have fun when joy is the last thing on my mind. When I'm low, I don't want to feel better; I want to dig my way down to hell and feel the worst way imaginable. Because the only way to get rid of the bad feelings is to make new worse ones.

I'M ON THE COUCH, LEANING BACK, LEGS SPREAD, PEOPLE-watching at this point in the party since everyone is sloshed. I'm not drinking tonight, too afraid of the repercussions if I lose control of my emotions—and I'm guaranteed to lose control with Nia around.

It's two in the morning, D is asleep sitting up in a dining room chair, her husband, Phil, is slaughtering Nancy on one-on-one pong while Venice, and Electric roll around with forty ounce beers duct taped to their hands. The rest are either passed out or gathered around the tv, pouring beer into shot glasses while they finish the night with a power hour. This isn't a regular Devil's Dame's gathering. This one feels like more, like no one is holding back because everyone is happy to enjoy themselves at this moment, consequences be damned.

Everyone but me.

I should just go home now that D is asleep. For the first time all night, my inner monologue and I are on the same page. Just as I go to stand, I notice the braided one fishing the plastic bag from her pocket before walking into the bathroom.

I bite my lip.

I fight the itch.

But it burns, and I need to understand why.

So, I follow her.

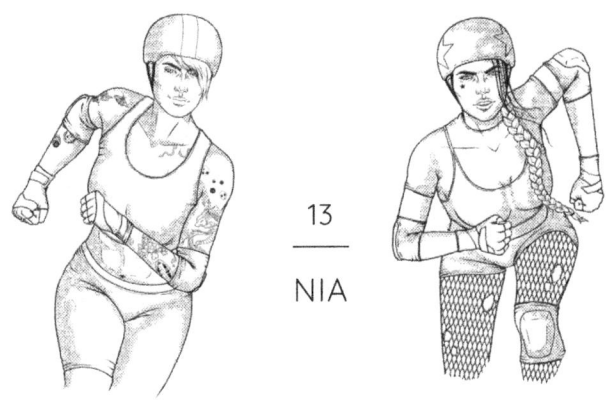

13
NIA

This is the longest I've been around Cat Harvey without skates on, and the tension is quite literally killing me. Without K around to be my shield, I feel exposed, vulnerable. My friends don't get it. They are also *her* friends, constantly dismissive of how intimidated I feel in her presence.

"She'll get over it and warm up to you soon. Cat doesn't hold grudges," Deandra said when she warned me that Harvey would be here tonight.

But every minute is long, and it's exhausting avoiding her gaze. She's fucking gorgeous, and the only thing keeping me from staring at her all night is the knowledge that she can't stand me.

I find reprive in the bathroom somewhere around two or three in the morning. I can't tell how late it is anymore, and though Kade offered to pick me up, I'm more than content just crashing on a couch here to avoid extra work on anyone's part.

I just need a break from everyone, from the social buzz and the noise that's not just external, but inside of me too.

I dry the bathroom counter to be safe before I dump out the pill I had already crushed earlier in the day.

I've been a good girl, and this is my last one.

After this, I'll be done.

I'm rolling up the dollar bill and leaning over the counter when the bathroom door opens. I'm not startled. It's a party; no one should bat an eye to see me putting anything up my nose this late in the night. But I am cursing myself for not making sure it was locked before starting. Cat Harvey closes the door behind her and crosses her arms over her chest, tilting her head in curiosity.

Her short blonde hair falls over her eyes, down her cheek, just a little longer than when we first met a few weeks back. Everything else is still trimmed short and neat, and the blonde is impeccably white. I thought her eyes were green before, but now that I'm closer, it's impossible to miss.

Like an endless lagoon.

She hasn't said a word, but she leans against the door behind her, one knee bent with her foot resting against it, almost as if it's to keep anyone else from entering. I raise an eyebrow, but it earns no reaction or response from her. Picking up my makeshift straw, I proceed as planned, inhaling the powdered pain pill until half of it is gone.

I'm ritualistically pushing up my cheek to drain my sinuses when I look back at her, her expression still unchanged, as if witnessing me putting drugs up my nose has no effect on her.

Good.

If she came in here to intimidate me, to threaten me, then she can fuck off. I won't pretend to be anyone other than exactly who I am, faults included. I spent far too much of my life afraid to be disappointing, and all I got from it was disappointments.

"What do you want?" I finally ask.

Her eyes narrow, and she bites her lip like she's thinking about the answer. My eyes are stuck there, watching the way her teeth graze over her skin before I'm hit with the blaring reminder that she's more likely to hit me before she ever kisses me.

"You're not scared I'll tell them? Tell Scott?" Her head shakes slowly from one side to the other.

"You would have done that already when you had proof." I dangle the empty bag in the air. "Now, you have nothing." I toss it in the trash and stick my dollar straw in my nose again, finishing the remainder of the "evidence."

Her expression remains unphased.

"Why didn't you?" I have to know; my brain won't shut up about it.

"I haven't—*yet*," Harvey clarifies, kicking away from the door and taking a step toward me.

I don't like the way my heart thumps when she gets closer, so loud that I swear she can hear, but if she does, she ignores it.

"I'm deciding what I'm gonna do about this." She takes another step.

"This?" I ask, swallowing down the bitter powder with a hard gulp.

"You," Harvey confirms, closing the distance between us.

"What about me?" My voice is quieter than I truly have the capacity to be.

Her hand cups the side of my face, lifting my chin up to meet her gaze, and I try to shift away from the heat of it. It's the thing I fear the most, being perceived from this close where I can't hide. Her stare is familiar, but it's hard and full of a hatred I can't begin to comprehend, especially when it's directed at me.

I do nothing when a tear wells in my eye, and with her in full possession of my face, I can only let it fall down my cheek. Her thumb squeezes against my jaw.

"Stop that," she says through clenched teeth, turning my head to the side, where the brand new scar is fully exposed by shaved hair.

"I have feelings," I snip back just as she lets my face go. She's still staring down at me, and it's overwhelming. I can't look away—I don't think I'm *supposed* to look away. "Sorry if you don't want to be reminded of that."

She lets out a humored exhale. "What happened to your head?"

I haven't told any of them yet, but for some reason, I tell her. "I hit a tree with my car."

She seems satisfied by the undetailed answer. "Looks bad."

"I'm lucky to be alive." I say the words for the first time since waking up from the coma, the same words countless doctors told me while I spent weeks recovering.

"I don't pity you," she clarifies.

"Wasn't asking for pity." I take a long, stuttered breath. "How did Lonnie die?"

It's like I've been holding in the question just for her. Maybe because asking the others feels a little like burrowing a knife slowly into someone I love, maybe because digging that knife into Harvey doesn't cause as much guilt, or maybe it's because I know that, despite how she feels about me, we both felt the same about Lonnie.

"Cancer." The word is heavy, and it begs no apologies as it falls from her tongue.

Lonnie deserved more than cancer. I can't fathom the image of them, worn and weathered, frail, dying of weakness. Lonnie was the epitome of unfaltering strength, a well of reserves for anyone who needed to draw from them. Lonnie was a goddamn Valkyrie, too battle-hardened to die from a sickness.

I forbid anymore tears from forming.

My final Roxy does the trick as it makes its way through my system, muting the sensation of the world around me and making everything just a little more tolerable. We don't speak for a few moments. We just stare, as if it somehow makes any of this more digestible.

"Is this a problem?" she asks, her gaze shifting to the plastic bag in the trash can.

"No," I lie, looking past her. "Why would you even care?"

"I don't," Harvey says without hesitation.

"Are you gonna let me go?" I'm quiet again. I don't mean to be, but I am.

"I'm not stopping you, princess. Just came to use the bathroom." She smirks.

Liar.

But I walk around her, only slightly disappointed when she lets me past her without incident. The party's fizzled once I'm out of the bathroom. D and her husband are nowhere to be found, which can only mean they're safely tucked in bed. Nancy and Bae are sharing the couch, and Electric is long asleep on the floor.

Everyone else is gone.

I fidget nervously for a few moments, deciding whether I'm going to find my own little corner to pass out in, or if I'm going to bother K and ask for a ride home. Though the latter is the more comfortable option, there's no way in hell I'm going to make myself that much of a burden, no matter *how* close I feel to them.

The sound of the door clicking behind me makes me wince, because I know exactly who's standing there. "Do you need a ride?" she asks.

I shake my head, not bothering to turn around to face her.

Her tone is irritated but her words contradict. "Come on. Let's go." She doesn't beg, and she doesn't look back to see if I'm following.

I know the invitation is only good for so long, and as much as I don't want to come back here tomorrow for my car, I want to sleep snuggly in my own bed before the bout tomorrow. Tonight.

Staying up this late fucks with my brain, with my logic.

Nothing good happens this late, everybody knows that.

Even my enemies are acting suspicious.

I follow, grabbing my shoes off the ground and scurrying toward the door behind her.

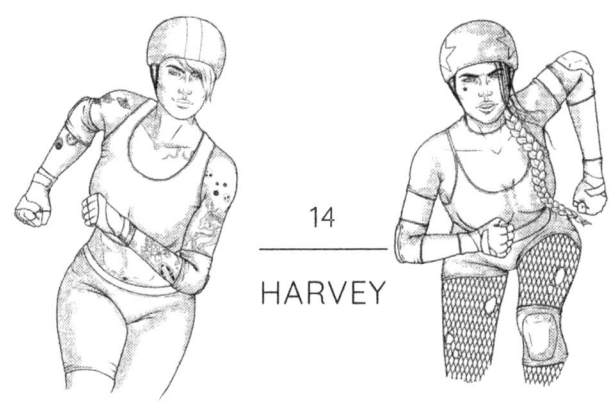

14

HARVEY

What the fuck am I doing?

I've asked myself those same six words on repeat for the last ten minutes we've been in the car. I despise this girl, and yet, I'm driving her home. The bubbling of feelings is too immense to ignore, but I'm certain this is hate. This is loathing, this is… inexplicably the most annoying person I've ever met, and she's stuck in my brain.

She doesn't even know it.

I have the music blaring loud. *Gorillaz* is drowning out any possibility of conversation, though I'm safe in assuming she isn't planning to start any. Nia stares out the window with a blank expression on her face; I can't tell if she's high, or if it's the same emptiness I feel too.

Funny how the same wound can cause two completely different reactions. She's filling that hole up with whatever she can to numb the pain. I'm carving it deeper, wider, until it consumes me, and there's no one and nothing left for me when I'm done.

She points every now and then, letting me know where

to turn until we've made it downtown. It's getting really familiar with every new turn, and then she says, "It's the red brick on the left."

"That's K-Otic's place." I've only been there once or twice to drop off Lonnie, but I wouldn't forget it, wouldn't get something like that confused.

"Yeah," she says, real quiet again, and the confirmation feels sharp in my gut.

When I pull into the driveway, she gives me a look full of hesitation, but then she shakes it off and reaches for the handle. It sticks the way it always does. I undo my seatbelt, reaching over her to pull it the exact way it needs to open the door.

"Thank you." It comes out of her in a breathy whisper that sounds too intimate.

"Hey," I call out to her before she has a chance to fully step out of the car. "Give me your phone."

Turning to face me, she says nothing, but she pulls it out and hands it to me. I enter my number, blocking out my own inner turmoil that tells me this girl is bad news.

I know she's bad news.

"Next time you go put that shit up your nose." The words are coming out of me before I have a chance to fully think through them. "Call me." I grimace at my own offer. "Or something."

"Yeah?" She furrows her eyebrows. "And what are *you* going to do?"

"Keep you busy."

She doesn't break eye contact, but she doesn't say anything else.

With a slight nod, she slams the car door shut and walks toward the house. She's not my responsibility, but I wait until she's through the door before I shift the car to reverse. Then, I drive home, to my miserable life, where every day blends into the next like some fucking purgatory Groundhog Day.

Except I'm not learning the lesson. I'm too afraid of what it has to teach me.

It's nearly five in the morning when I give up on trying to sleep. It's not my best attempt, but I can't waste my time pretending when my brain is going a hundred miles an hour. I roll out of bed and head for the kitchen, where my least favorite task awaits.

Opening the dishwasher to reveal the slew of clean dishes waiting to be put away, I mentally prepare myself with a single breath. Anything is better than giving my brain the peace it needs to overthink.

I'm uncomfortable in my head, tired of the way only *I'm* capable of making myself feel, and now, after seeing how clearly Nia hates *herself*, it's no longer cathartic for me to do it too. I begrudgingly put away each dish, fully aware it's doing nothing to stop the trainwreck of my thoughts, but at least now, I'm productive.

I sigh like this is the most laborious thing I've done in ages. It feels like it, because it's the task I dread most, but I know it isn't. Sitting in the car with Nia for twelve minutes in silence was nearly unbearable, yet this feels harder.

Looking over to the full sink of dishes, I let out one final, dramatic huff, as if anyone is even around to hear it. And then I begin to tackle the dirty pile of dishes. It's not even six when I finish. Not even thirty minutes. The thing

I've put off doing all week doesn't even take thirty minutes of my time.

I shake my head, frustration at myself and myself only.

I ordered pizza for lunch yesterday to avoid needing a clean plate.

My nerves are killing me. It's not the pressure of the bout tonight; it's something physically eating at me from the inside out. It's only when I've cleaned the entire kitchen from top to bottom that I feel the discomfort ease, and I can finally relax. The oven clock reads eight, and I finally consider resting.

I crash on the couch, turning on the tv and settling for subtitled *Inuyasha*. The minute my eye drifts from the screen and I lose focus on the story, I feel the wave of sleep hit me like a freight train.

And I finally welcome it.

Maybe, at least in my dreams, I can finally get that girl out of my head.

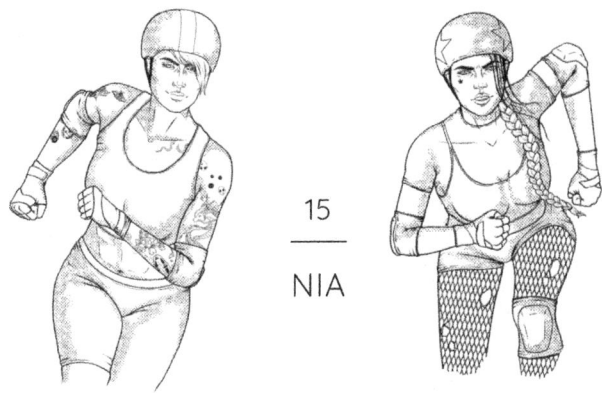

15

NIA

There are at least twelve things I could be doing other than driving. There's at least five things I *should* be doing other than driving *here*. And there's at least two things I *need* to be doing, but instead, I am parking.

Three blocks from his house, so as to not affect his relationship with his Karen neighbor, but I'm here nonetheless. Once again, at Ryan Lee's. I tell myself it's okay because I only got a couple of pills the last time. I tell myself it's fine because I don't need them. I just want them, and that's gotta count for something.

If it doesn't, I'm fucked.

I leave my phone in the car, grabbing only my wallet when I decide to make the three block trek on foot to his house. It's a nice day, spring on the horizon, which means from now until May, it could be anything from twenty to eighty-degree weather.

Layers are my friends.

I take the cardigan off just as I get to his mailbox, already dripping in sweat and regretting that I'll have to walk back to my car. I'm wrecked with soreness from yesterday's scrimmage, bruised to shit from every hit I took from Harvey, so conserving what little energy I have for the bout tonight is necessary.

I'm only not falling apart completely because I spent the last four weeks in physical therapy nearly every single day, rehabbing all the muscles in my body. The door opens before I can get to it, and the same dark-haired woman comes out, this time in a suit, all white from head to toe, except the red on the bottom of her heels. She doesn't spare me a second glance; she just unlocks her car and gets inside.

I try not to stare, but she's fucking gorgeous, and the car she's driving stands out in this neighborhood, despite Ryan wanting to blend in. I push my way inside the house to find a less-than-pleased drug dealer waiting for me.

"What? Was it me, or was it *her*?" I freeze at the door, unsure if my timing is bad.

"It's never you, squirt." He gets up to give me a hug, but once his arms are around me, I can hear the deadbolt locking. "What do you need?" He backs up and places the mask of a happy stoner back on his face.

I narrow my eyes in his direction, just so that he knows I'm well aware of how weird he's behaving. With a heavy sigh, I drop on the couch, kicking my shoes off at the last minute. "I don't know." I drag each word out.

"You always know what you want. You're just too embarrassed to ask," he corrects me.

"Fuck you. Always right about me and shit." I'm covering my face with both hands, but I manage to tuck some fingers in to flip him off at the same time.

"Should I be worried about you?" he asks.

He's never asked that before. I cut him a look, and he

raises his hands up in defense. "You want a dealer, not a friend?"

That cuts to my core.

"No. That's not what I want, Ryan." I'm annoyed with myself. "I'm just…" I linger on the thought. "I'm just not ready to stop right now. Everything still hurts."

It's a lie.

"That hospital really got you hooked, huh? How long did they have you on that shit?" He's staring at me like any of that matters.

"It's like you don't even want my money. You insult me before I'm three feet in the door." I'm turning over on my back now, crossing my arms over my chest and staring at the ceiling. "The whole time. I mean, I guess four or five weeks if you're only counting after I woke up. I was probably not on pain pills while I was asleep."

"Your money? When's the last time you actually paid me for something, squirt?" He gives me a look full of a knowing superiority I can't fight.

"Run the tab, drug man. If you remember it." I laugh, turning back on my side to face him.

"What's eating at you?" He gets serious, like he might actually just play therapist for a bit to entertain himself.

"What isn't? I'm a fucking mess." I groan, rubbing my hands over my eyes.

"What do I always say, Nia?" He gives me that fucking overprotective look I despise.

"Only commit one crime at a time?" I grimace, knowing it's the wrong answer as I sit up and steal the bowl of popcorn from the coffee table.

I snag a handful and throw it in my mouth.

It's stale.

"Yes, but not that rule." He reaches for the bowl and takes it back to the kitchen.

Blowing air through my lips noisily, I give him the answer he truly wants. "We get high to celebrate, not to escape."

"I knew you weren't dumb enough to forget." He seems more proud of himself for ingraining it into me than anything. "So why are you forgetting?" His tone is sharper at the end.

"I'm not forgetting, Ryan. I'm doing it on purpose." I look away, uncomfortable keeping his gaze when the following words fall out of my mouth. "I don't like being here very much right now."

"I'm not keeping you a prisoner in my house, Antônia." He's offended, but that's not my intention.

"That's not what I meant." I shake my head.

"Oh." Ryan finally gets it.

I sit up. It's awkward now.

There are friends you can share your dark parts with, the ones who hold space for you, the ones who can walk you through the darkness back into the light. And some friends run from it because they can't be responsible for the weight of that heaviness. Neither is good, neither is bad.

But mixing up those two can complicate things.

And right now, I'm not sure if Ryan is the first kind of friend, because we've never tested that boundary before. Getting high together doesn't require such deep thoughts and turbulent feelings.

"I'm sorry. I don't know—" I go to lie, to cover it up with something else so we can move back to the light and funny stuff, but he cuts me off.

"My dad killed himself." He shares something with me he's never dared to before.

My eyes blur with tears, but I hold them back. This isn't about me. "I-I didn't know."

"I don't talk about it. I was just a kid. People leaving like that, it fucks you up, you know?" He's staring past me now, like it's too much to look at me while thinking about this.

"I'm sorry." I say, but it means nothing. There's nothing that can fix the pain he'll carry until his very last day.

"This life, you get used to people coming and going. People ripping you off, people trying to catch you slipping up, or worse, take your place. Some of my favorite customers died too soon, and some of my least favorite made me rich." His gaze finds mine again before he continues. "I'd be *real* fucking sorry to find out you died from something I gave you, Nia."

Now it's awkward.

He clears his throat. "Promise me." His eyebrow raises, that brotherly stare directed my way again. "Celebrations. Not escape."

"Fine." I don't know if I'm lying yet or not. He's not wrong, and I should know better.

The problem is, I've found myself in that mental state where I just can't seem to care.

"How many do you want?" he asks, even though he's well aware I'm toeing a dangerous line.

"I don't think I want the pills this time," I confess, and he freezes.

"I told you that stuff's not right for you. How about some weed?" He pulls out his personal jar.

"Don't do that." I shake my head. "I'll just look for it somewhere else." Shrugging, I grab my bag and stand.

It's a huge bluff; I don't really know anyone else, not

anymore. Maybe once upon a time, when these were still my stomping grounds, but these days? I'm practically a stranger here now.

He's in front of me in less than a second, taking up more space than I remember him being capable of. Ryan's tall, probably six-foot-three, and now, in his thirties, he isn't some lanky little dealer, all bones from being high the whole day.

He's a big fucking dude.

"Do *not* fucking play with me, Nia." His hand is on my wrist, and it's squeezing hard. Too hard.

"Ow. Ryan," I whine but he doesn't let up. "You're hurting me."

"Swear you will not get this shit from anyone else. *Now*, you fucking brat." The nickname is playful, but his face is nothing but serious, and the pressure still on my arm confirms it.

"I swear, ow, fuck, Ryan, let go." I shake him off, but it's only when *he* decides he's satisfied that he releases me.

He cuts me a cold look, not bothering to apologize and ignoring me when I whisper curses in my mother's native tongue. I rub my wrist; it's red and the skin burns from trying to twist my way out of his hold.

"This isn't 2012 anymore, Nia. Every dealer on the street is cutting their drugs for profits. They aren't cutting it with Tylenol or aspirin anymore. They're cutting it with poison, with shit that *will* kill you," he warns. "Promise me you will *not* get it anywhere but from me."

He's so serious, it fucking hurts. It makes me want to dig a hole in the ground, bury my head, and disappear.

"I promise," I whisper, not daring to blink in case it's the wrong move.

He gets up and leaves the room. I could go, forget

about this entire interaction and chalk it up to game day nerves. Ryan would play along, and in a few days, when all the pills are finally out of my system, I'll feel better.

I wouldn't think about them again.

But I don't.

I stay, because I want to get high.

I want to forget.

I want to cease to exist.

Even if only in my own head.

He comes back with *The Lion King* VHS in his hand and sets it down on the coffee table before he asks me one final time. "You're sure about this?"

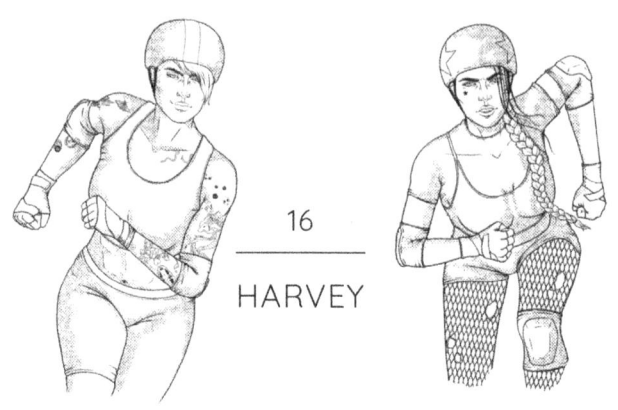

16

HARVEY

Am I obsessed? No. Can I stop thinking about Nia-Death? Also no.

I've convinced myself it's normal to think about my enemy, my *rival*, this often. But as we lace up our skates, side-by-side in the locker room before our first bout as an official team, I can't help but vibrate from camaraderie.

"How are you feeling?" StarScreamer asks her.

"I'm so nervous. Scott didn't tell me who we were up against." Her face is a little colorless, like the panic is very real.

"Wait, you *just* found out we were matched against the Wolverine Dreams?" Star looks pissed, her nostrils flared and her jaw set, like Scott has finally crossed the line for her.

She storms out of the locker room, and though I'm curious, I don't bother asking. I don't have to, because DreadPool does it for me. "What's wrong with that team?"

Nia looks uncomfortable. She stares off to the side, avoiding eye contact as she tells the story. "That's who we played against when I got hurt so bad that I had to—"

"Quit," DreadPool finishes for her. "Shit."

"He's such an asshole." Nancy pops the bubble on her gum as she slams her locker shut.

"No. I'm sure he didn't know," Nia defends him. "I can't expect everyone to know all my business."

She's not wrong, but skaters should have been informed of who we're bouting against long before the day of the bout. Nia *should* have been given the option to not skate today. There's not a single part of me that thinks she would have sat this out, though.

"Are you gonna be okay?" K asks her, their hand at her elbow, forcing her to turn to face them.

She takes a deep breath, staring into K's eyes before she nods.

K-Otic places a kiss on the top of her head, and there's a small part of me that hates myself even more than before because I can't stand how watching that makes me feel. I clear my throat loudly, clicking the plastic of my wrist guards together before I stand and skate out of the locker room.

Slam Night is a beautiful havoc. The rink is vibrating with energy. It looks great with the paint job, but it doesn't look like Skateland anymore. The grit was part of the charm, and now it looks… gentrified. Which is exactly the vibes Scott exudes with his Versace shoes and baby blue suit.

He's in the middle of the track, talking to one of the zebras, when I see Mo skating his way. The back of Morgan's shirt says "Coach" now. Not assistant, just coach. They deserve it, and if it's the one positive change that comes from all of this, then I'll celebrate it today. There's always time to mourn tomorrow.

Every skater has filed out of the locker room now,

standing behind the partition wall, waiting for the announcer to call our names. The visiting team always goes first, a kindness we bestow upon them. K and Nia are at the front; as jammers, they'll be called before the pivots and then the blockers.

"Give it up for *Reese Ender!*" The pivot for the Wolverine Dreams is called onto the track, and I see Nia stumble back. She's shaking her head, and in a second, she's skating right through the locker room doors again.

Star and K follow after her.

I follow them.

"No. No, I-I can't. Not with Reese." She's laboring through the words.

Nia's sitting on the bench, her head between her legs as she takes in heavy drags of oxygen through her open mouth.

"Should I tell Scott?" Star asks her, her hand making soothing circles on Nia's back.

"No," I answer for her, causing all three heads to spin in my direction. "You're not afraid of her. Let's go skate."

"I *am* afraid of her," she corrects, her tone sharp, like she's angry at *me* for not accepting it. "I had to learn how to walk again because of her."

"Yeah? Well, I hit harder, and yet here you are… still walking, skating." I cross my arms over my chest and lean on the door frame.

She's staring at me blankly, like she's thinking through it.

"It's up to you," K assures her.

"You've got my back?" The question is solely meant for me.

I should feel insulted. Fuck, I *am* insulted. A jammer asking their pivot if they have their back shouldn't happen.

It should be a given. But I've done nothing to convince her otherwise.

"Yeah, I've got your back, princess." I push the door open with one hand and gesture out to the track with my head. "Let's go."

She gives me a smile and nods, standing and skating past me just in time for the announcer to call her out.

"It's Nia-Death Experience!" The crowd cheers like they remember her. They probably don't, but the excitement is enough.

After K-Otic, I'm next, skating onto the track when he calls out for Harvey Dent-Her-Face. I take my place behind the pivot line next to Reese Ender, who doesn't spare a second glance my way. She doesn't need to. I'm the one sizing her up. I'm taller and my thighs are thicker, but we'll just have to see how hard this bitch really hits to make our jammer have that look on her face.

I look back at Nia, past the crowd of blockers between us to find her gaze locked directly on Reese's back. As if she feels the heat of my stare, she shifts to look my way. I give her a nod, a reminder of the promise I just made.

The referee blows the whistle, and we're off.

I'm skating, but Reese Ender stays back, and just when Nia is shoved into the wall of blockers, Reese hits Nia in the chest with her shoulder, sending her back. It's illegal contact, but the zebra can't see it, and every blocker on our team is too focused on clearing the opposing skaters. It's not until the pack has left her behind that she's able to get up. I'm skating backwards, lowering my speed so she can catch up, but just as I'm closing in on her, Reese hip checks Nia out of the boundaries of the track.

The Wolverine's jammer gets the first points.

We assemble behind our designated lines and wait for

the next whistle. I'm skating forward, but once again, Reese is heading for Nia. I'm too used to jamming, too obsessed with going for the offense to interrupt the way this pivot skates. She's made Nia her target. It's obvious.

Nia's ready for her this time. I skate backwards through the line of blockers again, and with StarScreamer's help, I'm through, but not in time to prevent Reese from throwing her elbow into Nia's chest. It sends her skidding on her ass over the track.

I pull my mouthguard out to yell. "REF!" I shout through the noise, but the zebra raises their hands up like they didn't see anything.

Bullshit.

"That's fucking illegal contact and you know it!" I'm skating toward the ref, who's just now blowing the whistle on the jam.

"I didn't see it." The ref shakes her head.

"Then you're the only one. Go get your eyes checked before you miss some more calls," I spit out, turning back to my line.

The zebra blows a warning whistle at me, like she has no problem dealing *me* a penalty for back talk even though she's the one ignoring perfectly clear calls.

Reese is already there, waiting for the next jam. She's practically in Nia's space, hovering in front of the jammer line with that smug fucking look on her face.

I want to be the one to wipe it off.

It doesn't take much to knock Nia off the track, but with every jam that passes, it becomes more evident that it's not Reese's goal to interrupt, detain, or get in Nia's way. Her goal is to injure her. Every block, every check, every shove, is delivered illegally and in a way that slowly leaves Nia less and less able to defend.

It's bully behavior, and it's getting under my skin.

By halftime, the entire team is aware, and Morgan is pissed. With enough complaints, we sub out the zebra and get one of the side-line refs to switch out with her. It doesn't help. Reese Ender plays dirty, and the only way to deal with players like that is to give them a taste of their own medicine.

We're barely ahead, but we're winning, which lets me know each jam is making the opposing pivot more and more desperate. All I need is for the ref to see it. The whistle blows again, and I time a hip check that sends Reese right off the track and buys me enough seconds to get to Nia before her.

She's there, in a low squat, doing her best to stand-off against the Wolverine's jammer as they smash their shoulders against each other. That's when I really see it: the strength she has. It's not weakness in her body. She's a little damaged—sure, but she's certainly not frail. I get behind her and place my hands on her hips, sending her forward with all of my protection to keep her standing, regardless of who hits her.

With the push of my hands, she's through the wall of blockers, grabbing StarScreamer's hand as I hone in on Reese once more. I don't have to guess; she's headed for Nia, but she's so focused, she doesn't see me coming, and my shoulder block sends her flying. I use the opportunity to get to the front of the blockers, expecting to see Nia through, but she hasn't made it yet. It's okay, though, because the Wolverine's jammer is still too far back to matter.

Nia is stuck, trying to wiggle through a solid wall of opposing blockers while our teammates try to get her past them. It's an impossible ask, and Reese Ender is heading for her again. Nia's gaze follows mine, and we both watch as Reese inches closer, pushing DreadPool out of the way like she doesn't even care about the rules anymore.

"Fuck," Nia shouts through her mouthguard, the frustration obvious, and we all feel it. "Harvey!" She demands my attention, and just as I turn back to face her, she's pulling the star panty off her helmet. The Jammer helmet cover. She extends her arm, and without thinking twice, I take it, sliding it over my stripe before the opposing team realizes we're passing the star.

She's passing the star.

In a second, I'm moving again, leaving the Wolverine blockers behind while I steal the win.

She passed the fucking star.

It's not unheard of, a classic derby move, one that requires trust amongst all teammates. One that requires the jammer to give up all semblance of an ego in order to hand all the glory of the win to their teammate.

She cares more about us winning together than being the one responsible for it.

Once I make a full lap, I'm able to call the jam off and take points for us. Just as my hands move to my hip to signal the end of the jam, Reese shoves Nia off the track, full contact use of her hands on an opposing player's body.

Nia's too stunned by the action to react properly. She tries to stand but doesn't have the time to correct. Instead, she falls backwards, landing on her ass. She screams, and I catch a glimpse of Reese's skate on her wrist.

It's intentional. I know it is.

The ref sees it, blowing the whistle and calling the penalty, shoving Reese Ender in the box for the first time tonight. Dread and Yaga help Nia off the track. She's holding her wrist to her chest, and she screams when Mo releases the Velcro straps of her wristguard. K-Otic steps on the track, grabbing the appropriate helmet covers and making the switch with Nia. Her pained sobs are loud, but Mo continues to examine the injury when the zebra blows the whistle for the next jam.

The transition with K is seamless. We move in sync with each other and clear the track, while I whip them through the wall of blockers. Without the Wolverine's precious pivot, we take the next jam without a hitch.

The penalty timer ends, and Reese Ender moves from the box to the bench, where her coach lays into her. I've disregarded the entire next jam now, skating on autopilot and hoping that K-Otic can carry the win with me doing the bare minimum. Maybe we've scored enough to have it in the bag regardless.

My focus is on the Wolverine's pivot and her only.

Reese throws her helmet on the ground and storms off, skating into the guest locker room without a care. I let the jam finish out before I pull the stripe off my head and toss it at Bae's feet, indicating a substitute is needed.

I'm no longer in control of my own brain or feet, I simply skate toward the visiting team locker room.

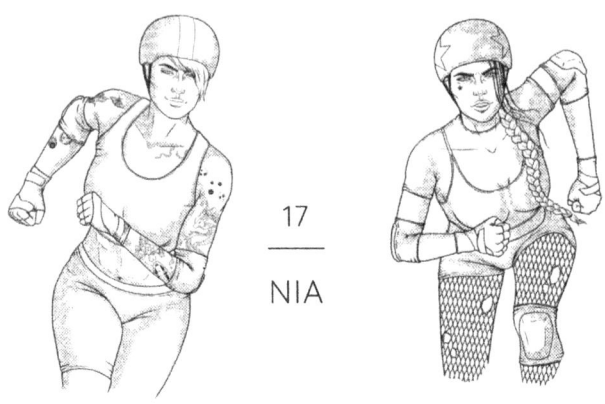

17

NIA

I press the bag of ice to my wrist, the purple and blue settling in so fast, there's no way I can avoid the hospital for this one. It burns, an agonizing ache that reminds me what true pain feels like when it's fresh.

When the jam ends, Harvey skates in the same direction as Reese, disappearing behind the locker room door. Mo and Venice eye each other, no words passing between them, but the look of concern on both their faces is enough to make the ongoing jam nearly meaningless. A small tilt of Mo's chin in the direction of the locker room is all Venice Witch needs to discreetly skate away from the bench.

I stand to follow, still clutching the ice around my swollen wrist.

The pull of my shirt's collar around my neck throws my center of gravity off, almost causing me to fall, but Mo's hand on my back catches me. I turn to see them shaking their head in a warning, but I disregard them, waving them off and following behind Venice.

She's already in the locker room by the time I get

through the door, reaching for Harvey in an attempt to pull her off Reese Ender. The swollen red lump around Reese's eye lets me know Harvey's already hit her at least once. She breaks out of Venice's hold and throws her fist into Reese Ender's face again, this time right under the chin.

"Harvey, that's enough." Venice holds her back by the arms, Harvey's chest heaving hard with each breath.

Reese Ender scatters herself back up onto her skates, legs wobbly and unsturdy as she skates away from Harvey. "Wait." She commands her to stop right before me. "Apologize to our jammer."

"What?" Reese doesn't look at me.

"Say you're sorry." Harvey gives her the same look she's been dishing out to me all week, but for some reason, it feels far more lethal when directed at her.

"S-sorry," Reese stutters out as she flies past me, holding her face behind her hands. Only when the door bounces back the third time does Venice let Harvey go, looking back and forth between the two of us before slowly backing up.

"I'm... gonna go let Mo know you're good," she says, her voice filled with pure uncertainty. "You're good, right, Cat?"

Harvey cuts me a look, that same vicious one that turns my spine to gelatin. Her gaze stays fixed on mine. "Yeah. I'm good."

Venice skates in reverse until her back forces the locker room door to swing, giving us just a peek of the crowded rink behind her. "You sure?" She checks again, but this time, she's looking at me for confirmation.

I nod silently.

It feels like minutes before the door stops swinging from

her exit, but it's only then that I can break away from staring at Harvey's face to notice the smaller details.

Like her knuckles.

"You're bleeding." I'm at her side in less than three strides, lifting her hand up to take a closer look at the torn skin.

"Didn't you see the other guy?" She gives me a goofy grin, filled with energy that feels so familiar, so natural between us, and yet completely out of reach.

My stomach is a nervous mess of butterflies any time I look at her.

She can barely stand to be around me.

Yet, here she is, settling a score on *my* behalf. What the hell is this?

The laugh bubbles out of me awkwardly, just like anything else in my life. "Like I said, I can't quite tell if you hate me or—"

She cuts me a look again. "Or what, princess?" The command in her tone forces me to shrink.

"You hit her for me," I whisper, just in case we aren't alone, though I know damn well it's just us.

"She was playing dirty, and she hurt you." She says the last bit through clenched teeth, her nostrils flaring, like thinking about it again is enough to piss her off.

"You hurt me too." I shrug, biting back a nervous smile.

"It's different," she says sharply.

I harden my gaze and challenge her, "Why? Because you think you're justified in your hatred of me?"

"It's just different. She's not part of *this*." Harvey gestures between the two of us.

I don't know what *this* is.

I don't think she does either.

"Oh, so only *you* can hurt me?" I ask, her fingers still in my hold.

She pulls them back, clenching her fist shut at her chest, her nostrils still flared.

Harvey frowns, and the rest of my confidence dissolves as I put distance between our bodies. She winces, a kind of disapproval she can't vocalize for some reason.

She's looking at my wrist when she speaks again. "You surprised me out there. You killed it."

My eyes widen, this conversation taking turns I didn't think possible for the two of us. "Are you… complimenting me?"

"I can admit to being wrong." She crosses her arms over her chest and looks me up and down.

"You're a better woman than me. I can't." I laugh at my own joke, though I know it's partially true. She doesn't laugh with me. Instead, she steps closer, her eyes glued to my lips. "Are you?" I ask, my voice so shaky when I continue. "Admitting to being wrong?"

Harvey lets out a humored scoff under her breath. "No." Her gaze shifts back up to mine as she takes the final step to close the distance between us. "I said I *can*."

I shake my head, not sure if I'm any less intimidated by her now that she isn't actively hating me. I release my bottom lip from the bite of my teeth, realizing I've probably been gnawing on it this entire time. "Thanks for having my back."

"Well, *someone* needs to have it. You're pretty fucking fragile." She sounds annoyed, but her expression doesn't match her tone. She's still all crooked smiles, and her eyes are soft.

"Still faster than *you*, though." I use my elbow to shove her away, but she grips my hip and pulls me into her.

She's hard and soft against me all at once, and my pulse quickens.

Her expression sobers as she looks down at my hand. "Let me see your wrist."

I pull away the ice pack, the bruise dark shades of blue and purple, the shape of the skate wheel almost visible if I squint hard enough. It's not the bruise that's concerning, though; it's how fast the swelling grows. My wrist is the same size as the rest of my arm now, and not even half an hour has passed.

"That doesn't look good." She grimaces as she inspects it, her touch so gentle, I can barely feel it. "You should get that looked at now."

I sigh, knowing she's right but dreading another hospital visit. After my post-accident residency, I was told it was normal to develop an aversion to health care facilities. I entirely loathe them. Even worse, I despise paying for them.

"You're gonna get that looked at, right?" She doesn't let me avoid her gaze, pinning me with a look that's full of concern.

"I don't know. Maybe?" I'm too flustered to do anything but answer honestly. A lie is a performance I can't quite nail down at the moment.

She exhales heavily. "Where's your shit? I'll take you."

"N-no, that's not what I meant," I try to counter. Owing Cat Harvey was the last thing I needed.

"You can't really drive while you're using one hand to ice the other." She starts skating toward the door before she turns back, uncertainty on her face for the first time since I've met her. "Unless you're waiting for K to take you?"

"What? No. That's fine, we can go." I don't need Kade to handle all of my problems. "They deserve to celebrate tonight."

"K? Socialize with the rest of us? Yeah. I'll pay to see it." She's arrogantly confident.

"Do they typically not?" I ask, realizing that while they've been warm and almost sibling-like toward me, I haven't actually seen Kade interacting with any of the other skaters.

"K has pretty much kept to themselves since they tried out two years ago, aside from Lonnie and Dread," she says before skating in my direction. "Sit on the bench," she orders.

Dropping to her knee pads in one smooth move, she begins to unlace my quads and undo the straps. I feel like she can probably hear my heart beating from down there, but I'm hoping she'll at least pretend she can't, for my sake.

She takes my skates in her hands, leaving me only responsible for the ice on my wrist. Harvey opens the door out to the rink, the bout finishing up, clearly in our favor. K-Otic is in the lead, and in just a few more minutes, the Devil's Dames will have their first official WFTDA win in five years. She goes through the doors for our own team's locker room to retrieve our things.

I stay back, watching the Devils secure the win.

It doesn't take her long to return with both our gym bags in hand. She gestures with her head toward the door, and I follow behind. We're exiting just as the final whistle blows, and thankfully, we're far ahead enough that we'll beat the exiting crowd.

"That's a nice hairline fracture." The ER doctor points to the X-ray, and I groan. "I'm surprised you're not in more pain.

"I'm in a lot of pain," I grit back, annoyed that medical professionals carry this expectation of their patients. I'm not here to put on a show; I shouldn't have to make a big scene to convey that something is broken.

"Could have fooled me," the doctor says under her breath.

Or maybe she can tell I'm still high, which is likely keeping me from feeling the full force of the break.

"So now what?" Harvey asks the doctor.

"Now, she can take this discharge paperwork down the hall to ortho and they'll make her a cast for the next six weeks, and this prescription down to the pharmacy on the third floor for pain management." She doesn't look up from the paperwork to deliver the news.

"Six weeks?" I shout, every possible plan and hope going out the window.

"If all goes well, yes. I'll take a look in six weeks to see if we need any more time," she confirms.

"Fuck." Harvey exhales. "Is she going to be able to skate?

"Does she need her wrist to skate?" the doctor asks her, like I'm not even here.

"No," I answer for myself. "I don't need my wrist to skate." I stand, annoyed, and grab the discharge papers from her with my good hand.

Harvey's following behind as I make my way down the hall to get my cast. "Are you okay?"

"I don't like doctors." It's not a lie; it's just a really simplified version of the truth.

"It's not the end of the world." She's trying to reassure me, and it feels odd coming from her. "It's just like skating with a bigger wrist guard."

I laugh. "Except if I fall, I break my wrist twice as bad."

"That *is* the gamble." She shrugs just as we get to orthopedics.

"You don't have to stay for this," I feel compelled to say.

"It's fine." The corner of her lip curls up, and she peers down at me. "I'm kind of enjoying seeing you in pain."

"Good to know that my misery is what it takes." I throw her a sarcastic look just as we get called back to the little office.

The doctor looks to be in his seventies, little tufts of white hair scattered at the top of his head, the only fullness on the sides. He wears round, metal-rimmed glasses and greets me with a warm smile.

"The swelling is pretty bad, so I'll have to make the cast bigger to accommodate since the injury is so recent," he explains. "You'll need to come back in a week or two for a new size, for comfort. By then, we may be able to get you in a softer cast."

"That would be great." I try to paint a smile on my face, to pretend I'm not in pain or that I don't want to just get home and blast my face off until I can't feel anything.

Anything.

Including the gaping hole shredding my heart, where I

can still hear Lonnie whispering of their disappointment in my recent decisions.

18

HARVEY

She's nothing like I thought she'd be, and the more time I spend in her presence, the harder it is to hate her. Instead, I want to fix her, fix the parts she's so obviously struggling to heal herself.

She's skeptical, and with reason. I kicked her ass not just a few days ago, and then today, I found myself splitting my knuckles over her on the Wolverine's pivot. Watching her get picked on activated something inside me that couldn't be held back anymore.

The thing I'd been fighting this entire time, ever since she came to Skateland after Lonnie's death. The very thing I tried to mask for contempt. It was just fucking obsession, desire.

Something even more.

She hasn't spoken since we arrived at the hospital pharmacy, the pain obviously setting in to the point where dissociation is the only thing keeping her together. Staring at a spot on the brick wall, her focus is on the furthest thing from herself. I'm standing at the counter, waiting for the pharmacist to come back with her medicine while she sits on a bright blue chair pushed against the wall.

"Alrighty, Antônia. Here they are. Do you need instructions for taking these?" He looks past me to ask her.

She shakes her head, coming to a slow stand.

He holds the bag out for her, but I take it from him and then, with one hand on her low back, I shepherd us out of the pharmacy. She's quiet, glancing at the prescription bag in my hand the entire walk to the car.

"Should I take you back to K's... or?" I had no reason to be saying "or." Or what? Or leave her behind? Or take her back to skateland? Or...

My house.

"K's is fine," she says with another quiet nod.

Vibrant. Full of life, energy, and confidence.

That's how Lonnie had described Antônia Da Silva. But now, with her here in front of me and our only connection dead and buried, there is no more painting her in lies. All I see is her truth: she's broken from her own chaos.

She is shattered by her own hand.

I blast the music, some old cover of a song written by *The Smiths*. The time on the radio reads nearly one in the morning; between the X-rays and the journey through the hospital to see multiple specialists, this wasn't a quick trip.

But I'm dreading the minute she'll be gone.

I can't stand the feeling.

She doesn't even try to pull the door open when we get there; she just gives me that blank stare. She knows it sticks, but asking for help isn't ingrained in her vocabulary, so she thinks looking at me is enough for me to guess her needs.

It is, but I don't tell her that. No, I just reach over to push the handle and let her out.

One more vacant look my way, the words probably itching at the base of her throat, but she won't say them.

"Do you need help?" I raise an eyebrow.

"Please." The vibrance, the confidence, is now meekness and self-consciousness.

I grab her skate bag from the backseat and toss it over my shoulder. Following her from the driveway up the stairs to K-Otic's place, I wait for her to fish the keys from her backpack with her good hand. She's a mess. The backpack's strap hangs off her cast, and it's gotta be killing her, but she hasn't asked me for the pills yet, and it feels like we're playing chicken again.

We both know she's going to abuse them.

So where do we go from here?

She unlocks the door and carelessly tosses the keys back into the abyss of her backpack before pushing the door open with her shoulder. All the lights are off, K obviously sleeping in their room, only the cat waiting for Nia.

He greets her with a loud mew, one that sounds nearly savage on a beast that size.

I drop to one knee to pet him, the purring a collection of bees in a jar, so loud and rumbly that it soothes. "Where do you want your bag?" I shift my gaze back her way.

"Um. In my room is fine. Thanks." She points to a door down the hallway.

I'm expecting to see K-Otic sleeping, but the room is empty. "Is K here?"

"Long asleep, I'm sure." She breathes out, and it looks labored.

She's in pain, but she's still afraid to ask me.

"Do you need anything else before I go?" I lean on the open door frame as she dumps the contents of her bag onto the floor.

"You've done too much already," she says but then doubles back. "Actually, do you think you could help me?"

"With?" I want to force the words out of her.

She gets by far too often with letting others assume her needs. Right now, there's probably nothing she can do for herself without her dominant hand.

"Everything." She lifts her cast. "I haven't showered yet, and I don't want to get in bed gross from the bout."

"Oh." I feign disinterest, my hands in my pockets as I take a step closer to her.

"Nevermind, actually." She's all nerves, too anxious to follow through.

"Don't you think you should ask Kade for help?" This tension between us feels immense, but I need the clarity. Even if K and I aren't friends, we're still teammates. I'm not stealing someone's girl out from underneath them.

She laughs, a summery sound straight from her chest before she speaks again. "Kade's made it pretty clear they'd rather be dead than see me naked."

And that's all I need.

"Their loss," falls freely from my mouth as she walks past me and heads straight across the hall.

I grab her good wrist, forcing her to turn to face me again. She stumbles back a step into the bathroom, biting her lower lip. Gripping her hips, I lift her up and place her on the marble of the bathroom vanity. Her eyes are wide, alert now, as she waits for me to make the next move.

"Lift your arms up."

She obeys the command, letting me grab the hem of her tank top and pull it over her head. Her sports bra clasps in the front, and I'm thankful, because it looks too tight to pull over her shoulders with the cast on. Nia's fully capable of undoing the clasp herself, but she's not. Instead, she's fixated on me, her eyes glued to my lips, shifting every few seconds to where my fingers sit.

I drop to one knee and pull at the top of her tube sock, rolling it down her ankles and then sliding it off her foot before repeating on the other side. Standing between her legs, I reach for the first clasp of her bra, and she leans closer. I undo the second, her chest rising with a deep inhale. The third comes undone, and the curve of her cleavage begs my attention. I give a hard tug, sloppy with the final clasp as I yank it free, her breasts spilling out as the bra hangs on her shoulders like an open vest.

She shrugs it off, and I back up, giving her space to hop off the counter. I stand corrected from all previous assumptions. What I had seen as scrawny and weak was a guise for battered and beaten. Her legs are a mapwork of scars, highways edging from one knee down to her ankle bone, some round scars the size of a quarter on the front of her shins. The other leg is not much better, and the work of the week is displayed on her flesh.

Purple, blue, green and orange bruising drapes her hips and knees, the array of colors making it evident that some are from me a few days back, and some are from tonight, already setting in. There's a bruise on her sternum, bright blue and small, about the size of an elbow.

I suddenly wish Venice hadn't pulled me off Reese Ender so fast.

She deserved more than what I laid out.

Nia's eyes are still on me as she stands there, all golden skin with nothing but sheer panties on. She's not covering up, but I'm only staring at her face now, at the way the brown of her eyes are so dark in this light, it feels like an entire night sky.

She fumbles with her left hand, trying to pull the hair

tie off her braid, but it gets stuck on a knot. Stepping closer, I take the bundle of hair from her hand and gently pull the band free from the tangle with minimal breakage. I slip it over my own wrist and run my fingers through the braid, starting from the bottom as I pull apart the strands and detangle.

Her eyes are closed, her head slightly dropped back like she's appreciating the contact. The "Thank you," is barely an audible whisper from her moving lips.

"Anything else? Or do you need me to wash you too?" The crooked smirk paints itself on my face too easily with her around.

Her eyes widen, and she brings her arms over her chest to cover herself up. "No." She shakes her head, and just as I'm about to exit the bathroom, she drops her arms once more. "But I want you to."

I freeze, half turned with my mouth agape.

Maybe not so meek after all.

"Will you get on your knees for it?" I challenge, my voice sharp as I face her.

She furrows her eyebrows at first, but she doesn't argue or disobey. She lowers to her knees, using her uncasted arm to support her on the wall. I close the distance between us, my boots practically touching her knees when she tilts her head up to look at me.

Fuck, she's a sight.

I bend down just slightly to cradle her jaw in between my fingers. "I think I *really* like you this way, Nia-Death." She shudders with her exhale, but she doesn't blink; she just waits for me. "Do you want me to take care of you?"

She nods, slow, but drastic enough that the movement forces my hand loose from her jaw. I use my thumb to caress the line before I move past her and turn the shower on behind her.

Nia doesn't move. She waits, like the burden of doing it herself is more than she can bear right now. "It's warm."

Her head doesn't even turn my way. "Get in." She begins to shift from the command, and I extend my hand to help her up and over the ledge of the tub.

She turns her back to the water; it's the only way she can stand in the shower and stick her cast out of range of the spray. Tilting her head back so that the water cascades down her hair, she closes her eyes and goes somewhere else.

I take the moment to squirt shampoo in my hand, and when she pulls her head from the water, I lather and massage her scalp. I hear a whimper when my fingers graze the scar, but I don't stop. I work through her hair and rinse the suds fully before I coat her ends in an excessive amount of conditioner.

Once I'm done, she opens her eyes. She's still in her underwear, though at this point, the sheer fabric is wet enough that it's a joke of an attempt to cover up. I loop my finger through the strap on her hip and pull, snapping it against her skin. She uses her free hand to lower her panties on one side, and then moves to the other.

It takes her far too long to get it free from her hips, but I don't help.

I watch.

I really enjoy watching her.

Doing a jiggle of her hips, she forces the wet fabric all the way down to her ankles, where I bend down to pick them up off the shower floor. She steps out of them, her eyes stuck on me. "You're getting wet."

I bite my cheek to hold back the smile, because I don't think she even recognizes the double entendre.

"Yeah," I say, looking up at her as I toss the panties behind me. "Are you?"

She hides her face from me like she realizes what she's said, biting the smile back. I stand and grip her chin, forcing her to look my way.

Her tongue slides over her bottom lip before she bites it again.

"Are you?" I ask one more time.

It's one small nod, and she hasn't blinked in ages, a little deer in headlights, and it makes me wonder if she's ever been with a woman before.

It wouldn't matter either way.

"If you tell me I can touch you," I warn her, stepping into the shower, boots and all, "everything changes."

That small jerk of a nod again.

"I like routine, structure, things a certain way. Are you going to be a part of that?" It's like my brain is warning her off before my mouth can save us from destroying this before it starts.

But I have to know.

I slip my shirt over my head, leaving my sports bra on.

"And you'll take care of me." She doesn't ask; she parrots the same words I granted her as she tilts her chin to the side.

"Yeah. I'll take care of you, princess."

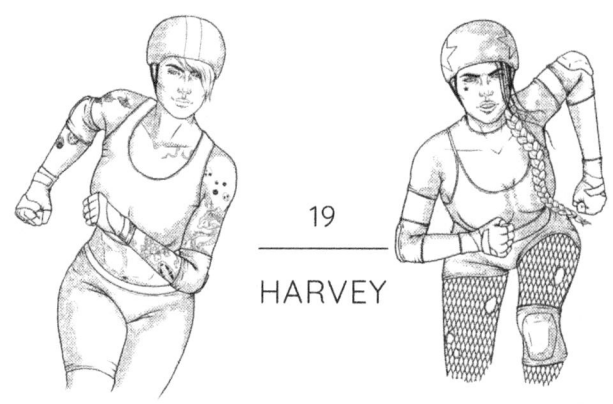

19

HARVEY

It's a terrible idea letting this mess of a girl into my life, allowing her chaos to disrupt the very delicate structure I built for myself in order to survive. I see through all her bullshit, because I'm the same way. Two faces on the same coin, just slightly altered from twists of fate. I had to grow up too soon, and someone tried to keep Nia from doing it at all.

Not intentionally maybe, but parental neglect sometimes comes in the form of doing *too much* just the same as it can be not doing *enough*.

Where my brain goes off at the speed of light with tumultuous thoughts any time I'm *not* in control, for her, it's the opposite. It's the need to decide, the need to perform according to expectations, that's drowning her. She's desperate for someone to relieve her of the burden.

Nia's putty in my hands as I run the loofa over her body, and I don't bother to not look. My eyes explore every inch of her just the same as the soap. I scrub her legs, her feet, and then I move up to her arms. She stops breathing when the loofa touches her stomach.

I don't move.

"Do you want me to stop?"

"No." Her dark eyes burn into mine.

Dropping the loofa, I reach for her, my hand sprawling across the width of her stomach before I decide If I want to move up or down. Her breasts are small, with perfect brown nipples that I'm aching to touch.

"Please," she whispers when I still haven't moved.

It's just us and the beating of water against the floor.

Slowly, I walk my fingers down her stomach, past her belly button, all the way down to her center. My eyes are on hers, and she knows better than to look away. "Breathe," I remind her, and her chest moves on command when her lungs inflate.

Then, I slip my fingers through her folds. The sticky arousal waiting for me is dripping down her thighs, and she gasps as I make contact with the little rose bud, swollen and coated in her juices. I want to taste her, but I'm already in over my head.

Not tonight.

I squeeze two fingers around her clit and rub them together, an audible squeak falling from her lips as she drops her casted arm over my shoulder. She's tired of holding it up, and it's probably heavy. I walk her into the corner of the shower, getting us out of the spray of water, and when her back touches the wall, I finally push the two fingers inside of her.

"Oh!" She grabs at my shoulder, and though I should have expected it, I'm not prepared; I can't help but tense.

Her face scrunches up like she notices the change, and then her hand is off me.

I focus on her again, rubbing my fingers over the ridged spot inside that has her moaning from the depths of her chest. She's not as quiet anymore, and I'm going faster with each stroke. My fingers don't just move back and forth, but spear inside, stretching her, the base of my palm hitting her clit.

Nia's teeth dig into her bottom lip, the color draining from the spot the harder she bites down, the more I fuck her with my fingers.

I swipe my thumb across that swollen button, pressing down with rough circles while my middle and index finger continue their torture. Deep, methodical strokes have her practically sobbing for release with each movement from me.

Her knees buckle with the climb of her orgasm, and I brace to bear her weight. "You can let go," I tell her, and she accepts permission, collapsing onto me. I'm still stroking her; the pulsing doesn't stop, so I don't either.

She's biting back a moan that sounds almost painful, muffling it with her face on the front of my sports bra until she finally stops. Wave after wave, her body finally gives, and she's limp in my arms. It's a kind of satisfaction I can't explain. I can only appreciate how it makes me feel.

I'm still shouldering her with one arm when I reach for the towel hanging in the rack. I wrap it around her and then carry her to her room. She's burnt out, all the adrenaline from the injury fizzled out of her, nothing but exhaustion and pain taking its place instead.

Her eyes are closed when I get her on the bed, and I hesitate, wondering if I should try to clothe her or not. I'm brushing a wet strand of hair off her face when she lets out a small sound, a hum, something like appreciation.

I grab the brush on her nightstand, pull all her hair over her shoulder, and begin to brush the ends. Working my way up slowly, I detangle the long mess to completion, feeling her stare on me.

I do my best to collect all her hair and divide it into three strands. I haven't braided anything in sixteen years, but I try anyway, crossing the chunks of hair over each other until something is slightly assembled. It's not pretty, but it'll do.

I cover her with the blanket and walk toward the door, flipping the switch to turn the lights off.

"Don't go," she mumbles out exhaustedly.

"I shouldn't stay." I don't owe her anything, but I say it for myself.

"You said you would help me." Her mumbles turn a little more clear, like she's coming back from the high of the orgasm and returning to coherence.

"You need help to sleep?" I toss sarcastically.

But she fucking nods, eyes closed, smile stretching over her face.

Is this girl for fucking real?

And why am I absolutely crazy for it?

"Let me get you water for your medicine." I walk out and grab a glass from the kitchen cabinet, filling it up from the pitcher in the fridge.

She's already asleep when I come back, so I lay the pill on the bedside table and place the water next to it. I close my fist around the prescription bottle. I could take it. She *needs* me to take it. But I don't.

Because she also needs to want it on her own.

I put the orange plastic bottle next to her glass and go in search of my shirt. It's still damp, but I pull it over my head anyway and ignore the discomfort. Just as I flick the bathroom light off, I feel something, like I'm being watched. I turn to the end of the hallway to see K standing at their open door, too dark to make out any expression on their face.

I throw them an awkward wave that they don't return before I head for the door and leave.

Staying here would be a mistake.

Because if I stay, she'll think I can offer far more than I truly can.

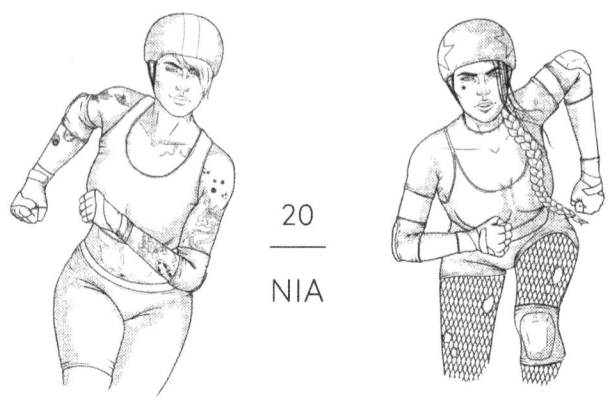

20

NIA

I'm still wrapped in a towel when I wake up. My phone is charged and plugged in next to me, and the clock reads nearly noon.

Every.

Thing.

Hurts.

Down to my fucking soul. The nausea is the worst, and I don't want to get out of bed or even open my eyes, but I know the longer I go without treating it, the worse it'll get. I scratch the sleep out of my eyes and see the glass of water and the pill waiting for me.

I check the dosage on the bottle and laugh. They may as well have given me nothing.

But Harvey left the bottle.

The way she was quick to reach for the bag at the pharmacy made me think I wasn't going to be in control of *this* anymore. I shouldn't, by any fucking means.

But I am.

I try to open the plastic container, but my cast makes it too hard, and the damn child proofing is impossible to beat one handed. I bite at the lid, a dull ache through my teeth as I try to pry the top off. Clenching my jaw in frustration, I settle for what's available, drinking down the weakest oxycodone to ever exist. It gets stuck in my throat; they always do, and it's an indescribable agony to go through.

It's why I normally prefer just burning away at my nasal cavity with it instead. My tongue keeps throwing the pill everywhere but down my throat, and the water eats away the coating of the pill to the point where I taste the bitter powder on my tongue. It's the worst, and I almost want to spit the pill out.

I don't. I take another long gulp of water and then another to wash away any traces of it from my tastebuds. The water is too much, too heavy and filling on an empty stomach when I'm already starting to feel dopesick.

Laying on my back, sprawled across the bed, I wait for it to pass. I breathe through my nose and out through my mouth until the need to vomit travels fully through me.

I hear a knock at my door.

"Yeah?" I answer, sitting up and tightening the towel around me.

Kade has likely been up since at least five, always having to catch a jog with the sunrise.

"Morning," K says, their eyes floating down to my cast. "How you feeling?"

"Like I was run over by an angry pivot last night," I laugh. "You won us the bout!"

Kade scratches at the back of their head, blue hair falling in front of their face to cover their embarrassment. "Yeah. I mean, you did most of the work."

"Don't sell yourself short." I smile, putting on my best face for them.

"Hey, uh… Cat Harvey was here last night." K says it like it's a fact, but I'm almost positive it's a question.

"Yeah. She was." I bite my lip before continuing. "I needed help last night."

"Oh. Well that's… nice of her?" Kade questions their own words. "Glad you two are turning over a new leaf."

I choke on my own cough. "Something like that."

The memory of last night comes flooding back. Of me in the shower, unraveling in her arms. The way she made me feel, not just physically but more than that, taken care of. That wasn't the same Cat who hated me so much that she couldn't stand to be in the room with me, and certainly not the same Cat intent on laying me out to prove a point. So if all of that was the way she hated, then what was this?

"How's your wrist?" K strays from getting too personal, a skill they've mastered.

"Fractured." I blow out a huff of air through my lips. "Looks like you'll be first jammer for a while."

K laughs. "Yeah, right. Scott would rather you break the other wrist before he sacrifices all those points you score."

"We'll see. This is probably for the best, anyway. I need to get a job before I burn through the rest of my savings. I can't be spending every second at Skateland," I admit, and it's mostly for myself.

The reality checks always come when I'm sober.

With a click of their tongue they lift a finger. "Actually, that reminds me. You said your degree was in social work?" I nod. "The girl who does my hair said her kid's school needs a counselor."

My eyes widen, and I lean forward, a new burst of energy filling me temporarily. "Wait, really? That's perfect!"

"It's a private school, though. Background checks, paperwork. Can you be on your best behavior?" Kade laughs like they know me.

They only know what I let them see but it's enough for this assumption, so I give them a smile.

"I can fake it." I promise with a low salute.

"Great." They're still amused by me, gripping the door handle to give me privacy once again. "I'll leave all the info for you on the counter. I'm heading out for the day."

"Okay. Have fun." Living with Kade is easy. They don't pry, don't ask too many questions, and we really get along on a fundamental level. "Shit. Wait!" I shout, remembering the opportunity.

K opens the door and pops their head in with a raised eyebrow.

"I can't open my meds. It's time for me to take my pills." I give them a cheesy grin. "Help," I cry pathetically.

K smiles and walks my way, opening the bottle with ease and pulling out one pill before they close the cap again.

My heart sinks, but I swallow down the feeling and paint a thankful look on my face before I accept the pill, chasing it with water, this time much more successfully than the first go-around.

"Bye." K pats my head and ruffles my hair before leaving for good.

I lean back against the headboard and swipe meaninglessly through videos on my phone until the pills kick in. I wait for the throbbing in my wrist to subside, for the burning to ease, for the relief to wash over me.

It doesn't.

My tolerance is too high, and I know why.

I pull the drawer and reach for my old copy of *The*

Divine Secrets of the Yaya Sisterhood. I open it to the middle, where the tiny Ziploc baggie is pressed flat with the light beige powder inside.

My heart thrums violently just staring at it. Long ago, this had been a bottom line for me, yet here I am, casually consuming it for breakfast. *Just a little bump*, never more than that.

My hands tremble as I dump a small pea-sized pile of the powder onto my nightstand then reach for a cut up straw somewhere in the back of the drawer. The sting is minimal compared to the pills, and the relief is instant.

I
sink
into
the
bed.
I sink into the bed.
I sink into the bed.
I sink into the world.
I
escape
my
mind.

THERE'S A BRIGHT LIGHT I CAN'T LOOK AWAY FROM. It burns with intensity, but it's so close, it's overwhelming.

"Hey. Twerp." Ryan's voice is abrasively loud and stern, and I hate when he tries to wake me up to move me to the bed.

"Just carry me," I whine, but he shakes me.

"Gimme a better sign of life, Nia," he says, and I flutter my eyes open, the flashlight still pointed directly in my eyes.

"Fuck, turn that shit off." I push it away with my braced hand.

Ryan is standing above me, and next to him is Bobby C, a guy who's been recently coming around. He's annoying, but Ryan trusts him and doesn't mind that the guy only comes by for free shit.

I guess I'm kind of doing the same anyway.

Bobby is in a stained gray sweatshirt from the same high school I attended, except his says class of '03 on the front. "Oh good, she's up. Thought I was gonna have to give you a second dose." He waves a little plastic bottle before shoving it back into his pocket.

"What happened?" I ask, and just then, the bile rises up my throat. Jerking to a seated position, I push past Ryan, running into his kitchen just in time to spew my vomit into the sink.

I heave a few more times until only bile is left, along with its bitter aftertaste.

"You OD-ed." Ryan's voice is stern as he stands behind me.

I'm still bracing the sink, sweat glistening at my back and a cold chill wrapping around me. I don't say anything. The vague memory of the day sets in, of me driving to Ryan's at the peak of my high, of being offered another bump from his stash and graciously accepting it. Of nodding off in front of the tv.

"What time is it?" I ask him.

"It's almost midnight. Nia, *why* did you overdose?" His voice is sharp and full of anger, disappointment, all the things I hate from the people I've parentified in my life.

"I don't know. You're the one dealing it out, Ryan," I snap at him, though I know I'm the one fully in the wrong. "How was I supposed to know it was too much?"

"Bullshit. I gave you one little bump."

Fuck.

"What else did you take, Nia?" When I don't answer, his hand slams down on the counter next to me, and I flinch. "What else?" It comes out too loud of a yell, louder than my own father had ever gotten with me.

"I forgot, okay!" I cover my ears like a child, overwhelmed and overstimulated by his outburst, his emotions and the situation. "I took my pain pills for my wrist."

"Shit," he hisses, and I turn back to see him palming his face with frustration. "I should have known when you walked in here with that cast that they'd given you something for it."

"Don't. Don't take the blame for it." I shake my head, hating that I've somehow put this burden on him. "I'm sorry. It was stupid and I won't do it again," I promise him.

"You sure won't. You're cut off." He crosses his arms like it's the final step for the foot he's officially putting down.

"What?" I explode. "Are you fucking kidding me?" He raises a sarcastic eyebrow, like whatever I'm about to say is of no interest to him. "So fucking typical of you, Ryan. Get your little addicts all hooked so that you can cut them off. What's your plan? Have me beg you to pay double, triple for my next dose?"

His face falls flat. "If that's what you think, get your shit and get out of my house."

"Gladly," I scoff, grabbing my wallet, my keys, and my phone and heading to my car.

I feel for the little baggie in my pocket, the one I came here to buy. It's still there, and I sigh a little bit of relief in knowing that.

And a dreadful feeling wraps me up in something bitter.

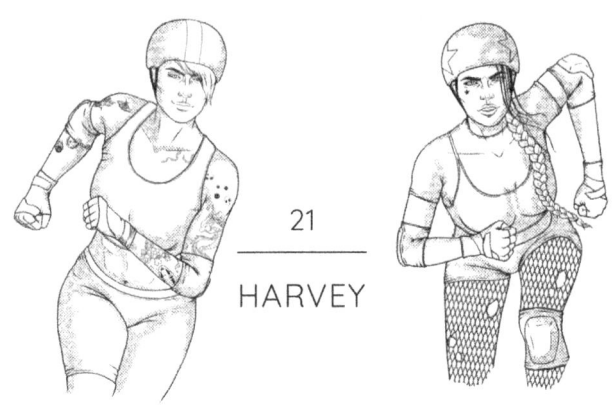

21

HARVEY

I'm thinking about her so often that by the time Monday comes around, I'm desperate for practice. I hang around the rink all day, hoping she may show up for some time to herself. Work was a drag the previous day. Every time that front door swung open, I hoped it would be her coming through them, but it never was.

She doesn't look great when I see her, though. The same shitty braid I fashioned two days prior still hangs down her shoulder. She looks out of it, sickly and lackluster. Either she's using, or this is the effect of not using. No one seems to either notice or care, though.

I do.

Scott forgives her for being slow and sloppy during practice, chalking it up to the injury and benching her for the remainder of practice. She looks pissed, and it's only slightly adorable. I take her place as jammer and get beside K-Otic, waiting for the blow of the whistle to start the jam, but Venice Witch is taking too long with her water break.

"Harvey," K says amicably before placing their mouthguard back in.

I nod my chin at them, wondering if they're going to ask about the other night. Surely they'd already talked to Nia about it.

But they say nothing, and the whistle blows. Already too used to blocking, I focus on the defensive instead of going for the win. We go a few more jams before Scott calls it quits for the night, asking the skaters to line up for their measly little royalty checks from the last jam. It's nothing, probably fifty bucks per player, but it's enough to excite the skaters. Before this, we were paying dues monthly to keep the league going. Now, we're getting paid.

I hate admitting it, but somehow, this asshole knows a *little* of what he's doing.

Getting rid of him isn't going to be so easy, but now, I'm not sure what my options are.

No one else here can help, and even if they could, the majority have their own very real problems to deal with. Skateland can't be all of our burden to share. I look over at Nia again.

She's a mess, falling apart.

Unraveling at the seams.

This grief devours you whole, and Nia is in the belly of the beast.

Scott hands Nia her check first, letting her skip the line, and then he passes me one as well. I don't focus on the rest of the players and what they do next. No, I zero in on the five-foot-nothing jammer skating toward the locker room.

We haven't spoken since I tucked her into bed after the hospital.

Is she going to pretend she was too out of it to remember?

In the locker room, her gear is already off and thrown in her bag, her helmet peaking out, the plastic dull and dented, like it needs to be replaced. She stands there, in front of her open locker, watching me remove my skates, but neither of us talk.

The tension is borderline fucking painful.

I want to speak, but I need to maintain some sort of control here.

She just stares, and eventually, every single piece of my gear is off and put away.

It's the longest game of chicken we've played yet, and she plays it well. I tilt my head to the side, as if to say *what's next, princess?*

Stepping backwards, she keeps her eyes on me until she hits the wall behind her. She gives me a single look, pulls the curtain open in one of the shower stalls, and drops her clothes to the ground. First the fishnets, then the spandex shorts, and when the shirt goes, I have to remind myself to close my jaw.

She walks into the stall and leaves the curtain open. The only skater in here is Bae, who's oblivious to us with her earpods in. The others will be in soon.

Fuck it.

I pull my practice tee off and leave it on the bench before I do the same with my gym shorts and my underwear. Then, I walk in her direction, closing the curtain behind us.

Her back is to me, her casted hand lifted out of range of the water, and she doesn't turn when she hears me join her. I wrap my fingers around her hips and pull her to me, one hand traveling north, up her side, while the other simply holds her.

She glues her spine to me, like she can't help but get closer. I pull her in even tighter, and she melts. My fingers twirling the hardened bead of her nipple while the other hand dances lower. She lets out a soft whimper just as I hear DreadPool's loudmouth enter the locker room.

"Can someone tell Scott to just shut the fuck up?" they yell like they've been holding it in all practice.

A trail of laughter follows, the rest of the skaters packing in behind them. "You were saying 'thank you, daddy' two seconds ago when he handed you your check," Nancy calls Dread out.

I don't let the distraction take me, and I don't let it take her either, my fingers sliding through the sticky heat waiting for me. She's so wet. Even with the water washing it away, she's still soaked, her arousal dripping down her thighs.

Nia lets out a squeak when I spread her lips, sliding past her clit and pushing all the way inside, my fingers curving and hooking.

"Shh," I whisper in her ear. "Do you want them to hear you?"

Their voices drown out in the background with their normal post-scrimmage conversations and plans for the night. The loud beating of the water makes it impossible to know what anyone is saying unless they yell.

But that doesn't mean they can't hear *us*.

I'm moving my fingers slowly, savoring the build up this time until I have her bucking her hips with each stroke. She's moaning, and it's nearly audible. If anyone is suspicious, they don't make it known. The stalls are tall, but it would only take someone looking in the gap beneath the curtain to see both our feet.

I flip her to face me, lifting her up by her hips and pressing her against the wall. She instinctively wraps her legs around me, holding herself up. A desperate, hearty moan falls from her lips once I move my fingers inside her again.

I cover her mouth with my free hand, but within seconds, she's wiggled enough to move it out of the way, biting it. Her teeth wrap around the outside near my pinky. She doesn't make another sound, instead, she bites harder the closer she gets to her release.

I take it as a challenge. The more pain I feel, the harder I fuck her.

Her explosion is catastrophic, a tidal wave of pleasure that pulses through her so violently, I can feel it in my own soul.

Satisfaction.

It's the only high *I* chase.

Somehow it's become intrinsically entwined into her existence.

I pull my fingers free once I feel she's fully down from the climb, raising them past her to my own lips so I can finally get a taste.

It's everything I knew she would be.

Now, I'm twice as fucked.

Her eyes are locked on mine, and she hasn't blinked. I lean closer, a quiet hum in her ear. "Now go try to pretend I didn't just fuck you again." Letting her down, she gives me one last look before she grabs a hanging towel and slides out behind the curtain.

I look at my hand, instant gratification at seeing the blood pebbling out from the mark her teeth left on my skin.

"I thought Cat was in the shower," I hear Bae asking loud, her headphones probably still on.

"Oh—uh, I think she's showering too." Nia's voice trembles just outside the stall, and the smile curves itself on my face like it belongs.

I wash, not bothering to relieve the ache between my own legs but still savoring the taste of her on my tongue. The water pressure sucks here, but it's enough to get the sweat off and do what it needs to.

When I'm done and dried, the locker room is clear.

I don't know if I'm relieved or disappointed.

It's Friday night practice now, and I've seen Nia Da Silva exactly two times since the bout. Monday and Wednesday. She's making a habit of sneaking out of practice early enough to get in the shower before anyone notices, always leaving the curtain open for me to follow behind.

I make her come, she sneaks away, and by the time I'm done, she's out of sight.

Tonight is no different. She's got her teeth wrapped around my hand, her eyes lasered in on me while I fuck her with three fingers. She grips the wall, the shower caddy, anything to hold herself up as she comes undone with tonight's orgasm.

But we still don't talk.

I open the curtain, already wrapped in a towel, but I'm startled when I see StarScreamer standing on the other side, waiting.

"Just so you know, I am one hundred percent invested in this." She grins like an idiot.

"What are you talking about?" I give her a side-eye before walking back to my locker and pulling clean clothes from my bag.

"Oh, I'm sorry, are we still in the pretending phase? We all assumed since you two were getting it on in the shower all week that we were good to talk about it." She shrugs, staring off into the distance to give me something like privacy while I throw on my clothes. "We're *all* talking about it, so I figured you'd at least want to join the conversation."

I don't answer her.

"Fine," she says dramatically, like she's the one exhausted of *me*. "But I'm thrilled about it. I think you're perfect for each other."

"Leave it alone, Stella," I warn her, not needing to complicate things any further by adding a peanut gallery to our situation.

They thrive on inner-team gossip, and there hasn't been a relationship in the team since Venice and Lady Yaga screwed around that one summer.

At least they can stand to be in the same room again.

Star waits for me. It's standard to not let a skater leave the rink alone at night. The walk to the car is brief, but you never know when a weirdo might be lurking. The rest of the skaters have gone, but Nia is sitting on the hood of her car, biting her thumb nail as she stares at her phone. Her hair is unbrushed, tangled, haphazardly thrown into something like a bun at the top of her head.

Because she can't put it in a braid.

"Nia!" Star chirps, her tone full of dramatic suspicion. "What are you still doing here?" She gives me a sly grin and elbows me, like she thinks this is part of some plan between Nia and me.

"My car won't start." She huffs, and though she's looking at StarScreamer, it's the first time I'm hearing her talk this week.

I'm desperate for her attention.

It's a measly little crumb, and I devour it.

"Do you need a jump?" I ask, giving myself permission to initiate since it isn't a conversation about us.

"That'd be great." She just barely glances at me, and I'm not sure if it's me or if it's StarScreamer causing this reaction from her.

"Well, I'll leave you two to each other then," Star sings as she opens the driver side of her PT cruiser.

Nia's staring at her phone again, so I flip Stella off as I walk toward the trunk of my SUV. I grab the cords and get in my driver's seat, pulling the car up beside Nia's banged up little shit.

She's off the hood now, sitting on the curb, still staring at her phone. The nervous energy vibrates off her, evident in the way she bounces her leg to self-soothe. I attach the ends of the jumper cables, and she gets in her car. We both let it charge until she's satisfied it'll run.

"Call me if you get stuck," I offer, knowing she won't.

She nods again. Nothing else said between us.

It's torture.

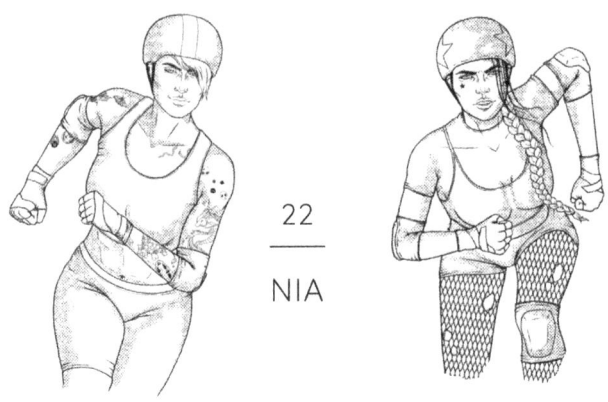

22

NIA

I coast through practice all week in a foggy haze from the mixture of pain pills and heroin that is starting to become such a common part of my day-to-day, I'm not even bothering to lie to myself anymore.

I have a problem.

Well, I have three problems.

The Cat Harvey-sized problem is growing by the minute, the one that shatters my confidence but keeps me wrapped tight in her chokehold. I don't know what it is we're doing, but I crave it, and every moment I don't have it, I need to be high.

She isn't the cause, though, and if I wasn't depending on her, I would just be using something else as another excuse to get high. My wrist became a new opportunity, but now, it's taking three times as many pills to do the job of a little bump.

I'm also running out of money, and my car keeps breaking down, which is an added issue I can't afford to fix. I'm running out of subject changes every time my father asks why I haven't answered my mother's calls since the accident. In a way, it almost feels like I'm running out of time, like I'm dashing toward some imaginary finish line.

Some sort of ending I can't bear to be a part of.

By the time Slam Night comes, I'm not interested in attending. I know I'm benched. I have to be, because putting me on the track is a liability Scott won't risk.

I fight the part of my brain that tells me to not go, and that I could just get high on the rest of my stash, figure out what comes next after I run out.

"You're not ready?" Kade asks, standing at the open door of my bedroom.

"Do I *need* to go?" I whine, sitting at the edge of the bed with my fishnets still hanging off my ankles.

"Is that even a question?" they deadpan. "Nancy Shrew and the Shrewdettes would literally put the bout on pause, hog-tie you, and stuff you into their trunk just to make you sit on the bench tonight." An eyebrow raises. "Or you could come willingly."

I exhale and drag out the word as it leaves my mouth. "Fine. Watch it, though. One snap of my fingers, and I'll have them dragging you along to the next social event too."

K's face is one of pure dread. "Kill me first, please."

Laughing, I start getting all of my things together. "You're not a fan of the team?"

"No, no. It's not that at all. Everyone is perfectly... perfect." They shove their hands in their pockets and shrug. "I'm just... not great with groups."

"I get it." I give them a reassuring smile. "I promise."

Kade leaves me to change, and I continue the ritual with my fishnets, pulling them up and then donning my Devil's Dame's black spandex shorts. I don't bother with anything other than my practice tee with my skate name on the back. I won't be on the track tonight anyway, which means I also take no care in slapping my roster number on my arm in eyeliner. The sixty-four is sloppy, maybe because I wrote it with my left hand, or maybe because I no longer care to tout my mother's birth date on my skin.

There I am, in front of the mirror.

Every flaw glaringly obvious.

I despise who I've become.

I'M THREE TIMES AS UNNECESSARY AS I HAD ORIGINALLY thought I was. Since Rae-Gunn passed their minimal skills test, Scott felt decent about moving the roster around so that K-Otic starts, and if needed, a switch could be made with Harvey.

But I'm not focused on the bout. I'm not focused on much of anything except my cuticles, which I've gnawed to death, and the itching at my chest from my last hit.

"You good?" StarScreamer slides into me on the bench as she takes a swig of her water bottle. She's dripping in sweat, but she's killing it out there. Stella is one of the best damn blockers I've ever seen.

"Just ready to be out there again." I weave another lie into my web.

She laughs. "Yeah, the bench sucks, but you'll be back jamming in no time." She gives me a playful shove before she heads back behind the pivot line.

At halftime, we're so far ahead that Scott is joking about putting me back in just for shits and giggles. Mo doesn't appreciate the joke and sets him straight. My neck and chest are covered in scratch marks, and I'm ready to get the fuck out of Skateland.

That's when Harvey stops in front of me. It's the first time she's acknowledged my existence today, and for some reason, it feels like a gift. The realization of what she's doing to me is both obscenely degrading and hopeless, and there's nothing I can do about it. I'm so small in her hands, so small in her world, and she's so big in mine.

All I can see is Cat Harvey.

Like she's not actually a problem but the *answer* to all of them. Her eyes lower to my knees, which are obnoxiously bouncing. She drops her hands to my thighs as if to keep them still, bending just enough so that her face is in line with mine. I think my heart's stopped, but I'm not positive, because all the blood is currently flooding down south. It feels like our entire team is staring at us, but I wouldn't know, because I haven't looked away from her.

Her thumbs squeeze the inside of my thighs, and then with one hand, she's reaching for a water bottle next to me. She finally lets me go, standing to get her fill of a drink.

I'm
a
speck
of
dust
floating
in
her
presence
again.

Mo calls the starting skaters to a huddle and delivers the final plays for the night before the zebra blows the whistle, signaling the end of halftime. I'm nodding in and out for the second half, but it's fine, because everyone is focused on the track, on the win guaranteed to be ours.

The team is vibrating with positivity. Two bouts in a row, and as I look around, Skateland seems to be fuller than ever before. This is good—this is amazing. It's everything Lonnie ever wanted.

Like pesticide, the thought of my dead friend kills all the joy that wanted to bubble around me, infiltrating every inch of my heart. I suddenly no longer desire to be on this bench, on this rink, or anywhere near this building.

I don't look at anyone. I just command my feet off the track, pushing past the excited spectators without bothering to head for the locker rooms. I'm sloppy taking off my skates, still too high to care to focus. There are judging eyes; I don't have to look up to know they're there, burning into me.

Once I've rounded up all my shit, I push out through the double doors, and the chill hits through the holes in my fishnets.

F

U

C

K

I didn't drive.

My heart sinks, all hopes of a sneaky early getaway evaporating into thin air. Pulling my hood over my head, I resort to slouching down against the wall and staring at the parking lot until time decides I'll have to do something else about this.

"Girl, where the fuck have you been? We've been looking for you forever!" Lady Yaga's loud voice wakes me up.

It's freezing cold out, and I'm still sitting on the ground in front of the rink, resting my back on a pillar. The parking lot is mostly empty now, like all the attendees who came to watch have already left.

Shit.

I rub the sleep out of my eyes, but I'm groggy.

No.

I'm high.

Looking down, I see my pill bottle in my lap, half open. I broke the child tampering lid the other day in order to stop depending on everyone else, so now it only barely rests on, half the lid split on one side. I think I took another while I was out here waiting, but I don't fully remember. Yaga doesn't notice the orange bottle in my lap; I quickly fist it and shove it into my bag.

"Wasn't feeling it. Sorry." I shrug sympathetically. "It's hard watching everyone else skate while I'm like this."

She laughs. "Maybe that's your lesson." I frown, but she doesn't stop. "I just mean, you never got hurt before. Not before the *big* one. You always started, always played, hardly got benched unless you were so exhausted someone else *had* to fill in. When you got hurt, you left. You didn't give yourself a chance to stick around and heal *with* us."

She's right. I ran away, tail tucked between my legs, because if I wasn't skating, then who was I? I couldn't let my team see me that way. And now, here I am, repeating history. Yaga looks at me like she can see it too.

"Don't leave again," she whispers, kneeling down to my level.

"I won't." The words come out, but I'm not sure I mean them.

"Promise?" She waits, an eyebrow lifted high.

"Yeah, yeah." I elbow her, forcing her to stand and then giving her my good hand to help me the rest of the way up.

"Party at Harvey's!" Nancy shouts coming out of the doors.

I'm guessing at this point, even the losing team has left, but I was out for most of it. I reach into my bag to make sure my wallet is still in there. Not like anyone would be stealing much anyway.

"Are you coming, K?" Dread asks. They're the only other person who seems comfortable communicating with Kade in a familiar way here.

"Come on, K, you practically won us the bout. Come celebrate," StarScream encourages.

Their face is uneasy, and I'm about to open my mouth to shoot off whatever random excuse I can come up with to get them out of this when Kade locks eyes with me and answers, "I will if Antônia comes."

Fucking traitor.

"Well, *of course* Nia is coming." Star links her arms with mine, and suddenly, my entire ability to speak and fight for myself is gone.

I search for Harvey in the pack and find her pretending like she's not listening while she fumbles with her keys at her car door. Her face is pure amusement. Her eyes find mine, and I'm so fucking obvious, it hurts.

"S-sure," I answer, looking back at Star. "Why not?"

Everyone cheers, but it's my roommate I'm blasting with a dirty look. "Fucking evil," I hum to Kade, pushing them with my shoulder.

"If I'm suffering, so are you, bitch." They laugh, shoving me back.

I guess we're doing this.

You can't grow if you don't leave your comfort zone. That's what Lonnie used to say, and though the words feel more like salt on a wound, they still attempt their intended job. Lonnie would say the pain is necessary; hell, they'd even find a way to make it sound poetic somehow.

Except Lonnie's in a casket under some dirt and I don't quite like poetry the way I used to.

I'm tired of leaving my comfort zone. I want to get wrapped up in it and never outgrow it ever again. That no longer seems to be an option. Skaters are packing into vehicles, most of them cramming and carpooling with each other, since everyone will likely be too drunk to drive. Instinctually, my feet follow K, but my eyes search for Harvey again, who's getting into her driver seat.

We lock stares, and she reaches over the empty passenger seat to get the door from the inside.

In some way, it's the same invitation I've been giving her all week.

My feet shift in her direction, and I take the first step, but then Bae hops over to Harvey's car and grabs the slightly open door, taking the passenger seat and buckling in. My face burns with embarrassment, and I dash to Kade's side as fast as I possibly can.

Fuck. I'm a goddamn tragedy in three parts.

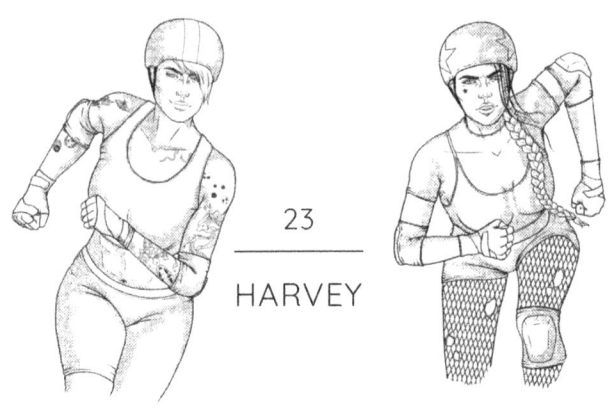

23

HARVEY

I blare my music and don't say a word to Bae the entire ride back to my place. Clitblocking on the most oblivious level, and it is one hundred percent her style. She sits there, little rainbow pigtails not even three inches long hanging from the top of her head while she bops along to *Cray* on the radio.

The song is catchy, but it doesn't take away my annoyance.

We aren't the first to get to my place, and the door is already unlocked. It looks like Mo's turned my dining room table into a poker setup, and DreadPool is trying to organize some sort of social media dance move to film on their phone with Nancy and Electric. I'm not trying to find *them*, though. No, my eyes are darting back and forth across my living space for the girl with the braid.

There's still no braid, though, just a knotted clump of hair above her head that's so wild and unkempt, it reminds me of Helena Bonham Carter. She's leaning against a window, talking to K with a forced smile on her face. I'm finding myself walking in their direction, hoping that, along the way, I'll stumble into an excuse, or someone else to talk to who won't make me feel or seem so desperate for her.

Venice slides in ahead of me, handing both her and K a beer. Nia gives Venice a grin when she says thanks, but K-Otic frowns. "Should you be drinking?"

"What do you mean?" Nia pops the tab anyway and takes a swig.

"You're on pain pills." K takes the can from her hand and, for some reason, that irks me.

"I'm a big girl, Kade." She tries to snatch it back, but they don't let go and the beer spills all over Nia's chest.

Her nostrils flare when she yells out in frustration at being wet and then runs to the bathroom.

Venice looks between the two of us with wide eyes and then awkwardly finds the next person walking by to take her away from the staredown K and I seem to be locked in.

"You can't control her." I don't know why I say it, but the words come out of my mouth anyway.

"I'm looking out for her." K crosses their arms, annoyed that I'm suggesting otherwise.

"Sure, but someone like Nia doesn't respond well to having her choices taken away from her." I take a drink of my own beer.

"Oh, suddenly you know a lot about Nia, do you?" They suck something through their teeth and push away from the wall, walking past me and heading out the door.

I guess that's as long as they can bear to socialize.

I won't apologize. They can't force her to make the right decision. They can't take her choice away.

I don't check to see if K's actually left for good. Instead, I hover in front of the bathroom door, unsure if I should knock, if I should go in, or if I should just leave her the fuck alone. She's said nothing to me, barely a thank you after I gave her car a jump the other night.

Nia Da Silva is officially the hardest puzzle I've tried to solve. I'm starting to think she has no idea what she looks like when she's whole, so how the hell is she supposed to put herself back together?

After ten minutes pass and she's still in the bathroom, I rap my knuckles lightly against the door.

"What?"

I don't answer for a bit. I don't know what to say, and I'm not quite sure what I'm doing. "It's me."

There's no response for a solid minute, but then I hear the click of the door unlock. Nothing else, no call to come inside, no sign from her on the other end. I open the door anyway to see her there, sitting on the closed toilet.

Her shirt is drenched in beer, her eyes red, her war paint from Slam Night streaking down her cheeks. There's a hundred things I could ask her; she looks miserable, in pain, and not just physically. Instead, I opt for skimming the surface.

"Dry shirt?" I offer.

She doesn't look up, but she nods and then lifts her arms, almost childlike, as she waits for me to help take hers off. It makes me wonder how she's getting by at home, if K is helping her, if she's hurting herself to get her basic needs taken care of. I raise the shirt and toss it into my hamper before pulling my own off and then sliding it over her head. She closes her eyes, shimming into the oversized thing and inhaling hard as it comes down.

"You look like shit." I immediately regret my choice of words, the hurt on her face like barbed wire in my throat. "I just mean, it doesn't look like anyone has been helping you. With anything."

She scratches at the side of her arm, and it lasts too long for me to think it's just nerves. "I just don't like to be a burden."

"You need help." She knows I mean more than just with the wrist.

"No shit," she whispers.

"You're a mess. You need order, systems, routines. Your type can't function without it." She's offended now, and it's obvious on her face.

Nia laughs, but it's not from amusement. "My type?" She looks like she's about ready to go a round with me.

"Yeah. Forgetful. Impulsive. Dopamine seeking." She backs down once I name all her most apparent qualities. "I know because it's my type too."

"You seem pretty fucking together." Her arms cross over her chest.

"It's that or get swallowed by the chaos. We can figure out what works for you," I tell her.

Her sigh is exhausted. "Nothing works for me."

I lean closer and crouch down in front of her. "Stay the night." It's the closest I've ever come to begging in my entire life.

"You're asking?" She's finally looking at my face now.

"I'm telling." My hands are at the tops of her thighs again, just like earlier tonight. I give the same gentle squeeze with my thumbs, and her breath hitches.

"What are you doing to me?" That anxious tone laces through her words, those dark brown eyes burning into mine.

"What do you mean, princess?" I tilt my head, just the tiniest of a curl to my lip.

"I mean, you spend a lot of time getting me off, I guess it *should* all be the same to me because, in a way, *I'm* the one using *you*... but I think I'm just trading one thing out for another." She scowls. "What happens when you get tired of me? Or worse, when you realize you can't fix me because I'll never love myself enough to stop, and the only person I loved enough to care to stop *for* is now dead?"

I start to laugh but clear my throat so it doesn't upset her, "You think you're using *me*?" I can't help but sound smug.

"It feels like it." She says it like a confession.

It doesn't offend me.

I shake my head instead. "Unless you're at risk from coming to death, I don't think I'd call this trading addictions, Nia."

"What do you know about addiction?" She huffs.

That offends me. "I know that it's the only word I can use to describe the need I have for you." My fingers carve deeper into her thighs, her frown deepens, but she doesn't say she's in pain. "That I'm itching for you every goddamn day, waiting for you to ask me for help, to need me in some way."

"You haven't talked to me all week." She's looking down, like my stare is too much.

"That's a double-sided problem, princess. Have you talked to *me*?" My fingers dig in harder.

She finds my gaze again. "What are we doing?" she asks once more, but there's so much desperation in her voice that I'm compelled to answer this time.

I trace my thumb and index finger along the corners of her mouth. "We're friends." I lie, my only defense left to protect myself from her.

She scoffs before pushing my hand away. "You do this shit with all your friends?"

I don't fight the twisted grin. "Just my *very* special

friends." My hand slides past her ear as I cradle the side of her head in my palm. She relaxes into the touch, melting, relaxing, until she realizes what it's doing to her. Then, that scowl forms again.

"Stop fucking with me, Harvey." Her eyes are welling with tears, but she leans harder into me, like it comforts her. Her voice breaks. "I can't handle it."

"You've been using." I don't say it with judgment; I just state it plainly.

It's all over her face.

"You've had my number this whole time. I told you to call me, didn't I?" Her eyes widen with realization.

"I just thought you meant it in the way *everybody* says shit like that. *Call me if you need anything. Anytime*, or my favorite, *You're always welcome here.* I can't decipher that shit."

She's spiraling, so I grab her chin once more to gain her focus. "Hey. That's them, *out there.* That's how they live with their weird societal hoops they jump through and codes they talk in that only *they* understand. Me and you? I'm always going to be straight with you. If I say call me, *then you dial my fucking number*, do you understand me? If I say *anytime,* then I want you here without thinking twice. *If you need me?* Then I better already be around."

The words are barely out of my mouth when I sink into the realization that I've lost at my own game.

And
Now
I'm
Hers.

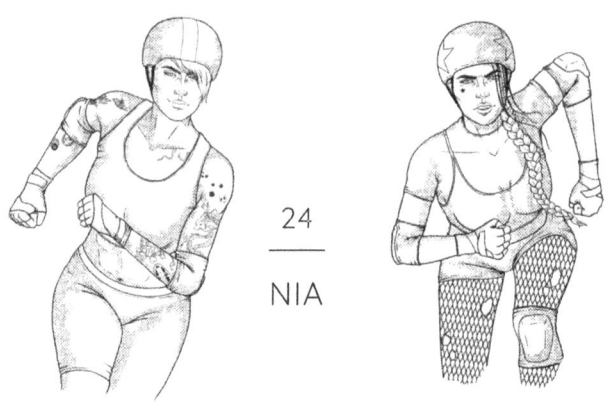

24

NIA

I'm trembling.

Some of it's the heroin, but most of it is Cat Harvey coursing through my fucking system. She's worse than a drug, because without the drugs, I'm miserable, but without her, I'm nothing.

"Stay the night," she says again, this time, her voice sure and full of dangerous promises.

I'm running out of oxygen.

"I-I don't know if that's a good id—"

She doesn't let me finish. "Is the alternative getting high?"

I don't know how to lie to her when it's this sudden. I have no script, no defense. I'm unprepared. Lying is a practiced skill. With my mother, I mastered it after learning the ways in which she could disarm me. With Cat?

It doesn't just feel painful.

I don't *want* to lie to her.

"Come with me." She gets up from her crouched position and extends her hand.

"I don't know that I wanna go back out there," I admit, shaking my head.

"K's probably already left. We aren't going back to the party anyway," she reassures me.

For Kade to have left me here is a swirling cluster of negative thoughts I'm not quite ready to process yet.

So I take her hand and stand, following her out of the bathroom. Harvey doesn't bother putting a new shirt over her sports bra; she just grabs her keys off a side table and waves two fingers at the crowd of skaters in the room. Some are paying attention, some already too shit-faced to care, but most are doing their own thing.

"We'll be back later," Harvey says to the room, still dragging me behind by the hand.

And then I'm in her car, shrinking to the smallest size possible as she fumbles with her phone to choose the right song. She notices the way my shoulders are hunched in, how I hold myself tight for warmth, and without a word, she blasts the heat on maximum.

Every song that plays is a new part of Harvey I'm discovering. She's eclectic, and her music taste is a kaleidoscope of her range. Six or seven songs pass, and I realize we've driven far enough that we're no longer in Devil Town. "Where are we going?" I finally speak.

"Does it matter?" she asks without looking my way.

I guess not, so I don't bother answering either.

It's another thirty minutes before she slows down, pulling into a dirt clearing. I officially have no idea where we are, which is a shock, because I know this state like the back of my hand.

She doesn't stop driving once we get to the dirt road. Instead, she swerves her monstrosity of an SUV into the grass itself and starts traversing the mountainside. I'm not sure how legal this is, but I know there's not enough funding in our area to employ someone just to keep us shitheads out.

Reaching for the volume control, she finally turns the music down just as the car comes to a rolling stop. We're still at a downward slope, but she seems confident the emergency break can handle the job.

"What are we doing?" I look at her until she finally turns and unbuckles her seatbelt.

"We're keeping busy." She smiles, hitting the button that slides her moonroof open.

The chill is unforgivable, but the view? The view is breathtaking.

Her seat slides all the way back, and with a singular look, she's beckoning me over. Biting my lip, I fumble with my seatbelt until she reaches over, and with a quick movement, she unclips me.

I practically fall into her arms, the seat somehow big enough for both of us, but with her arms around me and my body pressed to her chest, I'm hardly anything, just a fleeting feeling in her hold. I stare at her until I've memorized every freckle on her face, connecting them with imaginary lines until my own constellations form above her nose.

"You're supposed to be looking at the stars," she whispers without turning her head my way. She's got one arm folded behind her head now, but the other stays holding me into her, keeping me close.

"I am." It's still her face I see.

She squeezes my side.

I feel frozen, not from the cold but like a moment in time, like I could carve this one out and find a special place to hang it in my mind. It feels like the whole universe is on our side, giving us the space to be. I want to touch her, but I can't ruin this.

So, I just stare, and her hand once gripping at my side now softens, the tips of her fingers grazing up and down until the smallest hairs on my body have all come to stand. I'm impossibly aware of her touch, and if it's not on purpose, then maybe something is wrong with me.

Maybe this obsession is getting out of hand.

Each time her fingers travel, I pray they'll go further, maybe an inch higher, maybe a few inches lower.

"I need you to touch me," I whine, an embarrassing plea, but I'm burning with desire, and I want it from her.

"Not here," she hums in my ear. It doesn't feel like the rejection my brain would automatically go to. It just feels like a promise for later.

An hour goes by before she slides shut the glass of the moonroof and turns the heat back on. But we don't move; we don't ruin this.

The view *is* breathtaking.

"Lonnie used to joke about me and you." She finally looks my way. "They made you out to be this faultless, perfect little thing. Unbeatable, charming, undeniably likable."

"And the real thing must have been a let down, huh?" I laugh, snuggling into her side.

"When you blew in out of goddamn nowhere, you fucked all of my shit up. All my plans, every aspect of my life I had perfectly set up to get to the place where I finally feel safe and secure." Her honesty is starting to hurt, but I don't pull away. "I spent my whole life trying to feel that, and then *you*. But it turned out you were none of those things. You're self-conscious, you're fragile, you're so beyond damaged that *not* protecting you feels like a goddamn crime against Lonnie."

"You're doing all of this... for Lonnie?" The realization is like a splintering in my chest, and I try to pull away.

"Let me finish." She puts her thumb to my lip, and I fight the urge to bring it between my teeth. "I *would* have done it for Lonnie. I don't have to, though, because I'm doing it for me. I won't let you tear yourself apart anymore, Nia."

I shake my head. "I'm too good at it. It's all I know. I'm not sure anyone can stop me anymore."

She drops her forehead to mine, and the whole world shrinks to just us. "Try me, princess."

BY THE TIME WE MAKE IT BACK TO HER PLACE, THE PARTY has completely cleared out, and someone even locked up. Kade is nowhere in sight, but once I pull up my phone, it's enough to not make me worry too much.

CAN WE TALK WHEN YOU GET BACK?

THOSE KINDS OF TEXTS MAKE MY ANXIETY CLIMB TO NO end, but I respond anyway.

> SURE.
>
> I'M SORRY ABOUT TONIGHT.

Was I?

Harvey unlocks the front door and ushers me, closing it behind me then flipping the lights on to show the mess left behind by our friends. "Make yourself at home. I'm gonna clean up a little."

I stay unmoving.

"I mean it. It's not just a thing to say. Wander around if you want." She chuckles, shooing me with a free hand while the other picks up an empty beer can on the ground.

"Can I help?" I offer, fumbling with an itch in my cast I can't quite reach.

Her chuckle turns into a full blown laugh. "With your one hand? I'm good."

I walk down the hallway, and there's a third door I don't expect, the one that isn't the bedroom or the bathroom. "What's in there?"

"It's my hobby graveyard." She walks over and opens it to reveal a small office.

She calls it a hobby room, but it's an artist's space. There are a few paintings and drawings casually tossed over a table, some easels scattered on the floor. Some balls of yarn are falling haphazardly out of a box in the corner with a macrame wall hanging above it. It's the leatherworking desk that grabs my attention—beautifully detailed patches, belts, wallets, coasters.

"This is amazing, Harvey." I can't hold it in; it's a side

of her I couldn't have predicted, and I'm bewildered by it all. "You did all of this?"

"I go through phases. Some of this stuff is years old. I haven't touched a paintbrush in forever." She shrugs like it's nothing.

"It's still impressive; don't minimize it. This leather stuff is incredible." I turn to her, still fully dressed in cargo pants and combat boots. "Wait." I look closer, bending down to one knee. "Did you make those boots too?"

She's pink in the face, but she's trying to play it off like my excitement doesn't affect her. Knowing she has a physical tell feels like a superpower.

I affect her.

"What's that?" I point to one of the leather harnesses on the wall. It's two separate pieces, oddly shaped, doesn't look like something that would go over your chest or back, and doesn't look like enough leather to wrap around any normal-sized person.

She chuckles, stuffing her hands in her pocket. "A prototype. Never quite finished it. It still needs the final stitching."

"But what is it?" I'm no less confused than before.

"It's a harness," she explains casually. "For my boot."

"Why does your boot need a harness? I don't get it." I pull it off the wall, gauging to see if there's any reaction or if I'm overstepping by touching her things.

There isn't, so I bring it closer for inspection.

"This loop goes around the sole of the boot." Her mouth is so close to my ear, my skin pebbles at the contact. "Can I show you?"

I nod, my gaze locked onto hers as she takes the harness from my hand and slips the larger loop over the base of her boot like she explained. She tightens the strap around the back of her ankle to secure it, and there's a smaller, unbuckled loop attached right above the top of her foot. She lifts up the other, longer strip with a connecting loop and buckles it around her calf. It's fully secured to her leg now, but the two smaller loops right above her foot and in front of her shin stay empty. It's pretty, but I have no idea what the hell it does.

"What's it for?" I'm wondering why she only made it for one leg, but I don't ask that out loud.

"It's for when I need my boots to look nice and pretty." Harvey smirks, like she's waiting for me to ask her to explain further.

I hate feeling stupid, so I don't.

"Can I see how it works?" I ask instead, hoping to avoid the embarrassment of not understanding.

"There's only really one way for me to show you how this works, princess. And you'll have to ask a lot nicer than that." Her tongue flicks out to wet her bottom lip.

My face gets hot, suddenly realizing the intentions of the harness, even If I don't *fully* comprehend. I drop to my knees like I know she wants. One thing about Harvey is that she's predictable, in the way that makes her someone I can count on for consistency.

Something I can't bear to pretend I'm not desperate for anymore.

"Please?" I sweeten my voice, looking up at her through my eyelashes. "Show me?"

Her teeth graze her bottom lip and she narrows her eyes like she's thinking about it.

"Kitty?" I add to seal the deal.

Her stonewall façade breaks, and she points to the door

that leads to the hallway. "In the gray dresser, in my room. There's a white unopened box. Bring it here."

I stumble to my feet and pad away into the next room, opening the first drawer to find nothing but socks, but in the back of the second drawer, I find the long, rectangular box, still taped shut. I barely glance at it before I'm back in her hobby room, on my knees and handing her the box.

"Strap it in."

I'm confused at first, but when I look up, I finally see what she's holding. It's a vibrating wand.

"How?" I ask, my brain still struggling to connect all the pieces.

Cat bends down to show me, inserting the head of the wand into the loop just above her foot and the higher loop around the tail end, keeping it stuck to her shin. I catch on, tightening and buckling the straps around the head while she works the opposite end.

"Now?" I ask.

"Shine my boot, princess. I want to see you dripping on my leather." Her voice is husky, low and full of tantalizing promise as she flicks on the switch of the wand. The vibration buzzes loudly against her boot.

I let out a stuttered exhale, one knee placed on each side of her leg as I lower myself down to her boot. I'm in the same kneeling position as before, except now, there's a wand vibrating just below me.

"All the way down," she commands.

I look up at her.

God, I want her so much. I want to feel her in every crevice of my body, deep inside my soul. But I'll settle for this, whatever the fuck it is.

Lifting my arms up and without another word she helps the shirt come off. I slide off my derby shorts and panties, before I lower, the buzzing head of the wand hitting my clit just right and forcing me the rest of the way down, the front end of her shoe right below my cunt while I press into her leg. "Oh fuck," I gasp, the intensity almost too much at first, so I try to back away.

Her hand finds the side of my head and holds me in place. "Stay right there."

I'm overwhelmed and overloaded, and I feel the tightening in my core already winding, ready to unravel and explode in a frenzy.

"Can I touch you?" I ask, realizing she has yet to let me be the one who deals out pleasure.

"You can hold on to me." She grants me permission, but it's so specific, I dare not mess it up.

My fingers grip her thigh through the fabric of her pants as my other hand reaches up higher, holding onto a hip as the sensation climbs and I get closer to the edge of that cliff. She's tense at first, but when my hands don't stray, only grasp, she finally relaxes, looking down at me with those bright green eyes.

She tilts her foot up, the sudden change in angle sending a jolt through my most sensitive parts and ripping a drawl of pleasure from within me.

"Fuck," I moan, a muted gargle of noise through the fabric of her clothes I'm still pressed against.

"You're doing so good." The praise suddenly reminds me what all of this is.

A distraction.

Burning time to keep me sober.

She's done a great job of it, but now, with my heart in her hands, I'm not sure I can walk away.

When Cat Harvey is bored of making me come, where does that leave me?

Back at Ryan Lee's door for my next hit?

My thoughts are at war with my body, making it impossible to focus on the pleasure of the wand, the vibration starting to dull the nerves on my clit as my orgasm climbs further out of reach.

"Out of your head," she commands like she can read my thoughts and moves the position of her boot again, this time the head of the wand reaching lower and sending the vibration deeper into my center.

"Shit." My fingers are piercing into her leg and her side, but she says nothing about it.

Her hand is still holding the back of my skull, her fingers sliding through my hair, taking a fistful in her grip as she pulls my head away from her thigh and forces me to look at her. "Are you going to come on my boot for me, Antônia?"

I nod, and just like that, she moves her foot again, a shockwave of pleasure ripping through my entire body. It's the kind where I can't move, speak, or breathe—I can only wait for it to pass through me completely.

And it's a full detangling of my psyche.

I'm panting, still clinging to her leg with one hand while the other is holding me up on the ground, the wet sound of the vibrator stuttering against the pool of arousal on her boot is loud and awkward. It almost makes me feel something akin to shame for how I just got off.

But I don't flick the switch.

I wait for her to reach down and do it, and then I help her with the straps of the harness. It's messy, my cum coating the entire top of the boot, spilling over as it collects on the ground just beneath. As if she can sense my embarrassment, she reaches under my chin to lift my gaze back up to her.

"That's my girl." Her thumb grazes the side of my cheek.

I'm a puddle again, melting at the feeling of what it's like to be claimed as someone else's.

As hers.

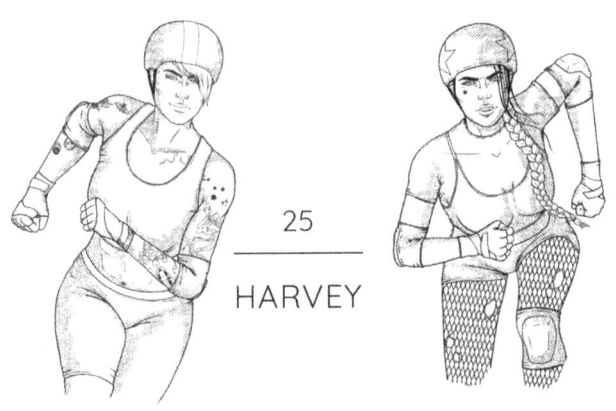

25

HARVEY

I've already washed her and tucked her into my bed before taking a shower of my own. I get off thinking about the way she melted over my boot, and it's all the dopamine I need to function with a clear head until tomorrow.

My phone buzzes on the nightstand. The text from Mo pops up on my notifications.

SCOTT HAS A PROPOSAL FOR YOU

I TOSS MY PHONE TO THE SIDE AND PRETEND LIKE IT DIDN'T come through.

She's wearing one of my old *My Chemical Romance* shirts that somehow manifested out of its coffin in my dresser. She's not asleep, though. She's restless because she's coming down, and soon, she'll be sick and then intolerable.

I crawl into bed with her anyway.

HARVEY

"Can I talk yet?" The question shocks me, because at no point had I thought I'd made her feel like she couldn't.

"What would ever make you think you couldn't?"

She's on her back, staring at the ceiling, hands nervously fidgeting.

"Well, it's not that. It just *feels* like I can't. I don't know how to really explain it. My head is a mess of thoughts all day long, most of them self punitive and destructive. When we're together, it's like all the thinking stops." She's trying to put into words what I'm doing to her.

"Good. That's the point," I reassure.

"It's peaceful." she admits. "I'm not used to that."

"I know. I see you putting your mask on daily, performing for people you've called friends your entire life, people who should know and accept all the parts of you." She's turning to face away from me now. "Hey. Don't ever feel like you can't talk around me."

"It's not you. It's—it's all me. If I don't talk, I don't have room to regret what I say. I always regret what I say."

I don't know how to respond to that, don't have a way to convince her that nothing she could say would turn me away now.

We've gone too far to turn back.

"Are you sure you want me here?" her voice is so shaky, I know it's taking everything for her to ask me.

"No," I tell her, feeling her trying to move away, but I wrap my arms around her waist and keep her in place. She feels hard, rigid, like she's dying to escape. She's still not facing me, not looking my way. "I *need* you here."

She softens, but a few moments go by before either of us speak again.

"You don't want to be touched?" she asks, and I pull

her closer into my chest, inhaling the sweet scent of my shampoo on her.

"We're touching now, aren't we?" I answer her sarcastically.

"You know what I mean, Cat." She's asking the question that takes most girls weeks to figure out. By then, I'm so burnt out of tolerating their touch that any romantic feelings are long forgotten.

She noticed immediately.

"No, I don't like to be touched. Not like that."

This is usually the point where they walk away or say it won't work. When they realize they can't make me into something they want. When the thrill of trying to convert me into a switch becomes sexual assault.

She doesn't turn around to look at me, but I can feel her chest expand with the nervous inhale. "Okay."

"Okay?" I'm a little stunned by her response. It's normally a long battle of me trying to advocate for autonomy over my own body to someone who takes it as a personal insult that I don't want a sexual favor returned.

"It has nothing to do with me?" she asks, slightly turning her cheek as if to look my way. "Like, you wouldn't be going to someone else to get it?"

I can't hold back the chuckle. "No, princess. I wouldn't be going to anyone else for it."

It's cute that this is the first place her mind goes, but even better is the feeling that she gets it, that she's not going to try to force it from me, as if I might change my mind about it *with her*.

"Can I ask what you do then?" She turns around, now facing me. "Do you not get turned on, or do you just miserably deal with a puddle in your underwear?"

I run my fingers along the side of her head. "Oh, I get

HARVEY

turned on," I say, gripping at a handful of hair to garner her attention. "And I take care of it."

"Hmm," she hums. "Sounds hot. Can I watch?" She bites her lip, but then her confidence shatters. "Erm—unless that's crossing a boundary for you."

I give her a crooked smile. "No, I think we can arrange that."

SHE'S NOT THERE WHEN I WAKE UP. I TRY NOT TO THINK about where she's disappeared to, and I'm hoping she's gone back to her own place. I think about texting Stella, about asking for Nia's number. She left because she didn't want to stay. What the fuck would I even say?

Instead, I scroll through the Roller Derby roster index Lonnie had created for us last year. I text someone else.

> DID NIA MAKE IT HOME?

> SHE'S NOT WITH YOU?

FUCK.

I only need one guess to know what she's doing. Except I don't actually have a clue where.

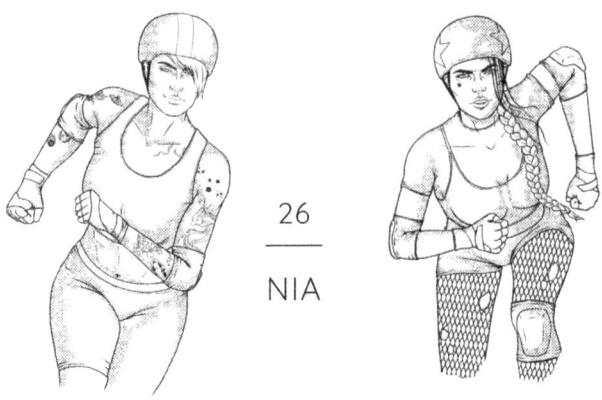

26
NIA

I found Bobby C's number saved in my phone under "Bboby wit beard," and all it took was a singular "Hey, it's Nia" text for him to invite me over. I think I've been here for two days now. I don't really know, because my phone is dead, and Bobby keeps his windows covered in aluminum foil.

"Was that the last of it?" he mumbles, fingers raising at a glacial pace as he leans slightly forward. He's trying to point to the missing pile of heroin on the table, where only specks of dust lie now.

I dip my head in a yes, but the movement is so small, I'm not sure he can catch it. It's not the last of it; the rest is back in a bag in my pocket, but we've both had enough, and if *I'm* the one saying it, it's gotta be true. His eyes are barely open, and he keeps nodding off, falling slightly forward and catching himself abruptly as he wakes. I reach for a phone charger and plug my phone in, hoping the end of the cord is attached to a wall somewhere.

I watch Bobby in a trance of my own, too high to wipe the drool that's starting to linger at the corner of my mouth as I spectate the way he fights the drugs coursing through his system. The tv is playing some old cartoon, the one with the road runner and the coyote who never catches him. Just as I hear the *meep meep*, Bobby does one final nod, and I'm positive he's gone too far.

My phone vibrates, and I confirm it's Tuesday, past noon. The text is from Kade again.

> ARE YOU COMING HOME?

HOME. HOME WAS A TIME, NOT A PLACE. HOME WAS A feeling I'll never get back again. Home was my youth, the ability to be reckless without consequences because there were people to catch me. Home was having somewhere to land regardless of how hard I fucked up. It was in Lonnie's presence, in their love and in their care. Home was a person.

I can never go home again.

I stumble my way to a stand, but I fall down with my next step. I decide crawling is fine— crawling gets me where I need to be. I shuffle on all fours to Bobby's kitchen, where he'd shown me he kept a generous stock of Narcan in a drawer. Smart addicts are addicts who stay alive.

One knee in front of the other, I struggle my way back to Bobby, though it takes twice as long as the journey to the kitchen. Grabbing a fistful of his hair, I yank, pulling back his head to expose his face. I shove the little nozzle into his nostril and press, delivering the opioid-reversing medicine to his system. Nothing happens, so I wait a little longer and deliver the medicine again.

It takes him a few minutes to come to, but when he opens his eyes, he doesn't bother getting up or moving to relieve himself. He throws up exactly where he sits, on top of his own chest.

Bile rises to my throat, and I fight the urge to vomit too.

"Fucking fentanyl bullshit," he mumbles angrily.

"Ryan doesn't cut his stuff." I furrow my eyebrows. We may not be on speaking terms, but I'm offended at what he's implying.

"I didn't get this from Ryan," he explains.

I try to swallow, but the lump in my throat feels impossible to work through. I can't stay here anymore, the stench of his vomit somehow waking my senses up, every smell in the house now impossible to bear. Something like fermentation, mildewy towels, and old pee. But Bobby has no pets.

I grab my things and head for the door to see my car isn't here.

Jesus fuck.

There's a rideshare driver less than four minutes away, so I don't stick around inside. I put a trashcan next to Bobby and a bottle of water in front of him before I leave.

Then, I text Ryan.

> CHECK IN ON BOBBY TODAY.

THE TEXT NEVER GOES THROUGH AS DELIVERED, THOUGH. He's blocked my number. I'm struggling to feel much of anything about it. I'm still nodding in and out during the ride, and though it's only a few minutes, it lasts ages. I'm pretty sure I went to high school with the driver, and he keeps trying to make small talk, even though I specifically requested a quiet ride.

The truth is, even if I wasn't high, I probably wouldn't remember him. I purposefully rejected most of that time out of my head, too fucked up from the damage caused by being the *one thing is not like the others* in a town of less than twenty thousand people. My parents were fresh off the plane with barely any English under them to survive, my mother pregnant with expectations for a child who would never live up to them.

I ruined a lot of acid trips by letting my mind take me to that place where I watched myself from my mother's point of view.

I wish I'd enjoyed the drugs back then. I never ended up making her proud anyway.

"Hey. You're here." The driver sounds annoyed.

It's probably not the first time he's tried to get my attention.

I thank him with a slurred mumble and roll my way out of the back. I'm pretty sure I tip him far more than necessary, but it's payment to deal with me. The inclined driveway up to the door feels excessively steep today, and by the time I'm there, I just want to sit and rest.

The door opens instead, and I fall inside, catching myself with the side of my cast to keep from hitting my head on the ground.

Look at that—I *can* feel pain.

And it's a splintering shock up my arm.

"Where the fuck have you been, Nia?" Kade's voice is so angry that I'm hesitant to look up, and when I do, it's worse than I expected. The look on their face is worry and disappointment and... rage. "Are you high?"

"N-no." I squint, using the back of my hand to shade over my eyes as I look up at them.

"I haven't seen you in days. I've been calling you since Sunday morning. You've missed practice, you missed your interview for the job at the school." The scowl on Kade's face is terrifying, and I've never regretted letting someone down so much. "And you're fucking *high*, Nia?"

K drops their head into their hands and takes deep breaths.

I'm so nauseous, I think opening my mouth would make me spew, so I just wait. And it's a lifetime. Kade slowly removes their hands; their eyes are almost lifeless, and I fight the urge to look away when they speak.

"You have two minutes to get all of your shit and get out of my house."

My blood runs cold.

"Kade." I'm not sure they can even hear me.

"I love you, Nia. I love you *so* fucking much. You get me, and I *thought* I got you. I told you I had one rule. I can't do this. I'm not going to watch you lose yourself the way I lost my sister."

My heart breaks into a million pieces; I can't ask them for more.

I somehow muster the strength to make my way into the house, the tears falling freely down my face with no hope of stopping. I'm not too unpacked, so it doesn't take me long to gather all my things and throw them back into the bags, but every item feels heavy, massive with the weight of my guilt, dense with the force of my mistakes.

It takes longer than two minutes, but Kade doesn't make an issue of it. I give Tolkien one final scratch under the chin, using the top of his head to dry my tears before I walk out of the house. I don't dare look in their direction, but I feel their grip around my arm, pulling me back in.

"You wouldn't rather just *try*?" they ask, but I can't answer.

They wouldn't like it. "Just let me go, Kade." I pull away, but their grip is stronger.

"No! I will not be the villain in your story. I'm your fucking *friend*, Nia."

I know they're right, but I shake them off one final time, and they let me go.

"No, you're not the villain. *I am*." Not daring to look back in their direction, I just keep going. I walk until I'm certain I'm no longer in view. I walk a block, and then another.

And then, I cry.

THE RAIN DOESN'T STOP ME. IT FEELS LIKE PART OF THE punishment, and at this point, I feel deserving of any pain that comes my way. My feet keep moving, my suitcase behind me, my backpack strapped to me and my gym bag hung over my shoulder.

Everything aches.

I don't stop until I get there. The rain's stopped and the sun already set when I'm at her door, reaching to knock.

She opens first, and I can't hold back the sobbing, my words barely coherent through my tears. "I didn't know where else to go."

"What the hell? Why are you all wet?" The look on her face is angry and confused. Harvey looks behind me, like she's trying to find my car. "Did K do something?"

"Nothing I didn't deserve." I wipe my face with the back of my hoodie, but it's drenched, the fabric coarse and scratching at my tender skin.

"They didn't know." She doesn't have to ask about what; we both understand. And now she realizes she's the only one who knows.

"It's not Kade's fault. They didn't ask for this." I know my words are dragging, and I'm staring at my feet now, too uncomfortable to make eye contact and borderline freezing.

"But you came to me." She's not asking. She's simply pointing it out.

I nod.

Opening her door the entire way, she jerks her head to motion me through. "Come inside. You look miserable."

I take enough steps in for her to shut the door behind me, nothing more, nothing less.

"When's the last time?" She tosses the words over her shoulder as she walks further into her living room. I've been here before, but it's the first time I'm really taking the place in.

The ceilings are tall, and there are exposed ducts and metal piping everywhere. It's industrial, with a shiny concrete floor and copper accents splattered throughout the place.

It's so fitting of her.

"A few hours." I'm embarrassed to admit it, but lying to her feels like an anchor chained to my foot.

I'm already drowning, so what's the point?

"Do you have your things?" I'm avoiding her gaze, but I can feel the burn of her attention on me.

"Yeah. Except my car," I tell her. "I needed to get the fuck out of there. I didn't want to risk it not starting." I feel numb saying the words, but the reality is, I'm shattered. Disappointing Kade feels too heavy for me to process.

"You walked here?" She's in my face now, fully in my bubble, and the scowl she wears is carved deep into her expression.

I nod again, but I don't tell her I'm only here because it was further to Ryan's, where I *really* wanted to be.

She looks at me and says, "You're overstimulated," like she can read me better than I can.

"Obviously. That's why I want it." I'm only slightly annoyed. I don't like playing these kinds of games, and I just want to get high. I'm not a kid anymore. I know *exactly* why I get high; I don't need to be analyzed about it.

And I'm starting to regret my decision.

"Drop to your knees," Harvey says, as if it's a completely normal demand at this point in our… relationship? No. This isn't a relationship.

I don't think either of us know what this is.

The questioning only happens in my mind, though. Her tone is enough to command my body to will itself to my knees, where I then lower my ass to my heels.

The line of her mouth barely curves at one side, and my stomach flutters. As she peers down at me, her hand cups the side of my face. It's a far gentler touch than I expect, but I don't say it. I don't dare open my mouth and ruin this moment with something as misconstruing as words. Her fingers run along the side of my head, and a sigh escapes me.

She's looking at me like I've done something so right, like she's proud I came to her.

Maybe I should be proud too.

Harvey lets out an appreciative hum. "Do you want my help?"

Her help.

I'll take anything she gives me.

I squeeze my thighs together, an urgent need starting to grow between my legs. The more she holds me this closely, the more I feel enveloped in her grandness.

Because she is. Cat Harvey is everything I'll never be. Confident, strong, *tall*, determined, and, worst of all, she's breathtaking. The bright green of her eyes and the soft pink of her lips against the drastic cut of her jaw—she was made to be admired, and from this angle, it's all I *can* do.

"Yes," I finally answer.

She squats down to my level. "Are you asking?" She's speaking low, even though she doesn't need to.

"Yes." It comes out almost mechanically, my body taking over and doing whatever I need to feel anything but this terrible anguish and burning need to get high, to soothe the discomfort.

She sees it too.

"Please." I'm not beyond begging.

She looks me over one more time before she speaks. "Undress," is the word of choice, and then she's gone from the room, leaving me kneeling on the floor as she heads down the hallway.

I'm only frozen momentarily, not paralyzed, stunned by the whiplash of the day.

And Cat.

Cat fucking Harvey, who invades my dreams, my showers, and now my real life. Cat, whose hatred felt heavy but whose desire feels explosive.

I'm sitting on my heels, hands placed over my thighs, when Harvey returns to the living room, a t-shirt in one hand and a pair of tube socks in the other. Her eyes widen for only a split second at the recognition of me being undressed and on my knees again. Satisfaction paints her face, though she's trying hard to not show it.

"Here," she says, handing me the *Job For A Cowboy* shirt from one of their early tours. It's probably just right on her, but it comes down to my mid thighs. "I don't think you're going to fit into my pants, so you can have these." She gives me the socks next, and I know she's right. Me in her pants would have been comical.

I unroll each sock up to right above my knees. These are Devil's Dame socks, color coded with black and blue stripes at the top and the logo of our Dame on each side. It's my team too, and I have my own socks, but for some reason, putting hers on feels different.

Like I'm trying *her* on.

And

she

fits

just

right.

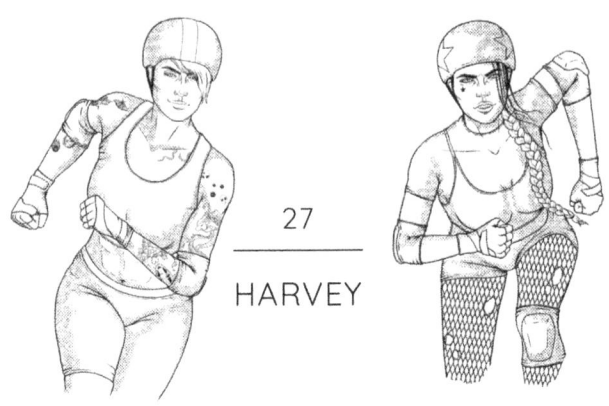

27

HARVEY

I knew something was wrong when she didn't show up to practice last night. Still, with no response from her and Kade giving me only blunt replies, I had nothing to go on.

"Can you eat?" I ask.

She shakes her head. If she used a couple of hours ago, she's just now on her way down, which means food is the last thing on her mind. I don't ask her anything anymore; she's past the point of making her decisions. That's why she came to me.

"When's the last time you ate something?" I just need to check.

"Yesterday, I think." She doesn't try to lie to me, and I appreciate that for what it is.

She trusts me.

"Come here," I tell her. "Let me fix your hair."

I grab a brush from the bathroom, and she sits between my legs while I get to work. She's fidgeting, anxiously bouncing and wiping her nose on the hem of the shirt. "I don't think I should stay here, Harvey." She's a little more alert now, and probably ready for another hit.

"Mmm. That's okay," I reassure her.

"No, I mean—"

"You're staying here, Nia." I pull on the braid, garnering her attention before I finish wrapping the strands over each other.

It had been years since I'd braided anything before her. That first braid had been a comical joke of an effort, and now, here, with a few practices under my belt, I wasn't going to lie that I wasn't a little proud of the smooth plait running down her back.

"Thank you." She runs her hand over it like it's a soothing mechanism.

"Let's go skate." I stand, giving her my hand.

"Are you joking? It's nearly nine o'clock on a Tuesday night." She laughs at me, but I don't put my hand down.

"And who's going to stop us?" I ask.

Biting her lip, she tries to argue, but nothing comes out when she opens her mouth. "How are we going to get in?"

"Are you telling me you don't have a key?" I scoff, knowing damn well I have my own.

She reaches for her backpack and pulls the tiny key out of the side pocket before wiggling it in front of my face.

"Then let's go skate." I smirk, grabbing it from her hold.

"Wait, what is that?" She grabs my hand, and I try to pull away, but she's already got it in her grasp, examining the red ink on the top of my hand. The tattoo of teeth.

"Is that…" A small smile curves its way over her face, and I pull my hand back. It's been there for days but this is the first she's noticed.

She doesn't finish and I don't confirm, but we both know the truth.

It's the mark she's left on me, and I'm going to wear it forever now.

THIS IS THE NIA LONNIE WANTED ME TO FALL FOR, THE ONE I get glimpses of every time she crosses one knee over the other and rounds the corner of the track. Her braid beats behind her, head chin tilted up, and her eyes are nearly closed. This moment is hers and hers alone, and I'm just privileged to get to witness it. She gets about three or four laps in before she notices I'm watching.

"Are you coming?" she shouts back at me, extending her arm my way as she passes once more.

I take her hand and let her drag me, knowing damn well it's more effort for her this way, but if she's not complaining, then I'm not either. She's pulling me, skating backwards now with a giant grin on her face.

She's fucking stunning like this, when all her feelings aren't being masked by the drugs she's trying to kill herself with. When she's allowing herself to be free, to do the things she loves. She knows it too; that's why the tears are falling from her eyes, drifting with the breeze and landing on my shirt.

We skate until she's so worn out, she's refusing to get up from the track. Her chest heaves up and down, and she laughs uncontrollably from sheer exhaustion. It's almost one in the morning. She rolls to her stomach and perches up on her elbows, panting to catch her breath.

"You didn't have to do this."

"Which part?" I don't know why, but I want to hear the words. From her, I *need* them.

"The part where you're trying to save me." She looks ready to break again, her eyes weepy, and I know it's the comedown fucking with her mood.

I pull her into my lap, laying her head across my thighs so she can look up at my face. "The problem here, princess, is that you're so fucking annoying with your self-esteem issues that you don't think you're worth saving, that I'm wasting my time on you." I don't wait for the nod that surely comes before I continue. "Well, get over yourself. I'm saving you for purely selfish reasons. I'm saving you because I want you for *me*."

She props herself up onto her hands, some of the weight sitting on her cast. If she's in pain, she doesn't show it. Her eyes don't move from mine. "You want me?"

I don't fight the smile on my face. "Isn't it obvious?"

"Not a lot tends to be obvious for me." She shrugs like she's embarrassed about it and looks away.

I place my hand on her cheek, cupping her face and turning it in my direction again. "Well, I'm telling you, then: I fucking want you." Throwing my helmet behind me before unclipping hers, I kiss her.

Her lips are soft and full, and they part easily when my tongue pushes its way through. A soft moan simmers the deeper I explore her mouth. It's the first time we've kissed, and for the first time in as long as I can remember, I don't want this moment to end. Her hand finds my neck, but the touch is brief—within a second, she lets go. Gripping her wrist, I bring that hand back to my neck and deepen our kiss.

I lock my legs around Nia to flip her under me. It's a

clean move, but she yelps in surprise once I'm straddling her. Reaching for the water bottle next to me, I take a swig and hold it in my mouth before lowering back down, her head lifting to meet mine. Just as she parts her lips, I spit the water into her mouth.

"Drink," I say.

Her eyes are jarred open now, pulling me into her as she swallows the water along with me in the next kiss. Nia grinds her hips upward, moaning under me, begging for contact.

I'm holding up all my weight, gripping at the hem of her shorts. I begin pulling them down with her fishnets, but she protests. "W-wait, I'm so sweaty!" She laughs through broken pants. I don't stop. I pull the shorts down to her knees, not breaking eye contact until she's fully exposed. Then, I shift my eyes to where the magic is. Sure, she's sweaty, but she's glistening with arousal, and I'm desperate to lick it off her.

"Do you think I give a fuck?"

Her eyes widen further with shock.

"I wanna know what you like, Nia," I say, our eyes still locked as my fingers play with the sticky mess between her legs, never fully committing to the touch.

"What I like?" She's already breathy, looking up at me with that lust-ridden look on her face. "Everything you do feels good."

Finally, I slide my fingers back and forth, making contact with the bundle of nerves between her legs and forcing a hiss from her. She drops her head back with closed eyes. "Look at me," I command. "I want you here, with me, fully aware of who's making you come undone."

She nods, surprising me and propping herself up on her elbows to get a better look.

But I'm still only teasing, just barely touching here and there, torturing her until she answers my question. "Please." It's barely a whisper.

"I'm still waiting." I space each word out along with my movements, making the torment nearly unbearable. "Tell. Me. What. You. like."

She's panting, squirming her hips, like she could possibly steal from me what I won't willingly give. I pull away, placing each hand along her hip and pinning her down. She's frustrated now, rubbing her legs for friction as she tries to fight under my hold, but it's useless.

"Cat," she grunts. "Just fuck me, please."

I'm laughing. I can't help it, and God, this girl is fucking hot beyond belief, even if she's a tragic mess. "Then tell me what you like, baby, so I can do it for you." I lean in close, until our noses are touching, and then I lean further down so that my mouth is in line with her ear and whisper, "No one else has to know."

I release a hip and run my fingers over her clit again, eliciting that gasp I've come to love so much. She bites her lip, shutting her eyes tight before she leans up as far as I allow.

"IIIIII…" She drags it out with so much hesitation that I lean in, hoping that if she doesn't have to say it loudly, she'll be brave enough to tell me all her dirty little fantasies. "I like to be stuffed."

I try to mask any sort of reaction, but I can feel myself getting wet at her confession. The smile gives me away, finding its rightful place on my face. I raise an eyebrow; I want the confirmation.

"Like… *really* stuffed." Her breath hitches when she says it, and then she lowers herself back down to the floor, covering her face with her hand and her cast.

I hover above her, pulling her arms back and pinning them to the ground, being careful with her injured side. "Not with me, Nia. You're not allowed to get embarrassed with me. Okay?"

With a small nod, she leans forward, pressing her lips to mine and initiating a kiss. It takes me by surprise, but then again, she always does. Nia Da Silva is unpredictable. I think it's why I crave her so badly.

She breaks up the monotony.

Everything I've ever desired waits for me, so I lower past her belly button, my tongue trailing its way to her center, licking up every salty droplet of sweat on her flesh. She's humming in approval, but she's burning with need. I know, because the minute my tongue laps up the nectar between her legs, she's crying out for me.

She

is

an

exposed

wire

sparking

in

the

rain.

I can't get enough. The taste of her ruins me, and the sounds that come from her mouth are programmed to destroy. The way she bucks against me—her fingers winding through my hair and pulling me impossibly closer while she fucks my face—is everything I'm jonesing for.

I can make her see stars, even inside Skateland.

Her quiet moans turn louder with every stroke of my fingers, her hips moving in sync, extending her pleasure in any way she can. She whines when I pull out, but it's only for a moment, just long enough for me to bring all four fingers together. She's tight, but I'm going to try anyway.

Bringing my fingers to her entrance, I push—just the tips—and when I pull out again, I go to the first knuckles. The gasp is more pleasure than pain, so I keep going, slowly pulling out and then inserting again. Each movement douses my fingers in her arousal as I push in further.

"Fuck." She's frantically gripping at my arms, my shirt, whatever she can when I have all four fingers in up to the second knuckle.

I slide my thumb over her clit with every push of my fingers, and she writhes in pleasure, knuckles white as she grips onto me while I send her off the edge. My fingers are flat now inside her, the webbing between my thumb and index finger meet with the base of her cunt; I'm as deep as I can go, and she squeezes around me so tightly.

She's a bright cluster of hot, molten desire. Nia *is* the stars inside Skateland.

The noises from her are unintelligible. She's so close to coming, I could breathe on her cunt and she'd fall apart. Instead, I lower back down, continuing the pumping of my fingers as I lock my mouth over her clit and suck. The death grip of her thighs around my head is all I need to keep going, and I don't stop until her pleasure spills out of her in a gush, dousing my hand and covering the track below us. Only then is my ego satiated.

Lifting up, I grin, watching her attempt to catch her breath under me. I wipe my mouth with the back of my arm before I roll off her to lay at her side, undoubtedly aware that this is my girl, and I'm going to take care of her at all costs.

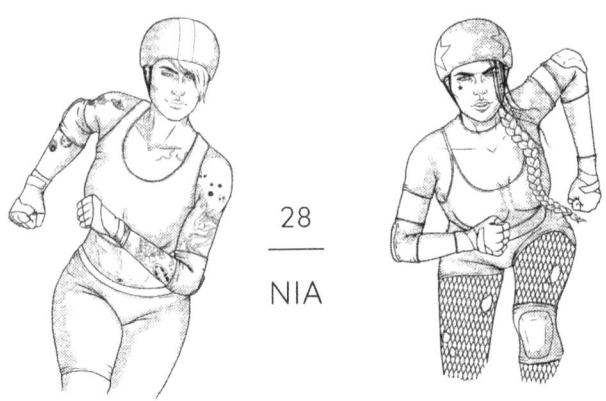

28
NIA

Cat's fingers entwine around mine, making it impossible for my brain to wander away from this moment, from the two of us. She's good at that. The distractions, the keeping me busy, the knowing just what my brain needs to not overcomplicate every moment of my life, to not rob the joy out of every second I breathe.

Cat Harvey is oxygen in my lungs when I've been drowning. Cat Harvey is a coma dream I never want to wake from. Cat Harvey is the hand gripping me as I dangle from the cliff. She wants to save me when I'm not worth holding on to.

But I let her anyway.

"We still haven't eaten," she says after my breathing has finally calmed. "Let's go get some trash."

"The only thing open at this hour is—"

"Waffle Station," we both say in sync and then laugh.

The place is chaos. The kind where you'd likely see a patron throwing a chair at a cook over the bar, and there's almost an unspoken law that you can't eat there sober or before midnight, but the food is the kind of mouthwatering greasy garbage that lights up your taste buds and puts Michelin star restaurants to shame.

"Fuck it." I laugh, lifting my hips up as she helps me roll my shorts back on. "I need to at least clean up before we go."

I start to stand, but she stops me, grabbing at my good wrist and shaking her head. "No. You can go like that." She grazes her teeth over her bottom lip, like she's remembering the way I sounded calling her name. "I want you sopping wet when I decide to fuck you at breakfast."

I swallow, doing my best to play it cool, like that wasn't the hottest thing anyone's ever said to me. I think she means *after* breakfast, but I don't correct her. Instead, I follow, hand in her hold as she leads me out of the rink, the mess between my legs ruining my underwear with every step I take.

Hunger is not a thing I'm capable of feeling at this time. Instead, I'm disgustingly nauseous, and the smell of fried eggs and bacon makes my jaw tingle with discomfort. I fake a smile, just grateful that when the hostess shows us to our booth, Harvey sits next to me and not across from me.

I'm safely tucked into the corner next to the window, but I'm leaning into Cat. She's got one arm draped around me. I've never felt more whole in my entire life. I'm learning that when she says she doesn't like to be touched, she doesn't mean always. She's never opposed to dishing out a beating on the track. She doesn't mind when I'm cuddling up against her like this. If anything, she *encourages* me when I'm gripping her to death, because I might just fall off the edge of the universe from her making me come.

But when it comes to sex, her body is hers and hers alone.

My brain tends to overcomplicate things. It loves to turn a situation that has nothing to do with me into a three-ring circus where I'm not the ringleader, but the main attraction. I almost expect my mind to begin turning loops, finding new ways to make it all about me and that I can't reciprocate how she makes me feel physically.

But I don't.

This somehow is the clearest thing I've ever come to understand. Harvey's already shown me all the ways she can love; it's not up to me to love her back in the same fashion. It's up to me to learn how she wants that love returned.

"Everything sounds good. What do you want?" She breaks me out of my thoughts, and I realize I haven't even looked at the menu yet.

Her hand drops to my thigh. I fumble with the napkin rolled around my utensils, but her touch is impossible to ignore.

My pulse is loud in my ears, her fingers casually fidgeting with the holes in my fishnets, entwining around each thread like she doesn't care if she rips them further.

I'm at that shitty point in the comedown where I would have dumped out my next hit hours ago. Instead, I'm tired, my mind wanting to sleep but my body fighting against it. I need to get high, but the thought of disappointing Harvey right now is too much to bear. Hurting Kade was a machete through my soul; I can't imagine what letting down Harvey would feel like.

It's like she can tell when I'm lost inside my head, diving far too deep into the depths of that aphotic swamp, the one that swallows up all the comfort in my mind and drowns me in sorrow. Her fingers scratch at the inside of my thigh. I hold my breath, only taking a tiny sip through tight lungs every time I feel her touch scale higher.

I can't avoid it; my face burns along with the rest of me. The anticipation only builds the more she runs the edges of her fingers along the bottom of my spandex shorts. *Legally*, they're shorts, but I've had underwear that covers more. It has never mattered on the track, but here, with her hand a fraction of an inch from where I ache to feel her, it's too obvious to ignore.

Finally, I look her way. She's still pretending to be looking at the menu, a crooked smirk painted across that devilishly good-looking face, that perfectly defined jaw that shadows at the edges every time she clenches her teeth.

"Orange juice or soda?" she asks, eyes still glued to the menu, her fingers invading their way into my shorts.

"Sprite," I exhale it out like it even fucking matters, her hand stopping just at the apex of my thighs.

Move your fucking fingers. I want to scream, but the server is back to take our order.

"What are you thinking?" Harvey asks.

Shrugging, I give her the truth. "I'm not super hungry. Can I just pick off your plate?"

She eyes me suspiciously, but she doesn't fight it, doesn't try to convince me to get anything. Still, she orders more food than I assume necessary for a single person.

I'm acutely aware of the way the server's eyes drift down from her notepad to where Harvey's hand grips my thigh. She blinks twice, registering the way her fingers are buried inside the crevice of my shorts. Harvey doesn't break eye contact with the server, despite the many times her gaze drifts back down to where her hand sits.

"I'll do the double sunshine special, with the hashbrowns instead of the side of fruit. An order of sausage on the side, and what's your pancake of the day?" Every word rolls off Harvey's tongue confidently, like she's not worried about the server's eyes or that she's a movement away from her fingers feeling the arousal I'm uncomfortably sitting in.

She does a double take. "The what?" Focusing back on Harvey and gripping her pen with a bit more rigor.

"The pancake of the day," Harvey repeats with a tilt of her head, her eyes doing all the smiling for her.

"Nutella and banana," the server answers with a clear of her throat.

"That sounds great. We'll do an order of those as well. I'll take a coffee too, and she'll have a Sprite." Harvey hands the server back the menu with her free hand and then thanks her.

She's barely turned on her heels when I feel her slide through my folds without warning. The moment is electric. Her fingers, the sensation, the fucking *restaurant booth*. I cover my face with my hand and my cast, dropping my head to the table. She doesn't stop.

Holy shit.

It takes no time at all, minimal effort for her to get me close to the edge. I was wet from my last orgasm, but the ten minutes we've spent in this booth with her teasing has me soaked. I hear a soft chuckle from her somewhere above me while still hiding in the shield of my own hands.

"Do you think if you can't see them, they can't see *you*?" Harvey asks, amusement dripping from every syllable.

I nod, head still down, breathing heavily as her fingers

move back and forth so lazily, so tantalizingly, that I can't help but squeak through my throat. And then her hand is gone, and my head is snapping up on demand, like I've been deprived of something I deserved.

She delights in the disappointment that's all over my face, but she nudges her head to the server coming back with her coffee and my soda. I pull the paper top off the straw like an animal, bringing the drink to my mouth and relishing in the way the bubbles calm my stomach. When I lean back into my seat, her hand finds the side of my face, turning my gaze to hers.

Her eyes dart over my face, like she hasn't taken in my features from this close up before. She has, but it's like this time, she's memorizing them. Harvey's fingers are still gripping at my jaw when she brings her mouth to mine, her tongue parting my lips and her hand reaching through the top of my shorts this time. There's no pause from her, no hesitation, no second to look around.

Her tongue is hot, tangling with mine and leaving me little time to react when her fingers reach back in, forcing me to shift as she pushes her way inside me. She's pulling her face away from mine, that cocky smile I love now plastered over her face as she works her fingers deeper.

It's too instinctual to fight, the casted arm slamming down on the table while the other hand clutches her thigh. The burst of pain is hot through my wrist, but it's muted by pleasure. The sound draws attention through the small diner, forcing a few of the patrons sitting at the bar to turn their heads in our direction. Harvey doesn't stop, but she shifts in her seat, keeping me from anyone's view but hers.

She presses her forehead to mine, her body enveloping me in the little corner of the booth as she forgoes any sort of shame or decency. Neither of us have looked away from each other, the scrunch of her eyebrows mirroring the angry expression she used to dish my way that I now see clearly as focus.

Fucking me fast and curling her fingers into a hook that hits my g-spot, she destroys me. Every pull is shallow, barely moving out of me, moving only deeper and further to stroke that spot that has me squirming and biting my tongue to stay silent in the booth.

Her thumb presses against my clit just as she asks, "Can you come for me wherever I want, princess?"

My jaw goes slack, and I rest my head back against the booth.

My body tightens with the urge of the release, my nails digging into her arm, and soon, I'm shaking under her, fighting to keep my breathing silent and my whines contained with every quake of a climax that refuses to dim. I open my eyes, a pleased look on Harvey's face as she wets her bottom lip with her tongue, pulling her hand from my shorts and leaning back against the booth regularly again.

I can barely catch my breath, but once my thoughts are no longer muddled by the loud beating of my own pulse, I'm able to look around and see that the customers seem to be none the wiser.

Harvey casually runs her tongue along the back of both fingers that had just been inside of me before shoving them in her mouth. Pulling them out with a loud pop, she then wraps her arm over my shoulder and pulls me in. My chest is still rising and falling hard, and I'm still processing the comedown of it all.

Almost every moment with Cat is like that, like jumping off a bridge and still somehow getting caught before the splash. It almost sours the euphoria when my brain likens the feeling to a high. She's beginning to feel like that, and it almost seems like she's trying to compete with the drugs for my attention.

I lean my head against her shoulder, and with her free hand, she brushes my hair out of my face. I'm sweaty, a mixture of the amped up heating system in this tiny diner and the blissful orgasm cocktail delivered straight to my brain.

She sips at her coffee slowly, and the minutes go by until it no longer feels like my own brain is too loud for my head. Then, the food comes.

It's torture.

The pancakes overwhelm me, the sweet stench far too heavy for my empty stomach this early.

This late?

This *sober*.

The agony starts when the sweet, gray-haired server drops the sausage and bacon in front of me. I take deep breaths through my mouth and fight through the nausea, but it's too much to handle

"Can you let me out?" I try to keep my cool, but she can see it on my face that I'm not okay.

I run to the bathroom just in time to get all my vomit in the right place. The cold sweat runs down my back, and I know soon is when hell begins. I need to be as far away from Harvey before that happens. I gag once more just from the memory of the greasy smell, but once it's out, I feel a lot better.

Splashing some water on my face does nothing for me. I look exactly like I feel.

Withdrawing.

I walk back to the booth anyway, attempting to avoid her eyes, but I know she sees it on me. "Should we go?" Harvey asks, always so fucking thoughtful.

I shake my head. She just ordered food; I can sit through this.

She gets up from the booth anyway, walking up to the checkout and talking to the hostess for a bit before she comes back my way, holding her keys out to me. "Do you want to sit in my car?"

Nodding, I take them from her and walk outside. I wrap my arms around myself once the chill of the wind hits me, but she's parked close by. I don't bother trying with the passenger side. I don't want to fight with it tonight.

This morning.

Whatever the fuck time it is. I open the back seat and crawl inside. It's somehow colder in the car. My teeth are chattering, I'm sweating my metaphorical balls off, and if I pull a mirror out, I bet my complexion would be reminiscent of a Victorian child suffering from plague.

I cry out in frustration, uncomfortable in this fucking prison cell of a body and desperate for release, desperate to be free from it.

I hate most that she's going to see me like this.

Once she gets in the car, I hand her the keys, biting my cheek and curling into a ball until we've arrived back at her apartment. The drive is moments between discomfort disguised as blinks. She wants to draw me a bath, sees how visibly sweaty I am, and I'm sure I don't smell amazing.

The thought of sitting in hot water makes me want to peel my skin off.

"Just turn the shower on for me?" I ask, no longer having the strength to pretend like I'm okay. She's already done all the work of getting me undressed and putting my hair up.

The water is closer to cold than lukewarm, but I don't

care. I sit there, my head hanging while the stream of water beats over me.

"Nia, your cast." Harvey comes in, flustered because I'm facing the wrong direction, my casted arm against the wet wall with no option but to stay doused under the spray.

"Hmm?" I look over, and by the time my head has fully turned in that direction, she's already pulling my body and turning me in the tub.

"Shit. Well, at least your swelling's gone down, so you're probably okay to ask them for a new one now." She's looking at me like she's anxious, like maybe she's not confident in what she's saying.

I nod. That's all I can do right now.

She doesn't force me to stand. Instead, she just washes me. It's not sexual, but it's caring, it's intimate, and I feel far too vulnerable. The weeping comes again, and I hate myself, reminding me that it's just the fucking lack of drugs. When she's draped me in an oversized shirt and tucked me into the luxurious fluff of her bed, I think I might actually be tired.

I don't let my brain ask questions like what time it is or what obligations I have. That kind of overwhelm would send me into a spiral I don't need to face right this moment. I don't quite make out what she says, but I feel her comforting touch as she runs her fingers through my hair, coaxing me into sleep.

I NOD OFF FOR WHAT FEELS LIKE SECONDS, BUT MAYBE IT'S longer. I'm sweating, and I can hear the tv in another room. My phone says three in the morning. I haven't slept more than an hour, I'm sure of it. I'm cold, I'm hot, but most of all, I'm desperate to get high.

Harvey isn't here.

Rummaging through my bag is my first priority after I roll out of bed. A weightlessness fills me when I find all my things untouched. I feel around in the smallest zipper pocket until I find the baggie. It feels like the smallest victory. I pour just a little—not enough to get high, but enough to feel better—of the beige powder onto the nightstand. I don't bother with a straw; I simply block the other nostril and lean down as close as possible until it's already practically in my nose when I inhale.

I put it all away before the powder makes its way through my system. I remember a stupid joke from some stoner kid who used to hang around a million lifetimes ago. He used to say if you snorted through the right nostril, it went straight up to your brain and got you high immediately. If you snorted through the left, it went down to your stomach and had to digest and process longer, so the high would be weaker.

It was one hundred percent bullshit, but to this day, I favor the right side, only opting for the left nostril if the right one is completely out of commission.

I slump down against the side of the bed, feeling comfortable in my own skin for the first time all day. I'm barely leaning my head against the headboard when a sound catches my attention.

It's a sound I've only ever heard in a dream, and I follow it, gracefully stumbling from the bedroom into the hallway. It's coming from the hobby room, and the door is wide open.

My lungs shrivel up, all the air pulled out of my body

at the sight of Cat sitting on a leather chair with her fingers inside herself. It makes every part of me feel weak, fluttery, needy.

And it feels incredibly violating.

"I-I'm sorry," I say, gathering her attention because it feels better than a knock. "I woke and heard something and—"

"Nia, it's fine." She smiles, tilting her chin up as if to summon me closer.

I don't think I have a single solid bone in my body to move, though.

"Come here."

29

HARVEY

The words come out, but I'm not confident in them. I'm nervous, self-conscious, and all I can do is wait for the bad to surpass the good. I brace for her to rush to me, for her to try take control or try to be the one who fucks me, just like they always do. I'm clenching my jaw tight while I wait for it, while I anticipate eyes that burn with judgment.

My heart races and my thoughts spiral, but when I come back to myself, she's not looking at my hands or down there at all. Her eyes are on mine, on my face. She's barely moved, just a few steps away from the door, enough to close it behind her and kneel.

The smile on both of our faces is proof we've gone too far.

Because I've never allowed myself to be with anyone else this intimately before.

Not intentionally.

Not willingly.

Her stare is everything right now. I rub my fingers through the slickness, shocked by how wet I find myself.

I'm desperate to get off, and her here, watching me, is now somehow making every nerve in my body a hundred times more sensitive. I bite my cheeks to fight any moans, but she can see what she's doing to me.

Every stroke of my fingers, her smile sets deeper, and I get closer.

"Can I taste you?" she asks.

I nod. "If you crawl to me."

Nia obeys and drops to her hands, her eyes narrowing as her gaze evolves into something so seductive, I nearly implode from watching her. She's purposefully moving slowly, her hips swaying side to side as she prowls toward me.

And then she stops at the base of the chair and sits back on her heels, mouth slightly parted, waiting. I'm on the edge of my climax, but I pull my fingers free and extend my hand, shoving two fingers between her lips. She sucks them into her mouth, swirling her tongue, the jolt buzzing through my core like a lightning strike.

When she lets go, I'm so close, I could come from just looking at her. She has one hand between her legs, and I realize that it isn't a show or an act to try to make me feel better. She's just as into this.

The need to shut my eyes is nonexistent, even though it feels unnatural when I'm on the verge of climaxing. I've never stared into someone else's soul during my own undoing. I can't look away from her, can't break free from this, and when I let go, clenching the arm of the chair with one hand, a rogue grunt escapes my throat despite my efforts.

"I think I love you, Cat." She's breathing heavy, like maybe she came too.

"Come up here," I tell her, and she's standing by the next heartbeat.

But it's not love in her eyes I see.

It's the drugs.

I try not to let the disappointment show, try not to let it ruin this moment, because it doesn't take away from what it means to me.

And it means *everything*.

My guards go back up. Despite how much I want to give this girl more pieces of me, I'm afraid of what she'll do with them. Discard them once I'm no longer of use? Sell them for her next fix?

She warned me herself, and if anything, *I'm* the stupid one here.

The one person I loved enough to stop for is dead.

The words remind me that while I've had almost two months to process Lonnie's death, it's still a relatively fresh wound for Nia. She refuses to let it scab, to let it heal. Instead, she's picking at the edges, stretching the cut open and prying her fingers inside.

She wants the new pain to take away the old.

It only works to a certain extent. The new pain distracts, but once the novelty wears off, they coexist together and hold hands to ruin.

And Nia is rubble at my feet.

"I wish you would have come to me first," I cup her face in my hands as I lead her to my lap.

She swallows hard. I think she wants to lie, but she's not prepared. "How can you tell?"

"You asked me what I know about addiction, princess. My dad died when I was little, only four. I don't really remember it. But my brother was almost fourteen, and it really fucked him up. Eventually, my mom remarried, and my stepdad kicked him out of the house because of the drugs. When I turned eighteen, my step dad changed the locks on me too." This all feels like way too much to be sharing when we're both so vulnerable from an orgasm.

But I can't stop, and she doesn't look at me like she wants me to.

"That's not a parent," is what she says instead.

"No, but I didn't need him to be my parent. I needed my mother, and she let both of us down. I came to Devil Town to skate, but I came here for my brother, hoping that if we were at least together, we could make it." The words turn bitter in my mouth, and I'm not sure if I want to keep going, but she nudges me with a look. "My brother was too far gone." I say the words with a wave of my hand, as if they come out easily.

They don't. Every syllable makes my tongue bleed with regret.

"Is he dead?" she asks, the soft look on her face like her own personal apology.

"He's dead *to me*," I explain, her grip on me softening. "Some people don't want to be saved, and that's fine, but he wanted to take me down with him too. I couldn't watch my brother dig both of our graves. I haven't spoken to him in years."

Her tears fall freely, and I'm not sure if it's what I've said or if it's the drugs. "What?"

She shakes her head, but she finally clarifies, "What makes me any different?"

"That's the thing about it." *Love,* but I don't clarify the *it* for her, because I can only give her so much, and right now, I'm not sure how much I have left. "There's *nothing* that makes it different. I want you, and that's enough to make a difference *for me*." I don't tell her that it's the best *and* the worst part about love.

We have no choice.

She drags in a long inhale, so stuttered that I'm not sure her lungs can take in any more oxygen, but she does it anyway. The tears never dry. "I won't stop." She shakes her head.

"I can help you," I promise her for the hundredth time.

"Don't let me do this to you. I'm not worth it." Her seams are unraveling, and she pulls each thread like it won't make her smaller.

She's ceasing to exist, and I'm starting to wonder if that's the plan.

"Says who?" The way I shake her isn't violent, but it's enough to rattle her, and her eyes jar open a little.

"I'm not supposed to be here anymore." Her body shakes with each painful word.

"What does that mean, Nia?" Maybe with enough clarity, I can get her through this.

"I just want to go home," she sobs. She's too high, and I'm not sure she's fully aware of the words she's saying.

"Where's home, baby?" I ask anyway, remembering every time I had to talk my brother down when his high would turn dark.

Her face is pressed to my shirt, my fingers running through her hair in an attempt to soothe.

"Lonnie."

It's muffled, but I can hear it. It takes everything not to break *with* her, to not fall apart as well. Instead, I hold her and let her cry for as long as she needs. And then, I decide to let my brain run its course, every possible plan unfolding simultaneously at the speed of sound. I can't catch up, can't listen to my own thoughts coherently.

I still try, because home is no longer an option for her, not if her idea of home is six feet under in whatever version of afterlife Lonnie is kicking around in.

Life is for the living.

The same words invade my brain again.

Death is a starting point.

Death is a door.

Death is a starting point.

And here we are, gates wide open, waiting for the flood to come through.

If I can't save her, she'll wreck us together and lock the door behind us.

"Help me," she finally begs, the words clear but still filled with her sorrow.

And that's all it takes to seal my fate.

It's almost sunrise when she falls asleep in my arms I've already texted Freddy to call in for my opening shift at the bar today. I don't know what to do, but I know I can't leave her alone. I think about texting Stella, or Bae, or even Venice, but it doesn't seem like any of them have a clue.

Nia's leaving those closest to her in the dark, because it's not a cry for help. She's already decided on how this is going to end.

The thought makes me squeeze her tighter. I contemplate moving us to the bedroom, but I don't shift. I don't shift an inch, though I know she'd sleep through it. For the first time in three years, my brother passed through my mind tonight, and now, I can't get him out. I think about calling, about sending a text, but I remember every previous time I've felt this way, the way hope painted a rainbow bridge to the idea that once I reached out, he'd be there, waiting with arms open to be the hero I always needed. The hero I never had. The hero I was forced to become for myself.

It only takes twenty seconds into a phone call for that bridge to crack like fragile glass, for his words to turn into fissures that spread until nothing but puzzled fragments are left. A single step toward him shatters the entire thought. I don't dial the number. I don't text.

But in the back of my mind, I wonder if he's still alive. If he's still an addict.

If he thinks of me.

And then I remember the last time we saw each other, how I wasn't of value unless I was buying from him, using with him, or giving him money. His memory turns sour in my mind, and though I *hope* he isn't dead, I wonder if closure would feel better than this, this *thing* we've left unfinished.

It makes me wonder if I've numbed myself to this kind of pain, if I've survived the loss of Lonnie because I've already lost everyone before. I've already practiced the pain and rehearsed the feelings of mourning every person I've loved.

I had over a year to grieve Lonnie before they'd actually died. The diagnosis took too long, by the time we found out, all we could do was enjoy the time we had together. The treatments became too costly, and no matter how much we all wanted to help them through it, they refused.

Dying on their own terms was a respect I could grant them, one that caused a tectonic shift between the skaters who couldn't accept Lonnie's wishes. I never cried in front of them, never told them how much I'd miss them or how much I wanted them to keep fighting. StarScreamer once called me dead inside for it, but she didn't understand that my brain spent every day we had left already mourning. By the time it came, it hurt just a little less.

So dead inside was fine. Was I supposed to prove my love in some performative way that showed them all how sad I was? Was I supposed to scream how I would have worked until my bones were exposed if it meant paying for Lonnie to stick around in pain just a little longer? It wouldn't have mattered.

That wasn't Lonnie's way, and had they heard, they would have paid someone to kick my ass since they weren't strong enough to do it anymore.

Once I've nibbled at my soul like a well-pecked carcass, I finally gain the motivation to move her. Her heart rate feels okay, and her breathing isn't shallow. I turn her to her side just to be safe, and I stare just a little longer. Just another hour, maybe two, before I go back into my hobby room and decide to sit at the leatherworking desk again.

It's been at least a year since I've fucked with any of it. This shit, these meaningless little hobbies; I don't ever really lose the knowledge when I learn it, no matter how much time goes by, even if I only learn the basics, enough to satisfy the part of my brain that likes to check off the box that says "skill accomplished" before we move to the next one.

I find a piece of leather in my scrap pile. It's white and just the right width and length for what's floating in my brain. Sliding the drawer open, I pull out the satchel of tools, brushing the dust off and finding appreciation for the things that draw me back to creating.

Like her.

I remove the edgers and the marking awl, and then I get to work with a vision in my mind. One hole at a time, I set them in before stitching the edges of the top. There's extra leather to work with in the middle, so I cut the bottom into a downward angle. It's not drastic, but it's enough that it's not the standard. No, that would be too boring for Antônia. Instead, I let the leather shape slightly into a point. Measuring would have been ideal, but it's not exactly necessary. Room for error here is large; it would be hard to fuck this up when I'm already so aware of her body.

I'm confident that the length is perfect, so I choose a gold buckle set with a thick matching loop for the front and begin to set it in. I find just enough gold studs to add to the trim every few centimeters, lining both the top and the bottom edges all the way around. It's nothing like I've ever made.

But I've never made a collar before either.

It's nearly noon when I look at my phone again. I haven't slept, or eaten, or peed, or taken a goddamn sip of water since we got home. As always, the task at hand takes precedent.

Never my own needs.

I throw the work in progress into the drawer, not sure that it's actually complete, but then again, none of my projects are ever finished. If I could, I would revise each piece until my final day, continuously updating them as I grow so that no one can ever see what I once was at the start.

The finality of calling a piece done is far too great a burden to bear, far too heavy to accept. It means being satisfied with myself and what I can do, something I know nothing about.

A quick check on Nia before I shower shows me her breathing is a little more erratic and her body is now drenched in sweat. She's better off sleeping if she can. She'll be coming down again soon, if she's not already.

I'll catch her as many times as it takes, but she has to let me.

Help me.

Her soft little words permeate my brain as the water washes over me.

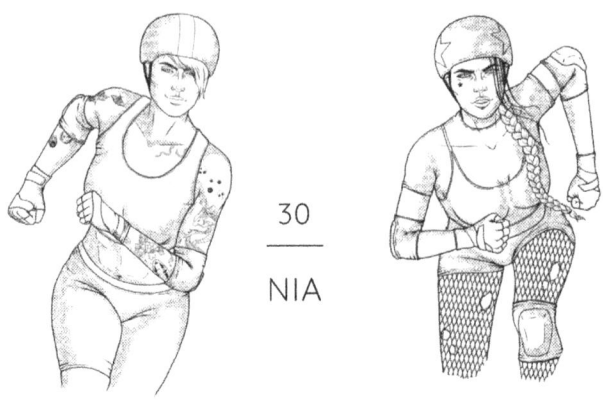

30
NIA

I wake up soaked in my own sweat, but it's the urge to vomit that hits me first.

My phone is nowhere to be found, but there's a clock next to her bed with a bright four staring me in the face. She let me sleep the whole day. My head pounds, an obnoxious sharp pain that's impossible to ignore.

Rolling off the bed as if it's the most laborious chore, I fall on top of a trash can already lined with a bag next to the bed. It's as if my needs were already anticipated.

I can't hold it back. I spew, heaving the little bit of liquid still in my body before the bile surfaces. Hot and cold wraps me all at once while vomit and snot mix together to drip down my face. I wipe my nose on the shoulder of my shirt before remembering that I'm not wearing one of mine.

It's not much better, the nausea only simmering instead of boiling over.

My head pounds with the smallest movements, but I don't want to be here. The carpet is too hot, and I can feel every fiber scratching at my skin. I crawl to the bathroom, only further worsening the dripping from my sinuses and the ache of the migraine.

Then, I remind myself it's not a migraine.

I'm withdrawing.

I'm fucking up my life again, and all it took was two months without speaking to my mother.

I want to call Ryan. I want to cry to him and tell him he was right, that I should have listened. I want him to make some stupid joke about the system, about how it gets us all in some way or another before he fixes this for me.

Because someone else *always* fixes it for me.

Except Ryan isn't coming, and the only person I haven't shut out doesn't know me well enough to realize I'm not worth any of this.

I'm shaky, no part of me strong enough to do anything, but I somehow muster the energy to get to the bathroom. I wipe my nose again. Fuck, it's rubbed raw, sensitive, and when I pull myself up to a stand, I look in the mirror and see why. My complexion is lackluster, but my nose is a bright rouge from rubbing. Scratch marks claw up my neck and down my arms from the sleep that clearly wasn't so deep.

This is just the beginning, though.

And it's exactly why I've already given up.

Gripping the edge of the sink, I stare just a little longer, just enough to hate myself a little more. My nose begins to drip again, and I go to wipe on my shoulder, but I catch myself before I somehow do any more damage to my face. Turning the faucet on, leaving the water cold and splashing it up into my face, I do it once then a second time before I feel a little less gross.

I don't know where my toothbrush is.

I don't know where any of my things are, but they're

here, in her house somewhere, and that's enough to alleviate my panic. I squeeze a glob of toothpaste onto my finger and scrub for a solid minute, deciding it'll have to do for now before rinsing.

When I come out of the bathroom, she's standing in the kitchen, putting away clean plates out of the dishwasher with a look of focus on her face. "Hi." I bid for her attention, still standing just outside the bathroom door.

Her head shoots up, eyes widening once she sees the state I'm in, but a placated smile quickly masks her face. She doesn't reach for another dish. Instead, it takes her just a few seconds to get to me, to hold me in her arms. It's not until then that I realize I'm shaking. Her squeezing me somehow makes it better, though, and her hand slides up to cup my face. I lean my cheek into her touch and close my eyes.

The feeling is starting to become too familiar, too reliable, too soothing.

She slides her hand past my face, fingers grazing the buzzed side of my head, where the thick scar raises. Her touch is gentle, explorative as she somehow makes the ache in my head nearly tolerable.

"How are you feeling?" Her voice is low and hushed, like she knows anything else would be painful.

My only response is a groan, leaning further into her as she continues to rub her fingers against my scalp. She pulls me into her body, and I'm suddenly no longer holding myself up, in her arms again. The thought that Cat is everything I've ever needed is both overwhelming and terrifying.

Because I still have yet to know what I am to her.

I think about her hobby room.

My mind takes me to that bad place, and I'm suddenly

convincing myself that I'm just her next project, the next thing for her to work on.

"Harvey." I open my eyes to find her staring straight through me. "What are you doing with me?" My breathing becomes shallow, and the words themselves churn my stomach.

"Isn't it obvious?" She smirks, her hand now back on my cheek, like she knows I can't help but be drawn to the touch.

It's my favorite place to be: held, protected by her.

She knows it, and she's trying to pacify me.

"I need the truth, Cat." I snap my eyes open and try to push her away, reserving the use of her first name so she knows I'm not happy.

She only holds me tighter.

"What do you need from me, baby? Reassurance? You have it. You're my girl." Her face is close, her eyes on mine, but I'm zeroed in on her lips.

"I *know*," I bite back, the coldness wrapping around my words. The idea of Cat being attracted to someone else doesn't even feel logistical in my brain. She knows that's not what I want to hear.

She knows, because she *always* knows what I want.

She's leaning over me, her forearm against the wall as she looks down on the shrunken version of me I've become. "Do you wanna ask me if *I'm yours* too?"

I look up at her, my heart thundering inside its bony cage. "Well, are you?"

She laughs, and it's the most genuine it has sounded coming from her. "From the very moment you surged out of whatever dream created you, I was yours and you were mine." Harvey shakes her head. "I don't know why I even *tried* to fight it."

I don't correct that it was *I* who dreamed her.

I don't think she'd understand.

She grips my waist, and I feel whole again. I swallow hard, her answer almost knocking the wind out of me with the way she owns her truth. "You promise?" I *need* the reassurance.

I'm desperate for it.

She chuckles. "I have something for you." She steps backward, her fingers still touching me until she's too far.

Then she turns around and walks into the extra room. She's gone for a second or so before she comes back holding something in her hand. It's only when she's back in front of me and opening her hands that I wipe the confused look off my face. It's a white leather choker. It's beautiful, adorned with gold studding perfectly spaced out, and the stitching is so flawless, it could have been done through a machine.

"You made this?" I ask, reaching for it, but she pulls it back, closing her fist around it.

I frown at the movement, but she responds to the question with a nod.

"When?" The word comes out almost like a laugh before I remember I've just been casually slipping through time in a drug-filled haze.

"This morning, today." She shrugs like it's nothing.

"Well… are you going to give it to me?" I look at her, but it suddenly feels too awkward, so I shift my gaze to the side.

"Here's the thing about this gift, princess, about belonging to someone," she says. "It comes with conditions."

"That doesn't sound like a gift then," I interrupt,

unable to shut my brain up from the incessant need to correct.

"Well, maybe it's not." She shrugs and extends her palm anyway.

It's fucking gorgeous, but I don't take it yet.

"Conditions?" I ask.

"You want me to be yours? Then I'm yours. But if you put this collar on, you are *mine* until you throw it back at my feet. Mine to take care of, mine to keep, mine to protect. Even if that means from yourself."

The promise is heavy, the obligation unspoken but so real, and my hand is in no way steady as it reaches for the white choker. "I want to be yours," I say, grabbing it before she somehow regrets it and decides to close her hand once more. And then Cat kisses me, enveloping me in all that is her.

Her lips stay pressed to mine, like separating might hurt one of us, until finally she pulls back, just enough to drop her forehead to mine.

"Put it on?" I ask, wanting to see what it looks like on me.

Her fingers are quick, nimble with the buckle as she slides the leather through it and then closes it to a snug fit around my neck. Harvey walks me to the mirror, standing behind me with her hands at the base of my throat, just below the collar.

It's truly amazing what she can do with her hands.

"Let me feed you," she whispers into my ear.

I groan walking past her, slinking my way down into the living room couch.

"Seriously. I haven't seen you eat anything in a long time. I know it's hard, but if there's something you *can* eat, then tell me," she pleads, following me.

Another obnoxious noise leaves my throat as I lay down fully on the couch. "Food is the enemy right now."

"Nia." Her voice is stern, like that's not an option.

"There's only one thing I can eat right now, and there's only one woman who can make it," I confess, knowing there's specifically only one dish I can stomach when I'm feeling this way, whether it's drug, alcohol, or virus-induced.

"I'll make it. I'll make you whatever you want as long as you eat it." She's squatting at the edge of the couch now, her hand a cool touch over mine.

I laugh, knowing she can't fulfill the challenge and finding a personal win in not being forced to eat. "Caldo de frango."

Smirking like I've won, I watch her eyebrows scrunch in confusion. "What does that mean?"

"It's Brazilian food. It's what my grandma used to make for me when I was sick. It's the only thing I can stomach."

"What do I need?" She stands so fast, it makes my head hammer trying to keep up. Pulling her phone out of her back pocket, she looks at me, then waits.

"What?" I'm not following her.

"Nevermind," she sighs, typing something on her phone and scrolling for a few seconds before she flips the screen to my face. "This?"

Damn.

But she's not just gonna try to cook this random thing she probably doesn't even have any ingredients for, and I'm certainly not in the condition to teach her or walk her through the steps. That would be insane. "Yes," I confirm with hesitation in my voice.

"Okay." She walks away, gaze fixed on her phone screen.

"What are you doing?" I turn my head back to see her standing in the kitchen, fridge door open as she rummages through what's already there.

She doesn't answer, typing something on her phone, and then she's looking in another cabinet.

"Harvey," I call for her attention, but she's ignoring me, still rummaging through her pantry for things.

No. She's not ignoring me; she has shifted all her focus to taking care of me.

"Cat," I call out, my voice a little more stern as I break her trance.

"Yeah?" Her head whips my way.

"What are you doing?" I ask.

"Ordering what I need to make this," she says casually before returning to the task.

"You're just *gonna make it*?" I toss it out mockingly, like it's just so easy to decide to do something and then *do it*.

Cat turns back my way, her eyes on me as she answers, "Yes."

31

HARVEY

I'm on autopilot, doing everything I can to remember what helped my brother go through this in the past, every single time he'd decide he was *finally* going to quit before he'd ruin our lives again two weeks later. I've got a cart full of things online, not just for food but for later, when the worst of it happens. It's too soon from her last hit, but I can tell she's already miserable. I add some children's electrolytes and nausea meds along with the ingredients for the recipe.

She's pretending to be doing better than she actually is. She's fidgeting, uncomfortable, and her red, watery eyes don't help the situation. But she's laying on the couch, head on my lap, while I look at sixteen different versions of this fucking recipe.

Nia thinks I won't cook it because I've never cooked anything like it, but that's never stopped me from doing something before. She's no help in telling me anything except which part of Brazil her family is from, and with that as a starting point, I'm able to do a few deep dives and find enough bloggers with English translations of the exact one I need.

It won't be perfect, but I can try to do it justice.

When the doorbell rings, I'm grateful that there's finally something to make me feel useful, *something* I can try to do. I tip the kid and don't bother to make sure the order is all there. She shifts on the couch, sweat glistening over her forehead as she watches me unpack the bags.

"You're really going to cook for me?" The realization that this isn't some prank is finally setting in for her.

"Why wouldn't I?" I don't bother masking my amusement.

For the first time all day, there's a real expression of emotion on her face, and hilariously enough, she's dumbfounded. I'm already walking in her direction.

"That's just... so crazy. I said this totally random food and you were like 'I'm gonna research and cook this.' And you've been at it for the last like two hours and—" I stop her train of thought with a kiss, running my hand through her hair to feel her roots damp with sweat.

I've gotten her to drink a few sips of water, and she seems to be holding it down. *For now.* We're still in the easy part of this, and now I'm kicking myself for ever thinking it *wasn't* a problem. She was already in too deep when she came into my work that first night with K.

I try not to blame myself, but I'm not dumb enough to pretend I didn't push her when all she needed was someone to share her grief with.

I shrug with my response. "I told you I'd cook whatever you wanted."

"Are you a Pisces?" she asks as I return to the kitchen to prepare the food.

"Fuck off with that," I answer, feigning annoyance as I set out the onion to chop. "But yes."

Her laugh is victorious, and the sound gives me hope.

I hope that she's truly my person when she gets through this.

Just as I'm getting all the ingredients prepped, my phone buzzes. I see a text come in from Mo.

> SCOTT WANTS AN ANSWER. COME TO PRACTICE EARLY.

> CAN'T MAKE IT TODAY. TELL HIM HE CAN KISS MY ASS THOUGH.

Skipping practice isn't a big deal to other skaters. They've all done it here and there, and no one bats an eye as long as we make it to the practices that count. We're required to show up to the practice before a bout in order to qualify to start; otherwise, we're benched and a B-team player subs out.

It's Wednesday night.

And though I've never missed a bout, I know this will get blown out of proportion.

> DON'T FUCK THIS UP, HARVEY.

HARVEY

I roll my eyes, annoyed and overburdened, draped in guilt for keeping too many things to myself. Then, Nia groans on the couch, and I'm back to focusing on her again.

I follow the recipe obsessively, reading the same sentence three times before it fully registers and completing the next step to make sure I'm doing it the right way. The way that will taste how she likes it. Peeling the yuca takes longer than I thought it would, and she's all smiles watching me deal with an ingredient I've never personally handled before in my life.

Once the root is peeled, I cook the chicken, then shred it and use the same water to boil the root. Once it's good and cooked, I put it in the blender before returning the broth to heat. I continuously season it, overly anxious that it's still going to somehow taste bland to her.

Taking a spoon, I blow, tasting it first. It's fucking delicious, but I also have no idea if this is the intentional outcome. With the green onions garnish on top, I don't bother asking her permission. I make her a bowl and bring it to her. I've never been more nervous in my life, but I don't show it.

She's forcing herself to a more upright position on the couch. There's a pained look on her face, but when I sit next to her with the bowl in my lap, it's not the same repulsed expression she had at the diner.

"That smells so good," she moans, leaning into me and dropping her head on my shoulder.

"You'll eat?" I can't help the excitement that comes through.

She chuckles softly before looking up at me with watery eyes. "I'll try."

I fill the spoon, bringing both it and the bowl closer to

her as she pulls her head up and sits a little more upright. I blow on it for good measure before I bring it to her lips. She opens, accepts, and swallows.

She closes her eyes and sets her head back on my shoulder, like that was entirely too much effort.

"Mmm," she hums with content. "It's so good."

I'm beaming, and before I can hide it, her eyes open just in time to catch me. I bite my lip, forcing the smile back while I wait for her to accept the next spoonful.

It doesn't take much for her to feel full, just a few bites and she's pushing my hand away completely. She looks a little better, less on-the-verge-of-death than before.

"Hey." I wait for her to turn my way. I don't want to leave her, but Mo rarely talks to me that way. Whatever needs dealt with at the rink can't wait. "I can't skip practice tonight."

Her shoulders slump in disappointment, and a look of worry drapes her face. "You don't have to come," I reassure her. "I'll tell them you're sick." She lets out a breath of relief, and I can imagine facing the team like this isn't something she wants to deal with.

"Actually," she says as I'm heading toward my room to change for practice, "I have some things I need to handle. Can you take me to get my car first?"

"I don't think that's a good idea, Nia," I say without turning around yet.

She clicks her tongue, the annoyance apparent in her tone. "What is that supposed to mean?"

I sigh, finally turning around to face her before I ask, "What kind of things do you have to do?" I try not to sound condescending, but there's absolutely no way she thinks I'm buying this shit.

Her face scrunches up. She's pissed, but she's trying to choose her words.

"What, because my life is just *this* now?"

Oh, yeah. She's withdrawing.

"*This?*" I ask.

She doesn't hesitate to bite back, "You being in control of everything."

"Stop it." I don't mean to sound stern, but I do. "Stop trying to create a problem where there isn't one. Don't make me say it." I shake my head.

With a scoff, she's standing and somehow managing to not look weak for the first time all day. "Don't make you say what? That you're keeping me here?"

"I'm not keeping you here, Nia. I'm *telling* you it's not a good idea." I don't look away. I just hope my words get through to her.

"But you're not going to take me?" It's not even annoying that her attitude is adorable, but the fact she gets this mean this fast... This is gonna be an even bigger challenge.

"Nia, you're withdrawing, you're dopesick, you just ate for the first time in days. What the fuck could you possibly need your car for, and what makes you think you're in any shape to be driving it?" I don't mean to be blunt, but I lay the facts out there.

"You're treating me like I'm a fucking kid, Harvey." She's trying to stand up for herself, but she's getting weepy, reminding me once again *why* we're doing this.

"I'm treating you like a *junkie*, Nia," I correct.

"I'm not a fucking junkie." The look on her face is pure anger, her eyes burning with intensity.

I can't help but laugh. "Oh babe, you're gonna have to take a hard look at yourself right now, because we both know once you walk out that door, there's only one thing you're gonna be looking for."

"Fuck you, Harvey." Her voice is cold, like she's shooting to kill.

I slap my hand to my heart and feign hurt. "*I'm* the one who does the fucking, remember?" It comes out as a breathy laugh.

She pushes at me like she wants me to back away, but I grab the gold loop of the collar and flick at it, reminding her it hasn't even been hours since she accepted it. The acknowledgment sets in on her face like she's been proven wrong, and she shrugs it off, crossing her arms.

"You're coming to practice," I tell her.

"W-what? There's no point. I can't skate like this." She lifts up the cast that didn't stop her before she started getting too high to skate.

"I can't leave you here, so you're coming with me." I shrug, changing into a pair of gym shorts and throwing on a clean practice shirt. I grab some clothes from her suitcase and bring them out to the living room with me.

"Come sit between my legs." I give her the clothes and sit on the edge of the couch, brush in hand, waiting for her.

The frown never leaves her face, and she doesn't bother going to another room to change. She's not wearing much of anything anyway. She slides on the sweatpants and grabs the hem of her shirt, her nostrils flaring as she makes eye contact with me.

She can't take it off on her own, but she's too pissed to ask me.

This isn't a moment I need to win, so I stand up and reach for her shirt to help pull it up and off her. Not bothering to let her try, I grab the fresh shirt myself and dress her in it. I pull her to me, pressing her against my body and gently tugging at the ends of her hair. She finally looks up at me.

"Let me brush it." I unravel the hair tie and slide it over my wrist.

She's gone quiet, and I don't know if it's a good or a bad thing, but she follows me back to the couch, where she kneels between my legs on the rug. I'm gentle, pulling the braid apart, and once it comes free, I rub my fingers across her scalp, a groan of satisfaction falling from her lips.

Nia cuts it short when she catches my grin, her personal protest in this tantrum. That's fine; if directing those raw emotions gets her through this, I can be that for her. She's been numbing herself for weeks, and now, Nia is going to feel the full force of every emotion she's been repressing since I told her Lonnie was dead.

I regret that moment to its full entirety now, wishing I'd done it differently in some way, that maybe if I had, it would have changed things. Maybe she wouldn't have chosen to lose herself in Lonnie's name.

It's too late to regret, so I braid instead.

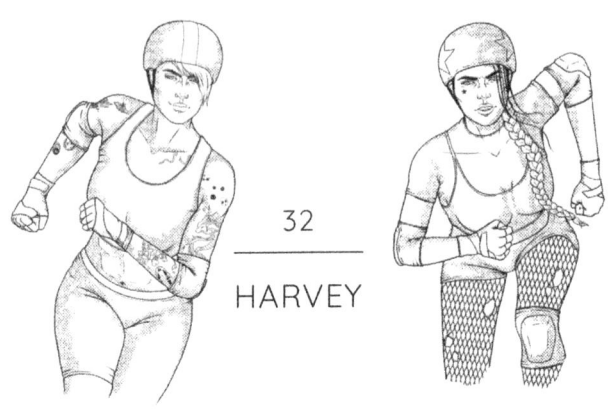

32

HARVEY

She's silent the entire car ride, but I'm not going to beg for words out of her knowing she's not in a good place. I blast my music, letting *Metric* play on the way to Skateland. Nia's incredibly skilled in masking her discomfort, and aside from the pink nose that can easily be excused for a cold, she truly *can* pass for sick.

We're just not specifying what kind of sick she is.

I feel bad that I'm bringing her, I know it's not fair, that she'd be more comfortable at home, but I don't plan to stay for the entire practice. I'll meet with Scott, run through two or three practice jams, and then go home.

It's both my obligation to the rink and to Lonnie.

"I wanna stay in the car," she rasps out, hugging herself with her arms. She's got a jacket on like a blanket since the other arm can't fit in the sleeve.

"It's too cold. You can lay down on the couch in Lonn —the office," I correct myself before I can finish.

She lifts the jacket up to her nose to wipe. "I don't want them to see me."

"No one goes in there." I bring a finger to her chin to get her eyes on mine. "I promise."

I use my key to unlock the office and sneak Nia in before any of the other skaters notice. Whatever energy the soup gave her seems to be fading quickly as her comedown sets in.

"You won't be long?" She looks up at me with those midnight-colored eyes.

"No, half the practice at best," I assure her, giving her one final kiss on the forehead before I wrap her in a blanket and place a trash can on the floor close by.

I lock the door behind me, knowing the only other person with a key to this office is currently inside of it.

I'm at the cubbies getting geared up when Star crashes into me on the bench. "Where's Nia?" she asks as I'm finishing lacing up my quads.

"She's sick." I don't put too much thought behind the words, but K lets out a sarcastic huff to my side.

Our eyes meet. There's indifference there, and clearly, K feels some sort of way about Nia's choices. That's between them. But K says nothing to me, only stands and follows DreadPool onto the track to begin warm ups.

"Seriously, though," Stella grabs my arm just as I come to a stand, "Nia was one of my best friends. I don't feel like I know this version of her anymore, and you've been spending all this time with her—"

I stop her.

"She's struggling with Lonnie. The way we all did, the way *you* did, Star. We've had more time than her. Just give her a little grace." It's not a lie, and I don't feel bad for saying it.

Maybe she's also not wrong. Maybe the friend she knew five years ago isn't the same woman here today. That doesn't have to be a bad thing. It just means she needs to get to know her again. Star nods, and we play-shove each other's shoulders as we slide onto the track for laps.

Mo has had me subbing for Nia since her wrist injury. Three weeks ago, I would have reveled in the feeling, bathed in it. Today, I'm glad she's locked away in that office and can't see me. I don't want to be another crack in what's already breaking her. Today, under these conditions, I just want to be her pivot again.

I just want to have her back.

The whistle blows, Nancy and Star doing their best to keep me from passing K-Otic. I'm practically pushing the wall of skaters as I try to move forward when K calls the jam. Mo makes some switches and blows the whistle again, this time Nancy and Stella blocking on my side to see the outcome.

It's the exact same. They form a wall, and K is unable to push through, having to skate forward at a glacial pace as I lap the opposing blockers and call this jam off. We keep moving the blockers around, but the result is the same no matter who's jamming or blocking, and I can't help but see the obvious difference.

We're missing our fucking jammer.

I'm dripping in sweat when I feel his hand tug the back of my shirt. "Cathrine," he calls for me, "let me pull you for a moment."

The less I want to do with this man, the more I somehow get involved with him, and it's no longer an annoyance I can tolerate. I follow him when I realize he's headed to the office.

But then I remember she's in there. "It's locked. Let's just talk out here."

"It's fine," he says, pulling a key out of his pocket.

"Where the fuck did you get that?" I block his arm from inserting the key into the hole.

"I found it when I had the crew clean out that room in the back." Scott says it so casually, but the entire sentence gives me whiplash.

"Say that one more fucking time, because I swear I thought you just said you had a crew of people in the locked *apartment* in the back?" My nostrils are flared, I'm clenching my fists, and every part of me is holding myself from exploding in this man's face.

"Someone left it open." He shrugs. "And I need a bigger office than this to run the team properly." He laughs in my face, like he hasn't done something incredibly violating.

Like he didn't steal a piece of Lonnie from all of us.

"This isn't your fucking rink," I remind him, my jaw practically clenched shut.

He sighs exhaustedly. "Cathrine, let's stop pretending. My offer won't last much longer."

With my hand still forcibly keeping him from shoving the key into the lock, he simply reaches over with the other, turning the knob and pushing the door open. "Oh." He laughs. "Look at that. Didn't even need the key."

What the fuck?

My heart sinks, my head immediately going to the worst possible place. Whatever Scott says next, I don't hear. I'm skating out into the parking lot to see if I can find her. If she left on her own, she couldn't be far. If she got a cab?

Fuck.

I try not to spiral, pushing the doors to go back inside. *Get my shoes on and my keys and go find my girl before she makes a terrible decision.* That's all I can think of.

Scott grabs my bicep as I skate past him, and he pulls

me back, throwing my balance off, but I'm quick enough to redirect the fall to my knees. I'm in panic mode, though, and anything he's saying isn't going to register until the noise in my brain quiets.

It won't quiet until I see her.

The pull I feel is nearly magnetic, and when my head twists to the side to find her standing by the cubbies talking to Mo, the weight is lifted.

But only briefly.

The look on her face tells me I've already fucked up everything.

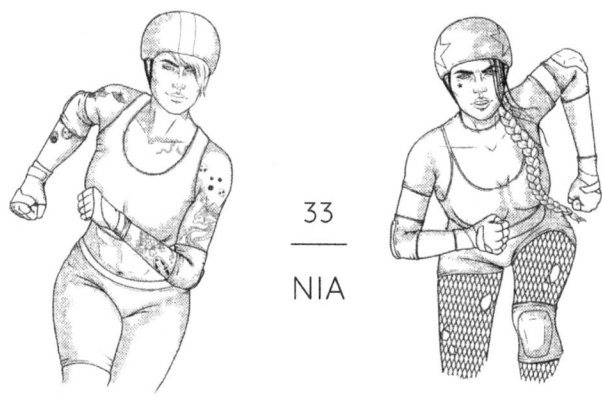

33
NIA

I'm restless, crawling out of my own fucking skin in that office and scratching the remainder of it to hell from the onsetting withdrawal. So I step out for a drink, and on my way to the water fountain, I stumble into Mo. Avoiding conversation isn't possible, but they're aware I'm sick and don't seem suspicious.

"Is your wrist at least feeling better? Hopefully that cast comes off soon. We barely got to scrimmage before you got knocked out of commission." Mo gives me an awkward side hug and ruffles my hair.

"Yeah, I'll be stoked to get cleared for contact, but that probably won't be for a couple more weeks. Scott will just have to suck it up." I shrug.

"I mean, in the end it's your call, now that you and Harvey are in love, and getting married, and having skate babies," Mo says.

I laugh, confused. "What do you mean, my call?"

"I mean, in the end, it's your rink, right? Or did you guys decide you were going to sell to Scott?" They frown.

"What the fuck are you talking about, Morgan?" I'm so confused, I don't know where the start or end to this conversation is.

"Harvey hasn't told you." A sinking realization splashes across their face.

"Harvey hasn't told me *what?*" My heart thunders a storm inside my chest, the thought of Harvey keeping something from me already enough to make me nauseous.

I've put *all* my trust into her.

"Well, you know how the rink is yours and all? Well, Scott offered to buy it outright. Own the Dames *and* Skateland." Mo stuffs their hands in their pockets uncomfortably.

"Back the fuck up to the part where the rink is *mine and all*." Every word is sharp, my confusion slowly turning into a burning anger.

"Harvey didn't—"

"No, clearly Cat hasn't told me a fucking thing, Mo. So why don't you enlighten me?" I'm so pissed, I can't see straight, dreading the words that are coming next even though my brain is already starting to piece it together.

"Lonnie left the rink to both of you. You and Harvey." Mo tugs at the top of their ponytail to tighten it, clearly uncomfortable with this whole exchange. Their gaze shifts up, and I don't have to follow it to see who they're looking at with that *oh fuck* look on their face. "I gotta go, I think. I'll see you later, Nia."

I'm dumbfounded, the other skaters continuing on with practice, too busy on the track to even notice me. My heart bubbles with rage, and I finally shift my eyes to where she stands with Scott.

My expression surely gives me away.

StarScreamer is skating toward us, trying to stop in her tracks like she senses the tension, but it's far too late. She stumbles into Harvey, almost knocking both her and Scott over.

And I'm too pissed off to keep what I'm feeling inside. This goes beyond our relationship, beyond whatever the fuck we are to each other. This is about her hiding something from me that Lonnie had meant to be mine. She had no fucking right.

Harvey's skates move toward me like anxious prey, unsure if she can approach or not, which is hilarious from someone like her. Except I'm not in a laughing mood. "Babe?" She lifts an eyebrow up, slowing down the closer she approaches me.

"Do *not* fucking *babe* me." The words feel cold out of my lips, and Nancy, who's three steps away from the locker room, does a 180-degree spin on her heels.

"Oh shit," I hear her say in the distance as she plops her ass down on a bench, like this is about to be the best entertainment of her life.

"Whatever it is, can we talk about it at home?" Cat asks, looking around, seeing that all eyes are now officially on us.

"*Your* home. I don't have a home in Devil Town. Oh—wait, except this fucking rink that you've failed to mention to me." I'm yelling, but I don't care. I cross my arms over my chest and immediately regret it. I'm so fucking angry, I don't know what to do with my limbs, but maybe it's better they're tucked away.

"Did Morgan tell you?" She takes a step toward me, but I shake my head in warning, stepping back as well.

"It doesn't matter who told me. What matters is that

you've been lying to me since fucking day one." I command every cell in my body to forbid the tear to form. Never in my adult life have I been in control of regulating my emotions, of *not* letting my anger turn into tears, but today, I will.

I will not cry over Cathrine Harvey.

"It wasn't supposed to be like this, Nia. You weren't—"

"Supposed to find out? Was your plan to just drive me away? Kick my ass until I gave up? Then you realized I was an addict and didn't need your help? You were just waiting it out?" I grit the words out, hating myself for saying them but unwilling to stop.

We're already standing in front of the meat grinder, so why not jump in?

"You get real nasty when you're withdrawing, babe. I'd really like to do this in private," she says calmly, like *I'm* the fucking one in the wrong here.

"Of course you would, you manipulative bitch. It's so much easier when you can just paint me out to be the unstable one." My arms break free from my own hold, and I clench my fists at my side.

"Ohhooooo, wow. Bite me, princess, spit in my eye. Whatever it takes, right?" She's smirking like she's amused, though I know she's not. Nothing I've said is worth a laugh. She's moving closer to me again, but I'm only getting more pissed off.

"Get that smirk off your face. You're so fucking condescending." I'm beyond my own control, overstimulated, angry, and approaching meltdown. She's in my space, and I can't help it. I reach out to hit, but she grabs my wrist instead, then the cast.

"It's not condescending. You're just kind of fucking

toxic, Antônia." She loosens her grip on the wrist that threatened her.

I lower it to my side, the sting of her words enough to quiet my voice so the others can't hear us anymore. "Then why are you still here?"

She clicks her tongue, as if I should already know the answer to that. "I guess that's just what I like."

She drops her forehead to mine, but I push away.

"How am I supposed to trust you when you've been keeping this from me, Cat?" And there they go, the weepy withdrawal tears ruining any chance of me maintaining my composure.

Making me weak instead of righteous in my fury.

"The same way I'm supposed to trust you to stay sober when you've already proven to me that you can't." She says it so plainly, but her truth is a leather belt leaving raised welts on skin.

She tugs at the gold loop of the collar like it's a reminder.

"Let's go home," I whisper, no longer wanting everyone's eyes on me.

IT'S THE FIRST TIME I'VE BEEN IN THE CAR WITH CAT WITH the music off. The drive feels three times as long, and all I want to do is reach over and hold her hand. In just a matter of weeks, she became my entire universe.

No.

She *made* herself my entire universe, and I can't help but let my mind tell me it was all part of some plan. This was orchestrated. Because it *is*. It is entirely in her nature to plan something out like this so craftily. Everything hurts, and I no longer care to be sober, to be hers, to be anything.

I pull my phone out and send the text.

> PICK ME UP

I SEND THE ADDRESS JUST AS I WALK INSIDE, HEADING TO the bedroom for whatever I deem essential. The collar itches at my neck, feeling too tight and suffocating. I don't ignore the symbolism of it as I fumble with the buckle, but I give up once I can't take it off one-handed.

She's still sitting on the couch when I come out of the room. This feels like more than just a fight, but I don't have it in me to lug around all my possessions. At this point, she can just toss all my shit into Skateland for all I care.

I only bring my backpack with me.

Feeling the buzz in my back pocket, I don't have to check to see who it is. The headlights against the window tell me Bobby's already here.

"Don't go, Nia," she says as I walk toward the door. Her voice sounds dry, cracked, and it's enough to make me turn toward her.

She's crying.

Typical.

I break everything.

Except for once, I don't feel as bad. Like a child who threw a toy at a wall too many times, I see the consequence of my actions.

I walk out the door, practically running into Bobby's car so I have no chance of stopping myself, no chance of ruining this perfect opportunity for self-sabotage. I haven't fucked myself over in a while, so let's make this one *really* good.

I wait at the passenger door for a split second, forgetting whose car it is and that the door works before I get inside. "Hey, pretty lady," he says, all smiles before his face really sets in on mine.

"Let's go." I wave him off, trying to get the fuck out of here as fast as possible. I can't help it; my eyes dart to the passenger mirror where I see Cat standing outside her door just as we leave.

"You look rough, girl," he confirms the obvious.

"Yeah, I know." I wipe the sweat off my forehead.

He nods towards the glovebox. "In there."

I open it, but there's nothing except car documents inside. "Manila folder," he says.

Maybe he's not as dumb as I thought he was. I shuffle through some of the documents before I find the bag of powder between the registration and the manual. I don't wait for the car to slow down or for us to stop at a light. I drop it to the back of my hand and shove the tiny mountain of dust into my nostril.

"Fuck," I whisper, pressing on the Ziploc and tossing it back into its hiding place in the glovebox.

The relief is immediate.

The physical.

The inside bits too.

The ones I can't put a word or category to, the ones I haven't quite named yet, only acknowledged. The ones shredding my soul everytime I blink and see Cat's face.

I lean back into the seat and close my eyes, disintegrating into the moment and finally getting some peace from my own head.

    I
can
finally
turn
it
off.

34

NIA

There
is
no
time,
only
anger,
sorrow,
shame,
guilt,
and
the
vast
emptiness
that
houses
it
all.
I
fill
it

until
I
am
no
longer
the
one
consuming
but
the
one
consumed.

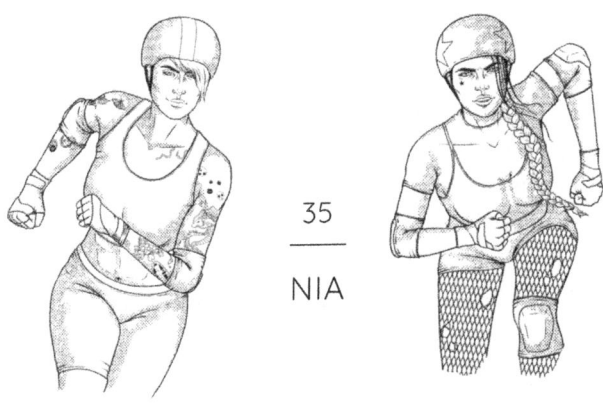

35
NIA

"Where's your money?" Bobby's voice is annoying in my ear, but it's his incessant nudging of my shoulder that forces me to open my eyes.

Not
asleep
not
awake
not
quite
here.

"Front zipper," I mumble.

"There's only forty here." His voice is stern, the paper bills fanning my face.

"Then you already took the rest." I push him away, my tone sharpening the more he invades my space.

He doesn't move though, his body turning into a solid wall. "You owe me money."

"Fuck off, Ryan," I groan, too high to do more than swat in front of my face.

"This isn't Ryan's house, little girl." He shakes me harder.

"You've done just as much of my shit as I've done of yours." I'm alert now, but I'm incredibly fucked up still.

"I'm missing at least a gram."

I'm having a hard time keeping my eyes open, but I can tell the look on his face is nothing short of displeased.

"Check your shit. That's not my problem." I'm trying to push him away, but at this point, he's patting my pockets and prodding his fingers into my pants. "Get the fuck off me!"

"Give me my shit, Nia. I'm not fucking around." He pulls up at my hips like he's trying to reach into my back pockets.

"Get off!" I send my knee up high and hard, hitting him right between the legs.

"Fucking bitch!" he shouts, cupping at his balls with one hand while the other swats at me.

I *know* I'm high as fuck because the sting of the slap doesn't register; it's the force of his hand against my face making my head spin. Crying out is pointless, but I do it anyway, scrambling back too slowly, my body trying to keep up with my brain and mildly failing.

My ears ring.

He climbs on top of me one more time, his right arm pinning my hip down while his left knee secures me in place. I squirm, try to push him away, but he's basically a boulder on top of me as he reaches into the front of my pants pocket again. My heart races, the feeling of being overpowered too frightening, nearly paralyzing.

Except my grandma was pregnant when she whooped my grandfather's ass with a chair for trying to hit her, and fuck if I was gonna be bested by this piece of shit. I remember the heavy cast that's been a pain in my ass for two weeks now.

"Bobby, stop!" I shout again, but I don't wait. I send my arm down over his head.

He's only stunned for a split second, his hand reaching for my throat while the other tries to invade my pants. Bobby's a fucking idiot, because he doesn't have enough hands to contain, kill, *and* rape me, and even high, I can send my wrist down over his head again.

It's a sharp pain, but it's short. Electric but it doesn't linger, traveling from my wrist to my elbow, coming back only when I strike again. It's enough to make him bleed, make him finally pull back and give me the space I need to kick him in the nuts again, this time harder and with more accuracy. I grab my backpack, stumbling off the couch and darting clumsily for the door.

I fall, catching myself with my bad wrist, and this time, the pain is a burning throb. I bite it back, ignoring Bobby's cursing as I run out of his house. I don't look to see if he's following me; I just pound my feet under me and move faster than I've ever moved.

Thankfully, he's in a shit part of town, and there's about three houses between his and a gas station. My lungs are on fire, but I don't stop until I can hide inside, making my way to the restroom and avoiding the clerk's stare from behind the counter.

I lock the stall behind me, holding my backpack to my chest and squeezing. In a way, it's almost soothing, like the rapid-fire drumming of my heart.

The nodding off is the best.

Or the worst.

Eyelids flutter.

Sometimes, they don't open.

Sometimes, they stay shut.

I blink, and my back is against the cold, tile wall, my head leaning on the side of the toilet tank. I'm still clutching the backpack, shriveled into the corner of the little stall. The confusion is brief as I piece together the last few hours. Stumbling to a stand, I hang the backpack on the door hook.

Lowering my sweats to my knees, I pee for the first time in what feels like ages. That's when the bag of heroin falls out of the other pocket.

I snort.

I guess he *was* right. He is missing a gram. I wipe and pull my pants up before I pick it up off the ground and dump a little on the back of my phone case. Digging through my bag for a piece of paper, I settle for an old pharmacy receipt and roll it up into a straw before I snort down my next hit.

It's time to go home.

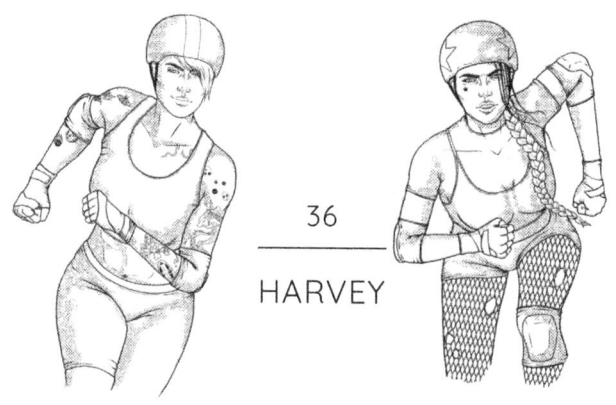

36

HARVEY

It's been nearly three fucking days. I've been blowing up her phone with no fucking answer, but with nowhere obvious to go looking for her, my only option was to wait for her to show up. Still, I drove around town in the middle of night, just on the off chance I'd run into Nia.

It's Saturday morning, and though I spent the majority of last night hoping she'd show up to the rink during scrimmage, I'm drawn back to Skateland today. I start to wonder if I'm strong enough for this, but it's too late now. I'm in love with her, and I can't let her do this to herself, though I don't know if that's enough to stop her.

There's not a single car in the parking lot, but something tells me that means nothing today. Reaching for my key is pointless, because leaning on the double door is enough to push it open.

It's unlocked.

My heart thrums, I'm only three steps in the building, but it's enough to hear the music coming from Lonnie's place.

It's a short-lived feeling of relief that at least she's safe.

The music is too loud for comfort, for *any* reasonable person. It causes a lump to form at the top of my throat, and I can no longer swallow it down. Not until I see her. I run to the little studio apartment our friend once called home, the music twice as loud once I'm inside, and there she is.

Everything suddenly moves impossibly slow. It feels like ages before my brain can make the connection. The way she sits on the ground with her back against the wall, her head slumped down to the side, her skin no longer golden but a pale, grayish color, foam pouring freely from her lips.

"Antônia." I shake her, my voice coming out a tremble.

Her eyes barely flutter.

"Nia, baby, what the fuck did you do?" I'm asking myself; I know she's not capable of answering.

I go through her things in a fury, tossing her bag apart, hoping that she's got something that can reverse a little of what she's done to herself, just enough to buy me enough time to get her to a hospital.

"Fuck!" I scream, rummaging through the backpack, but aside from her phone charger and her wallet, there's nothing else.

She moans like my chaos is disruptive to her high. I come back to her, lifting her eyelids by force. She's hardly there at all, and it feels like my world is ending faster than it took for it to come into existence. I no longer know what I have time for, what *she* can hold on for. I lift her into my arms, my keys still in my pocket as I thumb through my phone.

The number is there, saved. I don't know if it still works, though. He's had a million phone numbers, and half of them were burners. I call anyway. We're closer to his house than any hospital, and God knows an ambulance will take three days to get here.

"Catie?" The voice is shocked that I'm calling, and I haven't even spoken. He's kept my number this whole time too.

"I'm not calling to talk. I need your help. My..." I take a deep breath before I get the rest out. "My girlfriend is overdosing, and I don't know what to do."

He doesn't ask what I'm doing with a junkie, doesn't mock that I didn't have the tolerance for him but have the tolerance for her. He hears the panic in my voice, and he knows I need my big brother.

"Does she have any naloxone around?" he asks calmly.

"Is that Narcan? No. I looked everywhere." I've given up searching for anything in the barren apartment and resort to lifting her over my shoulder.

"You're gonna have to take her to the hospital, kiddo," he says with a sigh.

My voice is a pleading cry. "You're closer. Let me bring her to you." I'm not sure she'll make either drive at this point, and I *know* my brother. I know he can fix this.

"This girlfriend of yours," he says, "big scar on the side of her head?"

My stomach sinks so deeply, it feels like an abyss is created inside me.

He's her dealer.

Of course he is.

I'm loading her into the backseat while trying to process this information, but I don't want to accept it for what it is.

"Let me bring her to you!" I'm screaming. I'm so angry at him for once again taking the things I love from me with drugs.

First him, now her.

"No. Take her to the hospital. It's time for Nia to hit rock bottom." I'm pretty sure I hear him disconnect, but I'm still cursing and shouting.

"Ryan, what the fuck?" I'm sobbing from frustration and panic, but I don't have time to dwell.

This is exactly why I'd written him off, why I stopped depending on him, why I didn't want him in my life anymore. Ryan makes his own rules, his ego like God. He thinks he gets to decide who's the right kind of addict for saving and who's not, who conquers his gauntlet and who is crushed by it. I should have fucking known. My brain won't stop, but I settle on the passing thought that it would take twice as long for an ambulance, so I start the car.

I drive twenty over the speed limit, unsure how I don't crash, because my head is turned, checking on Nia every five seconds. I call to her every so often, but she only answers in mumbles. By the time we get to the hospital, she's completely unresponsive. I must look as desperate as I feel, because when I park in front of the emergency room doors, the medical assistants are scrambling out with a wheelchair.

It only takes three words to separate us.

"Are you family?"

The thought of lying doesn't occur to me. I'm in such a haze, all I can do is shake my head, the nurse's voice muted as she tries to explain that no one other than family can follow past the doors.

And then I watch them take her where I can't follow.

At least four staff members have asked me to sit down. The woman behind the front desk is beyond irate with me, and I'm pretty sure they've threatened security twice. I can't calm down, can't sit, can't think, can't stop.

I don't know how long it's been. All I can do is pace and nibble at the bits of dry cuticle that now bleed on nearly every finger. The skin is raw, red and torn, but I continue until it's butchered meat before moving on to the next nail.

I'm ushered back to a waiting room chair anyway, my anxiety uncontainable. Shifting my focus internally is the only way to stop. I pay attention to the thoughts now, no longer letting them serve as loud white noise playing on repeat, but instead picking each individual word out.

That's when I tell myself it's my fault, that I should have stopped her from leaving, that I should have seen that she was already so far fucking deep into this cycle of self-destruction from the beginning. That maybe if I had just been honest…

That I should have put my trust in her the same way Lonnie did.

I'm lost in the sea inside my head, but not too far under the surface to not recognize his voice.

"Antônia Da Silva, came in not too long ago."

Every hair on my body stands.

I'm suddenly afraid to look up, to risk making eye contact, for him to see me here. After denying me—no, denying *her* the help she needed?

"Family?" she asks just the same as she asked me.

"Yes," he lies, a wave of envy hitting me that I wasn't able to do that for myself.

I just want to hold her hand.

I just want to make sure she's okay.

"Need some sort of proof or something," the woman says with an air of annoyance, and just as I'm considering finally looking his way, to relish in the satisfaction of him being turned down access to her…

He's right in front of me.

"Are you coming?" His hand extends like he wants to help me up.

I don't take it, don't look at his face yet. I can't. He's the last person I want to see right now. He's the reason she's in there. I stand anyway.

"They're letting you in?"

He chuckles, cocky and poorly timed, but that's his style anyway. "Hard to deny that I'm family when I'm in possession of her government documents." He waves a folded up piece of paper in my face, and I rip it from his hand before opening it up.

It's her birth certificate.

I don't have time to ask him how or why he has this, though; the nurse takes us through the double doors, and her room is the first one to our left. I still haven't lifted my eyes from the paper, avoiding the prickly stare of my brother's gaze.

"I'm not sure how she survived that," the nurse says softly as she turns the knob. "We've never had to deliver so many doses to one patient before." She bites her lip, fumbling with her chart once we get inside. "Your wife must have a guardian angel on her side."

The shock of her calling my brother her husband has

me whipping my neck so hard, it's almost impossible for me to recompose myself and remember that's what he said to get us in here.

"Will you be calling the police?" he asks, and I'm not surprised. That's all he cares about, probably only here to threaten her not to open her mouth about where she got it.

"No, we don't do that here. There will be a caseworker coming in to check on her and talk to her about overdose prevention and steps to take so this doesn't happen again, once she's a little more alert. After that, you can take her home, and that's when the hard part begins." She's ignoring me, her attention only on my brother, as if he even gives a shit about her.

"What's that?" I ask, immediately regretting and knowing the answer before it comes out of their mouths in unison.

"Detox."

"Why is she not awake?" my brother asks.

"She'll probably come out of it soon. Every reaction is different. Once she's awake, we can start the discharge process," she tells him.

A slightly sleepy groan pulls my attention back to Nia, and I don't care that the nurse is here. I rush to her side, grabbing for her hand.

"Give us some privacy?" Ryan asks her.

I don't turn around to watch her leave, my whole world right here in front of me. She closes the door loudly enough that when the latch clicks shut, my mouth is moving on command. "Why the fuck are you here?"

"Closure," he says from the chair in the corner of the room, as far away from Nia as possible.

As if his plan is to just sit there until she's fully awake.

"For you, or for her?" I ask.

I still haven't looked at his face.

"Does it matter, Catie?"

I can't help but reject the nickname with my entire body.

I was never a fucking Catie, except when I was his sister.

I hope it tastes like saltwater on his tongue.

I hope it dries his mouth out.

"She didn't OD off my shit." He says it so plainly, and I'm not sure if he's trying to clear his name or his conscience. "I cut her off almost two weeks ago."

Him not being to blame doesn't make any of this better.

"Are you the one who got her started?" I finally turn my head and take a good look at his face. I hate how much we look alike.

He chuckles like the asshole he is. "Nia has always been smart enough to know her limits. I made a bad decision, but I'm not the bad guy here."

"She was fucking falling apart when she went to you. You might as well have just given her a gun." I know my words hurt, I know they remind him of our father and that while it affected me, it didn't define me like it did him.

My voice is devoid of emotion, but it's a mask. I *need* him to think he's not affecting me.

Because inside, it's tearing me apart.

"Mãe?" Nia's voice is weak and raspy.

"It's me," I say that like it means anything, like I'm not just someone she walked out on.

"Cat?" She squeezes my hand, finally opening her eyes. They're immediately flooded with tears, and all I want is to hold her in my arms now and tell her she's safe.

"Fuck." It's all my brain has the power to come up with. The relief of hearing her call my name is everything.

Her eyes dart past me, and her expression changes too suddenly for me to think anything other than she's noticed him.

Ryan.

"Get out." It's barely a whisper from her lips, but every hair on my arms comes to stand at hearing her say those words.

They aren't for me though. They're for him.

"Oh? And here I thought I was coming to say goodbye to *you*, squirt." He laughs it off, standing up from the chair and walking toward her despite her request.

Nia's eyebrows furrow in the middle, but she doesn't ask for clarification. He drops his hands to the bed's metal support bars. "You broke my heart too, kid."

"You can't be my friend and my dealer," Nia says without breaking his stare.

With a nod, he turns to walk away but freezes.

The scene is like something from a movie, and I'd laugh if I wasn't on the verge of crying.

"Proud of you," he says to her, letting go of the bars before he shifts his gaze to me. "Proud of you too, Catie."

And then, he's gone.

For the first time ever, I hope it's for good.

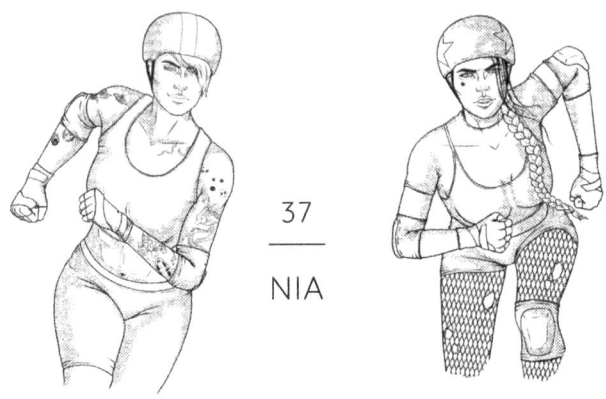

37
NIA

The social worker is an asshole with no empathy, making me wonder if, one day, I'll become desensitized to the very people I want to help once I'm in my field.

It's the first time I've had a thought about my future since…

Since finding out about Lonnie.

I've held myself in a permanent state of limbo ever since, unsure if my place was here in Devil Town or if I was ready to bolt once more and start new.

Discharge takes hours, and by the time Cat has me in the passenger seat of her car again, it's dark. "What time is it?" I ask her.

"One in the morning," she says, sliding the key into the ignition.

"What day is it?" I ask the better question, my teeth starting to chatter, and while I'm convincing myself it's from the brisk chill of the night wind, I'm not stupid.

I'm already withdrawing now that the Narcan has run its course.

"Sunday now," she tells me.

"It was Slam Night." The realization is meant to be internal, but it comes out of my mouth anyway.

She missed a bout.

"Let's get you home, Nia," she says, as if the rest isn't important.

She says it like I have a home.

Fighting her words is an impossible task. The leather collar still grips at my neck, proof that, without her, I can't even undo what we've become.

I don't know what we've become, so I lean my head on the window and wish the thoughts away.

It doesn't work.

I'm standing awkwardly at the door, unsure where to go from here. She's already in the kitchen doing whatever Cat Harvey thing is next on her never-ending list of things to get done.

There's an entire planet between us, hundreds of conversations we haven't had yet, a galaxy of things we've both shattered that need mending.

But all I want is to be held by her again.

No—all I want is for her to *want* to hold me again.

She's wiping the counters, clearly amped-up from dealing with my shit all day, and it's running through her now like three cups of coffee.

"Harvey?" I say her name, but it's quiet. I'm not fully sure myself that I *want* her to hear me.

The emptiness inside of me finally explodes.

I drop to my knees, only to brace myself with my casted hand—a new, searing pain reminding me of the giant crack splitting along the side of the plastic. I'm hyperaware of every single ache and throb in my body, and this one is no joke.

The thing with Bobby is already a fuzzy memory in my

mind, but the break in the cast reminds me that it might have saved my life.

That's when I piece together that it took no time for the same environment I had safely grown up in to turn hostile. The difference? Ryan Lee. His name scratches at my throat now that I know it in its entirety. Ryan Lee Harvey.

Seeing them there, in the room together, I don't know how I didn't see it before. They could have been twins, with just a slight difference of hair color and the scruff on his chin to set them apart.

It makes the guilt I'm already drowning in even more unbearable to swim through.

"Cat," I call to her once more, this time a little louder.

When she finally turns to me, she freezes.

"No." Her voice is harsh, and it stings.

She's walking towards me, and I swallow a hard lump, waiting for her on my knees. "There's no point in doing *this*," she waves her hand over me, "if you're just going to self-destruct every time things get hard."

"You lied to me," I remind her, still staying on my knees.

I wanna scratch, I need to puke, and I can tell I'm three words away from tears falling.

It doesn't matter.

I *have* to heal this.

She squats with one knee on the ground as she looks me over, the disappointment on her face is so fucking sobering that if the naloxone hadn't already done it, she could. She reaches toward my neck, like she's gonna take the collar off.

I slap her hand out of the way with my cast, wincing at the sharp pain, my teeth clenched when the words come out. "You said I'm yours until *I* throw it at your feet." Her eyebrows raise, and she pulls her hand back with a nod.

"Do you trust me?" she asks, like nothing else matters but that.

"No." It's the truth; there's no point in lying. "But that doesn't mean I don't want to figure this out."

"Because you have no other option?" She's defensive, and I deserve it.

I still laugh anyway, as if I'm not the one in control of my mouth. "I *always* have an option. That's the thing about me, *babe*." I throw the nickname at her the same way she uses it with me. "I'm *resilient*. I don't need you," I remind her.

Hating that I'm already going to that dark place, but unable to stop myself when I'm there. The jabs, the hurting her so I can ignore what's hurting me—but I'm also not wrong. I've survived everything that has been shoved my way; what was once my biggest fears are now monsters slain at my feet.

"Stop it." She's grabbing at my face, holding my cheeks in her hands. "Just let me fucking love you." Her voice cracks as she pulls me into her chest.

I fall into her, enveloped into her grandness once again, and the overwhelming hot light in my head finally dims, even if it's just for a little bit. I'm sobbing, but I can feel her shaking too.

"I ruin everything good," I warn her between hiccups.

"Who said I was anything good?" Her words are muffled, her mouth pressed to my temple, every part of her body touching mine, like she can't get closer, but wants to try.

I pull away, just enough to look at her face again,

before I speak. "I'm not a hyperfixation. Some day, you might just have to accept that you can't fix me."

"Fix you?" she asks, a small smile on her face, like she can't believe what I just said. "You were never broken."

I wish I could believe her.

"You sure this isn't just your next hobby?" The wounded look on her face makes me almost regret what I've said, but I need to know.

We need to do this. *All of it*.

She shakes my shoulder like she's trying to knock some sense into me. "Just the same way that I'm sure you aren't meant to be an addict. You're lost. We all get a little lost in the dark, Antônia. Even me."

"Even you?" I laugh a little in disbelief.

She's the perfect picture of composed, organized, kept together. She's everything I could never be, and that's when I remember who her brother is, what growing up with that might do to someone. But maybe we're more alike than I realized, it makes sense. Everything that she does is a coping mechanism.

Overcompensating to prevent the past from repeating.

"You will never get past this, not until you let yourself grieve for Lonnie." Each word hits like a six-foot blocker and leaves a sweltering bruise.

She's right. We wear the same cuts, but a wound never heals the same twice.

I'm just not sure I'm ready to feel the full impact of that pain.

No choice.

I'll be feeling everything in:

three

two

one.

The rush of nausea comes so fast, I'm borderline violent pushing her off me. With a higher power on my side, I make it to the bathroom, the shirt stuck to my back from sweat and saliva pooling at my mouth as I hold back the next wave. Nothing but bile comes out. I'm scrambling, grabbing at every piece of fabric glued to me. Pulling the shirt over my head, I toss it behind me, ripping the sleeve when it snags on the sharp, exposed pieces of my broken cast. I'm shuffling my socks off and trying the same with the pants, so uncomfortable inside my own skin that all I can do is take things off, take things off until all that's left is me.

But I can't take *me* off me, and it's goddamn agony to be trapped in this body.

I lay on my side, pulling my knees into my chest, the cool bathroom tile somehow soothing just enough for me to close my eyes, but there's no urge to sleep. I shake—not from cold, not from hunger, not from fear. I just shake.

Because it's all my body can do.

Naked.

On the floor.

Of her bathroom.

The remainder of my dignity down the toilet.

A sliver of hope somehow still remains in the shape of a tiny bag of powder I've hidden in a jeans pocket.

That feeling turns into self-loathing, and I despise myself for knowing that I *will* use it. It doesn't matter what she does. I've never gone this far, never walked so far into the tunnel, and now, it's too dark for me to see how long of a walk back it is to get out. There is no light on the other side.

I keep walking toward the luring abyss anyway.

My muscles clench and release painfully as I crunch into a smaller ball.

I try to disappear.

I want my fucking mom.

The thought is worse than a pill, worse than the powder, and twice as lethal as both combined. Calling her at my lowest only proves everything she's been saying all along.

I don't grow up.

"Nia?" Harvey's voice is soft outside the door.

"No." I drag the word out with a pathetic whine.

The last thing I want is for her to see me like this.

"Can I come in?" Harvey's voice has never been so gentle, so tender, and it only worsens the pressure bubbling inside me.

Guilt.

"Please don't." It feels like a sob, but I think I'm too dehydrated to actually cry.

"Nia." It feels as if she's right there beside me, but I know she's not.

"I just—" It's pathetic and weak and I don't have the energy to finish.

She opens the door anyway and drops to her knees, bringing me into her lap and cradling me in her arms like I'm not this disgusting, sweaty thing.

"I'm gonna take over now, okay?" she says, smoothing my hair out of my face in a way that almost forces me to look up at her.

Cat Harvey *is* the entire universe. I've known it all

along, from the first time I saw her. I think I saw her in my dreams when I laid in that hospital, my brain broken and unsure if it wanted me to come back to this.

What a wasted chance.

Lonnie should have had this, not me.

I'm sobbing in her arms again like the pathetic fucking shit I am. She's moving slowly, unwrapping me and peeling me off her as she comes back to a stand. "What's going to make you comfortable?"

My face is leaking from every possible crevice, my entire body hurts, and I'm nearly positive that if I had eaten in the last twenty-four hours, I'd be in a pool of my own liquid shit.

"Nothing," I manage to groan out, but I'm not sure it's even audible.

Breathing takes effort.

I should have died.

I'd been saying the words like a thankful prayer for weeks now, gratitude to whatever deity could hear me for letting me survive that crash.

I should have died.

I should have died when my car wrapped around that tree and my brain almost came spilling out of the side of my head.

I should have died.

Maybe this is what happens when we cheat fate. Maybe the universe is just righting the course and putting me back on my path.

I should have died.

Except the words are no longer a call for thanks, but an angry rupture, the feeling of missing what was destined for me. I *should* have died. Maybe my death guaranteed

Lonnie's life. I robbed them of it when it was meant to be theirs.

I'm so lost in my thoughts, I don't notice she turned the shower on and is sitting on the edge of the tub, staring at me. There's so much kindness in her eyes, and it only makes it worse.

The sobbing is beyond ugly, every piece of me picked raw by my own nails. "Why are you doing this?"

Falling for Cat becomes the largest obstacle in my path.

Because I see what I'm doing to myself reflected in her.

"Doing what?" She's upset too, in her own right. I can hear it in her voice.

"Why are you bothering? You could have just had the rink." I look up to see her eyes narrowed on my throat.

At the collar.

She reaches out and tugs at the loop, pulling me just a hair toward her. "I didn't lie when I said you were mine," she says in a hushed tone. "I fucked up. *So* bad. I didn't tell you in the beginning because I didn't know you, didn't trust you, and then I *hated you*." She laughs, but it's a nervous kind of laugh. "Then I thought I could take away the need to tell you, and it wasn't because I was trying to keep Skateland from you, Nia."

Her hands reach behind my neck, and finally, she undoes the buckle and removes the leather from my neck. It's been on for at least three days now. My hands reach up to soothe, but hers are there first, caressing the sides of my throat with thumbs that gently graze my jaw.

"I made a bad call because I let my history with my brother interfere with how I treated you and how I saw you. You deserved to know the minute you came back. I'll apologize for that until the day I die if it keeps you next to me."

Somehow, her saying sorry only makes me feel worse. Undeserving.

She picks me up as if I'm nothing and places me inside the tub. It's the shower that's running, the water the perfect temperature, and with me on the ground, it's just gentle enough for my sore body to tolerate. The comfort it provides me is short, and soon, the room is filled with hot, dense steam, and the nausea hits me again.

My breathing turns shallow, rapid, and I close my eyes, hugging my knees to my chest with my head under the water.

"Is it too much?" Cat asks like she's in my head, opening the door again.

She swings it open and shut a few times, like she's fanning out some of the steam, and the rush of cold air is exactly what I need to settle back into my body. Some of my muscles unclench from the warmth, and for a second, I feel relief.

"I can't do this." It's meant to be internal, but there's no filter anymore.

"You can." She says it like I haven't proved her wrong before, her confidence a fifty pound sledgehammer shattering my humiliated pieces.

"I should have died, Cat." I don't know which time I mean. This time, *that* time. At this point, I'm simply acknowledging I've lived past my expiration date.

She cuts me a look through hardened eyes, the line of her jaw becoming more pronounced as she clenches her teeth. Within a few seconds, she pulls her shirt over her head, and her pants are on the floor. The sight of Harvey in nothing but a sports bra and boxers has become top three in my head, but even right now, it's just a reminder that I'm not worthy of her.

Stepping into the stream of the shower, she pulls me into her lap, and I melt in the comfort of her hold. I close my eyes, but I feel her tug at my chin, the same cold look still plastered to her face as her gaze burns into me. "Is that what this was?"

I don't answer. I know I don't need to. When I try to shift my gaze, lower my chin, anything to escape the pain of her stare, she instead holds tighter, then speaks. "If you go, I'll go too."

That's all she says.

But that's all it takes.

"In my backpack," I tell her, watching the way her eyebrows scrunch in confusion. "The rest of it."

She squeezes me hard, like I've just given her the world back.

Maybe I have.

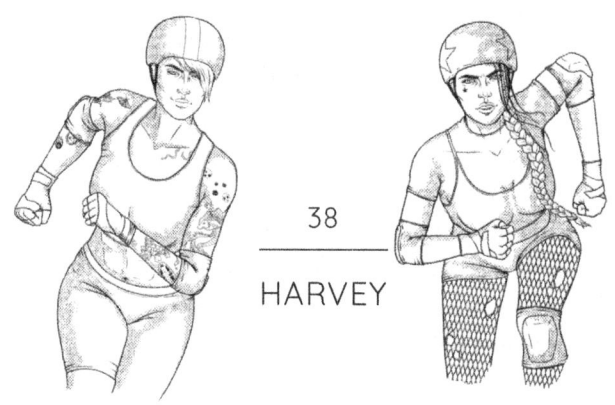

38

HARVEY

She's been on and off the last forty or so hours, bouncing back and forth between the shower and the floor. Nia's set up camp in the bathroom and the bedroom, unsure where she feels more comfortable. I found the rest of her shit, not hesitating for a minute before dumping it down the toilet.

Poor fish.

I've called into work the last two days, and now it's finally my day off. Freddy is frustrated, but he's known me long enough to understand something is up. I'm thankful to have people around me I can trust to lean on when shit hits the fan. Job security is not a worry for me.

WHERE THE FUCK HAVE YOU BEEN?

Mo's text is a reminder that the very thing which once consumed my life, I'm now seeming to run away from. Of course Nia took precedence over the bout when her life was at stake. Of course I've been blowing off the other skaters, unable to answer their questions or explain what's happening.

None of it matters right now.

I'll miss practice again today while we get through the worst of her withdrawal. I've prepared for it, ordering from a nearby grocery store that delivers so I could have what she'd need on hand when the time comes for it.

> YOU'RE BREAKING CONTRACT AND SCOTT IS PISSED YOU'RE IGNORING HIM. ARE YOU SHOWING UP TONIGHT?

IGNORING HIM IS A BLANKET STATEMENT. I'M FLAT OUT pretending the man doesn't exist anymore.

The sound of her dry heaving in the tub breaks me away from my phone and, once again, I have a new excuse to not respond to Morgan. I want to give her the privacy I know she wants, but I can't risk not being there if she needs me. I only run the bar of soap over her slightly, just enough to clean a little without overwhelming her senses.

Using the spray attachment, I rinse her off before I lift her out. I don't bother with a towel; she'll be shivering and sweating regardless. Instead, I just drape her over me and take her back to the room. Pulling at the hem of my shirt, I begin to lift it over my head to give to her to wear, but her mumbling stops me.

It's impossible to ignore the violence of her teeth chattering as she tries to talk, still clutching her knees to her chest as she sits on the bed. "No clothes." She shakes her head before she drops, still in the fetal position. I don't know whether to cover her or turn the fan on. I don't know how to help.

She's severely dehydrated though, and if that's all I can do, I'll do it well. Back in the kitchen, I pour the grape flavored electrolytes into a plastic cup and fill it with ice, breaking through the clumps with a glass straw as I push it all the way in. I don't find her much different from how I left her—same fetal position, just a little more still now. Her body tightens, muscles clenching in discomfort, the noises coming from her heart-wrenching and pathetic all at once.

"Can I sit you up?" I ask, but I don't let her respond. I just move her myself, a little limp doll in my arms with her head hanging low.

Climbing onto the bed, I position behind her, my back to the headboard as I pull her into me and hold her up. "Take a sip." I grab the cup off the nightstand and bring the straw to her lips. A loud gulp tells me to pull it away, but she lets out a pained groan like she wants more.

"I know, I know, baby." I kiss the side of her head, knowing she's likely parched, setting the glass back down while she whines for it. "Little sips for now, until your stomach can handle more."

WE SPEND THE NEXT FEW HOURS DOING THE SAME DANCE, and she throws up until I'm afraid she might actually die. I rehydrate her and give her some Dramamine to calm her stomach and keep some Gatorade down. The medicine makes her sleepy, which is great because I'm able to convince her to lay down and it makes her tame. I'll take the sleepy version over the asshole, pre-exorcist Regan MacNeil that comes out when she wants to give up.

The girl can get mean, and she knows just where to hit to make it hurt.

I don't blame her, and I'm trying to look past it. The only thing it tells me is that someone taught her that pushing others away to see if they come back was the only way to guarantee they love you.

I'll show her that I can love her regardless.

My phone is vibrating nonstop, and I'm not sure how much longer I can ignore it. It feels like the entire team is pissed at me, but if there's one thing I'm certain of, one thing I'm dead clear about, it's that it *will* take the two of us to fill the space that Lonnie once did.

Even if we don't fill it exactly the same way they did.

I need her. The team needs her.

My doorbell rings.

Fuck.

I'm wrapped in panic, my first thought is that this invasive snake of a man would have the audacity to intrude on my boundaries, come to my home, to discuss something as menial as business. When I open the door, though, it's DreadPool at the door with her derby-wife, D-Stroya.

Or should I say ex-derby-wife now that D's retired?

"Double Ds," I say flatly, looking at Dread first. "Shouldn't you be at practice?" The words are dripping with annoyance as I direct my next question to Deandra. "Shouldn't *you* be at the boutique?"

"I sent out the bat signal," Dread says, walking through

the door and pushing past me. "What the fuck is going on with the two of you?"

She's looking around for Nia, but this isn't my story to tell, and I'm set on protecting her privacy. I'm about to spin whatever lie comes out first, except Nia's dry heaving is loud, and Deandra is too smart and stubborn to be sold on my bullshit.

She raises a single suspicious eyebrow and makes her way toward the noise. I grab her arm to keep her from going, but she yanks away from me, and I can't stop her. D opens the door, her expression falling flat when she sees what's on the other side. She looks back at me, then at Dread, still clueless by the front door.

"Dread, take Harvey to Skateland." Her voice is commanding, like she can't help but slip into mom mode.

"Wait, what's going on?" Dread takes a step forward, but I stop them, my arm extended to keep them from moving.

"Go, Jade." She uses Dread's government name, such a rare occasion that it should be time stamped and logged.

Dread doesn't miss a beat, nudging their forehead toward the door, as if I'm even being given an option here. I look back at my friend, the one I trust the most. She mouths the word "go" once again, but this time, it's directed at me.

I know I can depend on her. I've never had a reason not to.

Nodding, I follow DreadPool out the door.

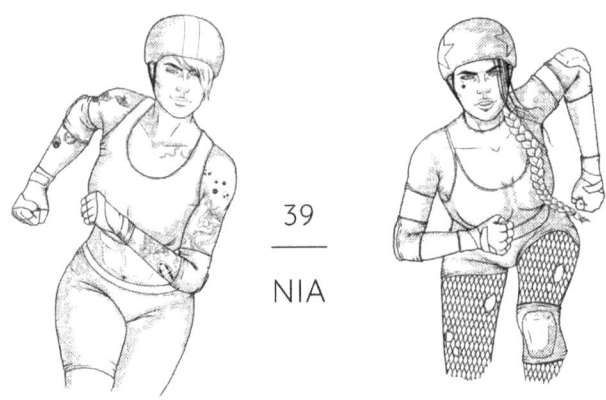

39

NIA

She waits for Harvey to leave before she moves or speaks. Once she hears the front door shut, her tongue clicks, and it's almost like I'm in the room with my own mother. "Antônia," she whispers, head shaking as she walks toward me.

Her voice is much kinder than my mother's, though.

I let my gaze drift. I'm sitting in sweat-stained sheets, wearing one of Harvey's shirts that are long enough to wrap my legs in. "Baby, why are you doing this to yourself?" The bed dips next to me as she sits down. I can't stand her seeing me like this, so I turn away.

"You know why." It's a whisper.

I feel her hand smoothing down my hair. Despite my rolling, sweating, and writhing around, Harvey has somehow managed to keep my hair brushed and knot-free.

"You gonna make me take my kid to *Titia Nia's* funeral?" She uses the nickname I once gave myself the first time I held her baby—now a full grown kiddo of almost nine.

"I don't know how to get out of this." I finally own up to it.

"Kiddo, you just gotta tell me how deep you've dug this grave, and I'll throw the rope down and pull you out." Deandra says it like it's so easy.

I turn to face her, shaking my head. "I don't know anymore. It's too dark to tell."

"Oh." She shrugs. "Well that's easy then." She brushes the sweat-drenched hair out of my face and leans down to whisper in my ear. "We can just make it up!"

The smile is autonomous and so are the tears, falling freely and dropping onto the pillow beneath my head. "Don't let me turn you into my new mom, D. I'll do it," I groan, my entire body feeling like the peach forgotten at the bottom of the fruit basket.

Moldy.

Bruised.

Putrid.

Oh, how I shine.

"We all need mothered every now and then. If I remember correctly, yours was shit." She chuckles under her breath before she presses her palm to my face. "I'll baby bird you, sweetie. You want me to chew your food up for you? Open wide, bitch. I'll do whatever it takes not to lose another friend."

She means it. I see the look on her face so clearly for what it is.

Desperation.

She helps me take a sip of the iced electrolytes on the nightstand. "What?" I ask, her face still full of woe.

"You look like shit, girl. If you were my kid, I'd be losing it," she says, shaking her head, and I'm not sure how I'm supposed to feel.

"Are you here to guilt trip me?" I ask, and the cackle she lets out is almost witch-like.

"Hell no. And I don't feel *that* bad for you either; you did this to yourself. I'm making sure Harvey doesn't lose everything she's worked for, and I'm making sure the Dames don't lose even more." Her expression sobers, and it nearly eats me alive.

"You're just babysitting." I don't hide my annoyance.

She winks before standing again. "Except you're not a baby, and I don't need to be your mother to tell you what to do. I just need to love you, so get up, you stink." Pulling her locs into a low ponytail and tying it with a thick band, she waits, but I don't move.

She claps three times, startling me and forcing my fight or flight into action. I stand, holding myself like a new recruit waiting for the sergeant's command.

D strips the sheets and pillowcases off the bed and balls them into a pile in her arm, brushing by me as she walks out of the room with them. "When's the last time you showered?" she asks.

I wait until she's in the room again so I don't have to shout. Even shouting hurts. "I'm in the shower all the time."

"Laying under the hot water while you hate yourself and wish you were dead doesn't count as a shower. Try again." She's out of sight, but within seconds, I hear the water running. I sigh, pulling the oversized shirt off and only coming close to a full blown meltdown when it snags on the broken piece of the cast.

"Fuck!" I scream, sobbing from frustration.

D runs into the room, helping me free myself of the t-shirt trap. Once the crisis is averted and I've breathed through the panic, I finally ask the lingering question, "What's going on with the rink?"

"Scott wants to buy it. He's realized how little we all care about any sort of input he may have, and he knows the only way to control the team is to buy the rink too." She says with a sigh, "I'm here so that Harvey can hopefully keep him from making things worse for us. I think if he buys it, he may just turn the property for profit."

"You said *we*." I grin, not daring to gloss past it.

She narrows her eyes at me, but it's a smile that's on her face. "Shush." She pushes my shoulder like she's herding me into the shower, and just as I start walking on my own, she grabs me by the arm. "I'm also here to make sure you don't fuck *this* up." Her tone is gentle but I cower under her stare.

"Fuck what up?" It's a silly question, because there are *hundreds* of things I'm fucking up at this current moment in time, but specifying which one would really help me categorize it in my brain.

"You and Cat."

For some reason, it's not what I'm expecting her to say. Fucking up my life—sure. Fucking up the Devil's Dames—absolutely. Fucking up everything I touch—well, of course. But me and Cat?

I don't respond, and I don't need to. She goes on without waiting for my permission or acknowledgment. "You two are so fucking perfect for each other. Don't let Lonnie's death ruin the best thing that might ever happen to you. If you can't stay sober for yourself, stay sober for her, for us—yeah?"

"That's a dangerous game to play. What happens when she leaves me with nothing?" It's my biggest fear. It's why I keep poking, prodding, creating new wounds where there weren't any before.

I think back to Harvey's words; I can't remember if they were days or hours ago.

If you go, I'll go too.

This kind of love, it's intoxicating, and once she's done with me, I'll never recover.

"I dunno." She smiles. "I'm kinda puttin' all my money on you two."

I breathe out a laugh. Maybe it's time I finally start planning for things to work in my favor instead of falling apart. I owe it to Harvey. I owe it to Lonnie. I owe it to every single one of my friends who deserve better from me.

I owe it to Kade.

Forgiveness isn't something we're entitled to, but I hope I can earn it.

I nod to one of my oldest friends, and I take her hand as she helps me step into that shower.

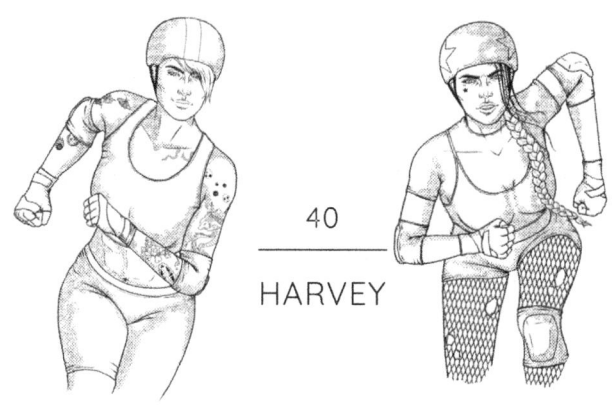

40

HARVEY

I've barely walked into the rink, and I'm ushered into what used to be Lonnie's office, where Scott sits behind the desk.

"Okay, I'm here. What couldn't fucking wait a few days?" I'm genuinely pissed. Every skater in this rink has had multiple emergencies, vacations, sicknesses, or job interruptions that have forced them to miss practices or even bouts.

I do it *once*, and suddenly, this motherfucker thinks I'm not capable of owning the rink?

"Twenty grand for the rink if you sign today." He pushes the contract over the surface of the desk toward me and then leans back into the chair.

"You said twenty-five last time we talked." I don't even know why I'm arguing. Either offer is a joke, and regardless, I'm *not* entertaining it.

"That was when I had more patience, when I had a rockstar jammer and a solid pivot who were reliable. Look around, Cathrine. I'm not really getting my money's worth here." He laughs, tossing his feet up on the desk and resting his arms behind his head.

"Why the fuck would I sell you Skateland?" I don't bother with politeness now. I've been holding it in for weeks, and I'm ready to get this asshole out of my face and out of my life.

"Because without *me*, you're going to end up spending more money to keep this place standing, and you'll be *wishing* you sold it for twenty grand, because a demo team is going to want thirty to clear this land before you can sell. Either way, the rink stays, you lose money, the rink goes, you lose money. Or you can sell to me."

I hate that every word he says is logical. Because he's right—without him, we weren't making it work. Without him, we were spending our own money to keep the rink standing, and even then, we weren't even *WFTDA* regulated. We were just playing the nearby teams for fun.

Every dime of concessions went to keeping the utilities running, and when it came time to pay taxes, Lonnie figured it out, pulling extra cash from their day job income to cover the losses.

"Antônia also owns the rink. I can't make this decision without her." I can't consider anything until I tell her.

"Tomorrow. Nine a.m.," he says, getting up from the chair, packing up some folders and stuffing them under his arm.

"Or what?" I laugh, like this ultimatum can do anything. He can't force me to sell.

"You've breached contract twice now, and your lack of communication gives me the grounds to dissolve your place as captain on this team, which makes me strongly consider removing you from the Devil's Dames altogether." My world is already spinning before the words are fully out of his mouth. "Or, you can buy the league back from me, and I'm gone."

Fucking snake. He's going to sell it for more than what he paid.

Has this been his game all along?

Is this his con?

I'm so mad, I can't think straight, and the minute Scott walks past me, I'm fuming. Once he's gone long enough that I can assume he's not in the rink anymore, I scream, wishing to God Lonnie could come back from the dead and tell me what to do.

Instead, the Devil sends me Stella, who doesn't even bother to knock on the door before barging into the office.

"If that wasn't a cry for help, girl, I don't know what to tell you." She plops down on the ratty old couch and waits.

"Scott is fucking us over," I tell her.

"What do you mean?" Her expression falls. "I thought he'd be buying the rink, y'all get a bunch of money, we all live happily ever after?"

She doesn't get it.

"You think if Scott buys the rink, things will change for the better?" I'm not challenging her; I genuinely want to know.

I've always valued Stella's opinion, even when I don't exactly want to hear it.

"No, I don't. But I figured that kind of money would be life-changing, and I wouldn't blame either of you for doing it, just as long as we get to keep skating." She shrugs.

"Yeah, but do we get to keep skating? Every part of me tells me I can't trust this asshole. Lonnie wouldn't have left the rink to us to sell it. Would they have?" I'm at a loss, overwhelmed, lacking sleep, my candle burning at both ends.

Bilbo once said he was stretched thin, *like butter scraped over too much bread.* I felt it right now.

"How much?" She bites her lip.

"Does it matter?" I breathe out a nervous laugh, knowing that it should.

I'm not sure that any amount of money could make me sell this place, though, and I *know* that's why Lonnie left it to me.

"Twenty grand," I tell her anyway.

"Twenty thousand!" DreadPool shouts from the doorway where they're hiding behind the wall.

That's when I notice the rest of the skaters there, listening along.

It's better this way anyway. We're a team. They deserve to be included in these conversations.

"Twenty thousand? That's a fucking joke. The land alone is worth at least fifty. Anyway, that's not what I meant. What's the deal with our contract? The Devil's Dames. We aren't changing our names just to be free of this fucker. Lonnie named us. It's ours." I love when Star gets pissed.

"We're signed for a seven year contract. Or a thirteen thousand dollar buyout." I grimace, hating the way this asshole took advantage of Lonnie, that something they thought would bring salvation to the team is now possibly going to be the cause of our ruin.

"Do you have thirteen grand?" StarScreamer asks me.

"Fuck."

"What's the alternative? Seven awkward years with this asshole benching you, Nia, and whoever else upsets him? Throwing bouts just to prove a point? Replace the team one by one? There's only so many skaters in Devil Town,"

Nancy Shrew says with a laugh, like the options are ludicrous.

They sound ludicrous, but for some reason, I'm still scared shitless.

I barely know who I am off this track anymore. Seven years benched, and I'll be ready to retire by the time I even get a chance to scrimmage again.

"Yeah." I nod, trying to give them a sliver of hope.

"We can figure this out. We do what Lonnie did back in the day. We rent the rink out on non-practice days. We open to the public more than one day a week. We breathe life back into this place. We can make thirteen grand happen." I'm not confident, but the least I can do is pretend.

Dread is already on their phone, likely texting D everything we're saying like a court transcripter.

"I can't do anything until I talk to Antônia," I tell them.

"Is she even capable of handling this kind of decision right now?" K leans on the doorframe, not committing to fully entering the room yet.

"I don't know. She's not a child, though. She's just struggling." I cut them a look, one that says *it's fine if you won't put your trust in her, but don't judge me for doing it.* "Once she's feeling better, we can figure it out—"

Venice interrupts, "Do you have that long?"

"No." I sigh. "He wants an answer by tomorrow morning."

It feels hopeless.

A problem with solutions we cannot physically achieve.

By the time I get home, Nia is on the couch, sitting with D and eating a bowl of reheated caldo. It's a fresh batch. Once I realized she wasn't kidding about it being the only food she could stomach, I didn't hesitate to make more. There's a little bit of color back in her face, but she still looks two stone throws away from death.

She's alive, though.

And that's enough for me.

I smile, walking into the room and heading for my girl.

She crawls into my lap like it's the only place she belongs, and I'm soothed by the feeling of her in my arms again. I press my face to the top of her head, smelling the apricot scent of my shampoo on her hair. "You smell good." I grin, looking at D, who's taking full credit for Nia not looking like hot garbage sitting out on the curb.

"D's helped put some things into perspective for me." She smiles back at me, and it's the first time she's said something positive in days.

It feels huge.

"Anything I should know about?" I can't help but be curious.

"Nope. Just between old friends." D sticks her tongue out, then looks back at Dread. "Take me home; I gotta chat with Phil about all this."

I sigh, knowing the gossip's traveled all the way here through DreadPool's texts, and now Deandra would be taking it home to her husband. "Is *everyone* up to date then?"

Even Nia nods her head.

"What do you think?" I ask her.

"Skateland is home." Her eyebrows furrow like it should have been obvious to me.

It should have.

But what the fuck do we do?

Once Deandra and Dread leave, Nia and I stay exactly as we are. I settle into the couch, pulling her into me and turning on a movie. Something old, with an airplane crash, time travel, and a guy in a rabbit suit. I don't get it, but it's one of her favorites, and the distraction is simple enough.

It's such a small moment, so normal, so *boring*, so human. It's exactly the proof I need to know this girl is more than a hyperfixation, more than a hobby, more than an addiction. This right here, it feels good, feels *right*.

I could do it with her for the rest of my life.

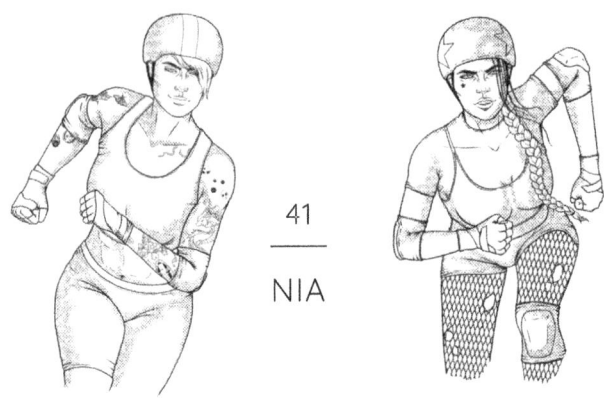

41

NIA

When I was little, I used to get stomach bugs all the time. I'd be sick for an entire week, head in a trashcan and my ass on the toilet. My mom would call me her little *norovirus* affectionately. By the sixth or seventh day, my brain would wipe all memory of previous life from my mind, as if sickness was all I knew.

I'm not quite there yet.

Still in the trenches, stuck between *it feels like I'll never feel good again* and *I don't even know what healthy feels like anymore*. But I'm not giving in this time. I don't just need Harvey—I *want* her, and I want to be someone deserving of her. I want her to be proud of me and look at me the way she does when she's admiring me.

I want *everything* with her.

What I don't get, though, is sleep. She's passed out on the couch. I'm only still in her lap because I don't want to wake her. The nausea has lessened now, and hopefully soon, I'll be able to get more than an hour of sleep at a time.

NIA

I feel like a leather saddle on a clothesline that had its time in the mud and rain.

Rode hard, put up wet.

Not quite the same.

Forever altered.

Still here for a good ride. I make myself laugh, a reminder that there's a piece of me who wants to be okay again.

The need comes in a violent wave. It's a rush I can't explain, a pulling of my own internal compass forcing me to move, act, right the course. I unwind Cat's arms from my waist, placing a soft kiss on her forehead before getting off the couch. Picking my phone up from the coffee table, dozens of missed calls waiting for me, I head for the door.

"Nia?" Harvey asks, like she's on watchdog mode and her body won't afford her the pleasure of relaxing if I'm not beside her.

"I just need a second." I look back at her, my hand on the doorknob. "I just gotta do something."

I don't think she trusts me, not when it comes to making good decisions for myself, but somehow, I think she sees that right now is more than that. She nods and closes her eyes again. I'm not fooled; she isn't asleep, but that doesn't matter.

Going outside is pointless; there are plenty of rooms to do this in, but it helps me feel better, less trapped, less boxed in, like I can somehow escape if the blowout is catastrophic. It's silly because all I need is a red button to feel safe again. To disconnect the call.

Instead, I hit dial, and it's only when I hear her voice that I'm able to slide my back down along the outside wall until I'm seated on the ground. "Antônia?"

"Oi." I'm already regretting it, heart rate elevating,

sweating out of my pits like I just did my speed test, and the nausea I thought I'd conquered comes rolling back in. "I just have a few things I want to say. You can listen, or you can hang up. I don't want to have a back and forth, though." I put the boundary in place and wonder if, for the first time in her life, she'll adhere to it.

Boundary is not a word our family understands. Boundary is not a word we acknowledge, respect, or accept. It might as well be a knife that severs our blood ties.

She doesn't speak, but the call doesn't disconnect.

"I understand now. I understand why you were the way you were, why I was the way I was, and what a mess *that* was together." It's almost a laugh, but I'm already crying. I don't make sense. "I know you did your best, and I'm grateful you kept me alive long enough so I could see that. But you have to stop calling me now."

My mother doesn't speak, the line staying quiet.

"You've hurt me too many times. I can't keep relying on the people who hurt me to fix me." I swallow hard, still waiting for the interjection that never comes. "I don't know if I'll ever be at a place where I want you in my life again." I don't tell her that I *need* her, that I'll always need my mother. "But I can't grow up if you don't let me. Maybe I'll never be capable of making the best decisions for myself, but I'm starting to realize that the right people will love me regardless."

I take one more breath. "I'll call you if I'm ever ready to change that."

I'm waiting for a barrage of frantic yelling in Portuguese, for the verbal lashing and the condescending that happens anytime my mother opens her mouth to me.

I'm waiting, but it doesn't come.

"Are you okay?" she asks.

The question is heavy; she knows I'm not.

She's my fucking mother—she can tell.

"I will be." It's the truth, and it's been a long time since I've been this honest with her.

"Okay. Te amo." The words aren't heavy with pain, like she has already mourned me before.

"Te a—" I don't get a chance to finish before the phone clicks off, and though the pinch in my heart is real. I can't blame her for it.

Can't blame her for not wanting to strap herself to the wooden wheel while I throw knives.

I fill my lungs with air, the inhale stuttering like every oxygen molecule is rubbing the wrong parts of me. But this time, it's not a need to shred or fall apart or break further that fills me. There's nothing there.

Not anymore.

I open the door to see Harvey on the couch, adjusted into a more horizontal position, but her eyes are open, like she's been waiting for me to come back inside.

"You okay?" She starts to sit up, but I'm in her arms in just a few quick strides, knocking her back down. She squeezes me tight, and the pressure is everything.

Security.

Safety.

Home.

"I will be." I repeat the same words I gave my mother.

I'm not okay now, but I will be.

Maybe that's enough.

I wake up in bed, not covered in sweat for the first time in what feels like days.

Harvey's already showered and tripping over her own foot as she scrambles to put her socks on.

"What are you doing?" I'm sleepy, groggy, and without the energy to even lift my head to talk to her.

"D is fixing everything." She laughs in disbelief. "I gotta go to the rink for a bit…" She doubles back as she's about to leave the room, and I'm sure she's wondering if she *can* leave me on my own. "Do you want to come?"

I think about it, and I nod. "Can you wait for me?"

"Wait for you?" She chuckles, coming toward me and scooping my face into her hands, "I'd make the whole world wait for you if I was in charge of the sun."

I push her away with a grin, but she doesn't back down, kissing me hard and setting the butterflies loose in my stomach. It seems like so long since I've felt anything at all, and now, all I *want* is to feel.

Feel whatever Cat wants to make me feel.

She wipes the tear from the corner of my eye, ignoring it as she focuses on the smile on my lips. "I love you. And I'm proud of you."

It's a heavy burden to bear, but I want it too.

She helps the shirt over my head and assists with the pants even though she knows I can do that on my own.

I shake my head. "Don't say that yet. I can still fuck everything up."

She's brushing my hair now, gathering up the pieces for the braid she's become so skilled at fashioning.

"Yeah? So can anyone else. *Anyone* can become an addict, Nia. I just need you to focus on today for me. Can you do that?" she says with so much confidence that I can't help but feel it in myself too.

"Yeah," I whisper in agreement, entwining our fingers together as we make our way to Skateland.

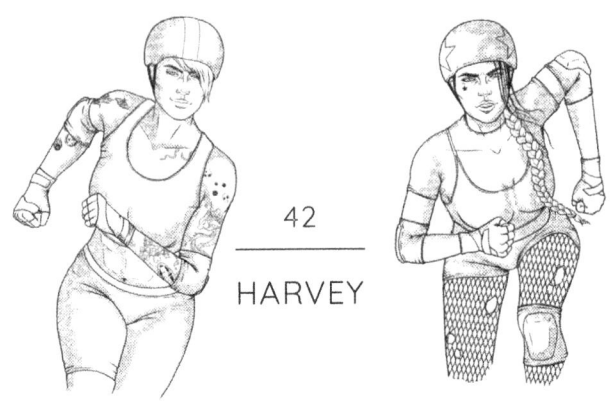

42

HARVEY

It's eight forty-five in the morning when we pull into the lot. The other skaters are already there, and it literally feels like it's a fucking showdown. Us versus Scott. Deandra called me at four in the morning saying she had a solution; apparently, she and Phil stayed up the entire night discussing logistics.

The smile stretches from ear to ear on my face when I open up those double doors like they belong to Helm's Deep, ready to slay my enemy. Deandra's waiting, a pen in hand and Phil next to her. Phil, her husband. Phil, our one trusty cis-het-man who has always been there for our derby shit. Phil, who never undermined his wife's need for community.

Phil, who volunteered his free nights as zebra until their kids were born.

Phil, the fucking *lawyer*.

I chuckle to myself.

The contract is the contract, and there's not much that can be done about that. What I *can* do is make sure this asshole doesn't fuck me over, and that's exactly why Phil is here. The skaters are packed into the lobby, no one bothers to space out or pretend to give a damn about privacy when it comes to Skateland.

It belongs to all of us.

I squeeze Nia into my side, more for her benefit so that I'm holding a majority of her weight. She's frail, weaker than she's ever been, and it's going to be a while before she's back to one hundred percent again.

"Didn't realize this was a team gathering," Scott says with an exhausted sigh as he opens the door to the office.

My fucking office.

"We do everything as a team. You would have realized that if you had taken a second to get to know us." I clear my throat, gesturing to Phil and Deandra to enter as well. I don't close the door behind us; the skaters can watch.

Nia sits next to me across the desk from Scott. D takes her place on the ratty couch while Phil stands.

"Did you decide then?" He slaps a hefty pile of *Helvetica* type eight font documents onto the table, the gust of it hitting Nia in the face and forcing a literal frown over her lips.

"We did," I tell him, nudging Phil over.

It feels like I'm holding a fucking sniper rifle pointed right at the crocodile.

"County law states no business transaction involving the sale of a trademarked entity can be inflated by more than ten percent within a six-month handoff," Phil states calmly, pulling the proof of his words out of a folder and laying it on the table for Scott to review. "It's been three months since the sale of the Devil's Dames, so the max you can request for transfer of ownership is…" He lingers on the *s*, pulling out his phone to look at the math. "Four thousand, three hundred, and forty-three dollars."

"Take it or leave it, asshole. I'm not selling you the rink." I lean back in my chair and cross my arms over my chest, nodding toward Nia. "*We're* not selling you the rink."

Her smile makes me melt.

"Maybe I don't want to buy anymore," he sighs, like he's been defeated but he's not done fighting. "Maybe I'll just burn you all out until I can get a fresh batch of skaters in. Maybe I'll just wait this contract out until you're all too old to skate." He sucks at his teeth.

"Unfortunately, this entire transaction has been recorded." Phil points to the nonfunctioning camera in the corner. "And bad faith contracts will be terminated immediately. Take your money, or leave with nothing." His voice turns a scary tone I've never heard before, and suddenly, I never want to end up on Phil's bad side.

"Write the check." The sour look on Scott's face is priceless, but it's Nia's panicked voice that has me swinging my head to the side.

"We don't have that kind of money," she whispers.

"No," Deandra says. "I do." She stands from the couch and pulls her checkbook from her purse.

"D—" I'm about to ask her if she's sure, to tell her that I don't know how long it would take to pay her back, but she's got her hand in my face to shut me up while the other writes the check.

"Get the fuck out," she says once Scott takes the check and Phil looks over all the signatures.

Only when he's gone does D finally talk. "That man doesn't get access to us—to our team, how we feel, and the shit we go through. *Only we do*." She sounds like fucking

Lonnie, but for some reason, the thought doesn't make me cry. It makes me feel good.

The other skaters file into the office, and it's immediately far too crammed for all of us, but nobody cares.

We're here.

Together.

We're home.

Nia is the first to break the silence. "I-I don't know if we can pay you back for this D—"

"You're not." She follows with a wink. "I own you bitches now."

"What?" I can't help but laugh.

"I'm gonna sell the boutique. I've been depressed for months trying to figure all of this shit out. Losing Lonnie didn't help, and then Scott came and changed everything. Made me feel like it was a sign that my time was up." She exhales loudly. "I read the wrong sign." She shrugs. "I'm not supposed to leave; I think my role has just changed."

"You're not retiring?" Star's voice is so full of hope that my chest swells.

"No, babe, I'm retired as fuck. These knees can't take a hit anymore," she jokes. "Lonnie was doing the work of like fifteen people, but maybe with enough of us to spread it all out, we might be able to do this."

"You love the boutique," Nia laments.

"No. I *loved* the boutique. Now, it's a money pit, and I'm lucky to get a sale or two a day. If I sell the inventory and the building, I'll make five times what I just spent on the rink, *and* I get to keep my friends. I'll pay the cost every day if that's what it takes, as long as someone tosses me one of Mo's old *assistant coach* shirts so I feel useful during practice."

I'm pretty sure every fucking skater in the room is crying, but they'll all swear they just have allergies later.

The fissure is gone, no longer an endless depth but a scarring wound where flesh regenerates.

We will heal.

All of us.

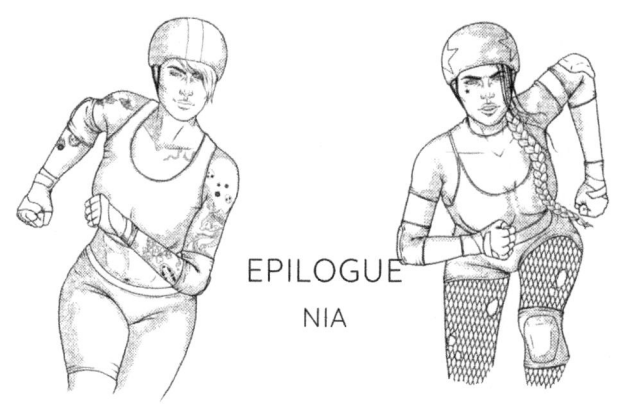

EPILOGUE
NIA

It's overwhelming how right everything feels. My heart is swollen, bursting out of my ribcage from the love in this room. This is my family, they've always been, even when I ran away because I couldn't fathom the idea of being broken to the Dames, they still took me back after all the heartache.

And in the end, I broke in front of them anyway.

I give Harvey a kiss before standing, and seeking out the one person I'm still undeserving of.

"You look..." Kade stops, giving me a once over and choosing their words carefully. "Alive."

"That's about as good as I can offer." I smile.

"That's enough." They nod; it feels like forgiveness, but I know it's not.

Because I haven't asked for it yet.

"I'm sorry." The words sound disingenuous, but I mean it with every fiber of my being.

I just can't muster the energy to perform right now.

"I am too. I should have done more." They tuck blue hair behind their ears, uneasy as always.

"No. Don't take responsibility for my mess. It wasn't your job to fix my shit. It certainly wasn't your job to tolerate it, and I'm sorry I broke your trust." It's the truth. "I should have been honest with you."

They nod. "Tolkien misses you."

"I miss him too," I admit with a soft smile. "I think I'm going to stay with Cat, though."

"Oh?" Kade raises an eyebrow, waiting for more juicy details.

Everyone around us is enveloped in conversation, small groups of skaters catching up and celebrating today's massive win. Deandra was so upset every time a text from DreadPool updated her on the situation yesterday, I knew there was no way she was going to stay out of it.

Having her here is everything.

It reminds me that Lonnie is still the glue, even though they're not here anymore. It reminds me that glue has the power to continue to hold even when it dries clear.

"Yeah. She just…" I'm trying to condense love into words that don't exist, and it fails me. "We just… make sense."

Kade nods, understanding perfectly somehow. They grab my shoulder. "Well, come over for coffee or something."

"I'd like that." I nod.

"What's your plan for today?" Kade asks, making me hopeful that there *is* genuine forgiveness there and a desire to stay friends.

It means more than I can explain.

"Meeting a new therapist." I grin awkwardly, like my physically broken head isn't enough, but the acknowledgement of my mind's fragility is too embarrassing to admit.

"Love that for you." They drape an arm over my

shoulder and pull me in, dropping a kiss to the top of my head.

"Maybe tomorrow?" I ask, my voice full of optimism.

Kade answers far too seriously. "Only if you bring those cheese bread balls."

"Deal."

Four Months Later

I'm locking up my office for the day at the junior high when Christa runs into me from behind. "Miss Da Silva, are you done?"

She's thirteen, a first gen kid, just like me. Her family just moved from a big city, and she's struggling to fit into this school. She's one of the reasons I'm glad I chose this degree and grateful I was able to snag this job. At her age, I would have killed for someone like me to give me advice. Kids like her give me even more reason to fight harder for myself.

So I can fight for *them* too.

I have to show her we can make it.

I don't know if I would have listened, but I would have still killed for it.

Looking at my watch, I realize it's ten till one, and though I normally don't leave until two, I promised Harvey I'd get to the rink in time to help set up the new lights. "Do you need anything?" I ask her, key still in the door, very much ready to re-open so I can help her with whatever she's dealing with.

"Not today. My mom wanted me to give you this,

though." She pulls out a Tupperware of homemade Argentinian treats from her backpack.

Catch me dead before you catch me turning down an Alfajore.

"Your mother is feeding my soul, Christa!" I moan with delight, clutching the container to my chest like it's gold.

It's becoming a common occurrence. She and the few other Latin American kids who frequent my office know food is my love language, and their gratitude always comes in the form of snacks. Quite possibly my favorite job perk.

She gives me an awkward side hug, and I add, "Maybe you can convince her to come to derby tryouts soon."

Christa laughs and shakes her head. "Mamá says she'll be skating on two broken legs if she tries. I'll probably be skating with you before *she* does. We'll be there to watch you tonight, though!"

"We appreciate the support. Stay out of that splash zone," I joke, like getting too close to the track would likely result in blood splatter stains.

My phone vibrates in my pocket just as I'm walking out of the school.

MEET ME AT HOME

THE SMILE SETS ON MY FACE WHILE I SHUFFLE THROUGH MY playlist for the perfect song to drive home to. I scroll in the heat of the car, ignoring the sensation until the sweat trickles down my back, and I resort to choosing a song I've heard a million times.

EPILOGUE

Predictable is good right now.

Predictable is safe.

When I get home, her car is already there, but when I open the door, the lights are off. "Babe?" I shout into the living room. "Let's go!" Anytime she asks me to meet her at home before heading to Skateland is so that we don't have to deal with the chore of two separate cars.

I assume today is no different.

"Babe?" I call out again when I don't hear her.

Walking all the way in and shutting the door behind me, I head deeper into the apartment. I open the door to our room to find her dropping rose petals on the bed. With a sigh, I tell her, "You're so romantic."

She jumps only slightly from the surprise, and I realize she's got earbuds in. Harvey pulls one out of her ear and grins before pulling the other one out too.

"What are you doing?" I ask.

"Well, my girlfriend is like seventeen weeks sober today, so a celebration was in order." That cocky grin fills her face up like she's so proud she was able to pull off a surprise without me finding out.

It's not that I don't like surprises—it's that I'm *always* capable of figuring them out before she completes them.

"I don't think that's a milestone." I laugh as she brings me into her arms. "They don't make a chip for seventeen weeks."

"Well, good thing you're not in a program then." Her lips press into mine, and I melt.

A program wasn't for me. The entire nature of it was far too nonsecular for my taste, and I couldn't separate it. Couldn't put everything in the hands of a God I don't believe in. The first meeting I stepped into with Kade at my side, we both looked at each other in horror once they broke out in prayer. We snuck off before anyone noticed us, and from that moment on, I decided to find something that worked for me.

There *isn't* a manual, and what might have worked for someone is certainly not a guarantee to work at all for me. I ended up coming clean to the team, feeling a mixture of relief and shame balled up together, and in the end, I only felt silly for not relying on them sooner. I wasn't met with judgment or criticism, but with more support and love than I could have ever expected. I have friends—the family I *chose*—who I will fight for.

I don't need to give it up to some higher power to stay sober when I can give it up to this incredible woman instead.

The *only* one I get on my knees for.

"Thank you," I whisper anyway as our kiss breaks, grateful for a partner who is proud of every little accomplishment I bring home.

I think she'd hang me on a shelf if she could.

I've never been anyone's trophy.

Not until her.

The End

In loving memory of Jeffrey "JB" Hirst
1991-2011

ACKNOWLEDGMENTS

To every person who picked up this book: Thank you. Telling this story was unlike any other for me. It touched old wounds that stretched deep, wounds that can finally scar. Moving on after this will be my hardest challenge yet.

To my Alphas, Betas and sensitivity readers. Thank you all for your dedication to the broken parts of me that I cannot stop spilling onto paper.

Smash, for guiding me through this one.

Angela, Crystal, Chris, Christina S, Christina C, Jenn, Louise, Shaye, Alex M., Nika, Jessie K, Jessie A, Erica, Dakota, - Thank you, to the moon and back for everything.

My editors, I am so proud to say I have the most fantastically gay team of editors imaginable, I hope my stories were worthy of you.

Alexa, for all of the everything that went into polishing the insanity that happens in my brain. My editor, my friend, my ARMOR. I love you.

R.N Barbosa, for the developmental edits, for making me feel like this book had purpose. For making my words matter.

Havoc, for the final proofread and making sure everything was squeaky clean and perfect. Thank you for being a part of this story.

Brianna, my friend, my muse, my partner in these

stories and my incredible artist. Thank you for imagining these girls with me. Thank you for a gorgeous cover.

Naomi Loud, I know for a fact now, that I cannot write a book without you, thank you for tolerating my existence.

Amy Oliveira, I love you. Thank you for holding my hand through this life.

The council, for all the counseling. Y'all know.

Margaret, for holding my hand and my leash. Thank you for keeping me together.

Hawk, for every hawking thing.

Chelsea C, for absolutely every single thing, but most importantly, thank you for being my friend.

The real life Cat. Thank you for growing up beside me, thank you for being my soul-person.

My amazing ARC team.

Good Girls PR for the continuous support.

Cat @thatrhgirly for inspiring the line "hit like a six foot blocker" because it was far too delicious to not include.

My infinites, for decades of love now.

The many people who cheer me on regardless of my faults, Haven, Erynne, Paula Jayne, Katie S, Tiara, Lori, Brooke, Eunice, Alyssa P, Jennifer R, Jennifer C, Susan C, Mila, Meghan, and if I missed anyone I'll just ruminate about it for the rest of my life.

To the real Ryan Lee, thank you for all the things only we'll ever know.

My husband, thank you for loving all the parts of me.

Hailey S., you make the good sparks in my brain go off and I'm grateful for your light.

Kris - The real Devil's Dame, thank you for letting me use your name for our roller derby league.

Hank-Her-Knickers-Off for carrying me out of that

track like a real-life version of the movie *The Bodyguard* when my leg turned into a noodle.

Brawly-Pop for forcing me to my first practice, SydVicious, Panama Crack and to every G-D*mn member of the C.A.R.D league who made me feel like family during my time on eight wheels.

I haven't been the same since.

ABOUT THE AUTHOR

Santana Knox is the pen name of a Brazilian author living in the United States.

Santana got tired of letting the voices in their head drive them crazy, and decided to write down the stories they were begging to tell instead. A lover of the unusual and a hopeless romantic when it comes to toxic villains, Santana's books should always be taken with a grain of salt, specifically the kind that keeps demons away.

To enter the cult, join the Facebook reading group: Santana Knox's Heathens

ALSO BY SANTANA KNOX

Crossed Over - A Sapphic, Roller derby, Coming out story

Dark-Romance:

Heartless Heathens -

A stand alone, why-choose, gothic-romance.

The Reina Del Cártel Trilogy:

Queen Of Nothing - Book 1

Reign Of Ruin - Book 2

Empire Of Carnage - Book 3

Diablos Locos Motorcycle Club:

No Place For Devils - Book 1 (Stand alone)

Novellas:

No Way Out - An Erotic Horror

Dreams Of Truth - A Dark Romantasy

Made in the USA
Coppell, TX
24 October 2024